LEGENDS AND LIBRARIANS

PANDORA PIERCE

LEGENDS AND LIBRARIANS

Copyright © Pandora Pierce, 2025

All rights reserved. Printed in the United States of America. No part of this book may be used or reproduced in any manner whatsoever without written permission except in the case of brief quotations embodied in critical articles or reviews.

This book is a work of fiction. Names, characters, businesses, organizations, places, events and incidents either are the product of the author's imagination or are used fictitiously. Any resemblance to actual persons, living or dead, events, or locales is entirely coincidental.

Cover Design: The Book Brander Boutique

Interior Illustrations: Della Claire

Formatting: Sara Vertuan of Stardust Book Services

Book Coach: Cathy Yardley

Book Coach: Rachel May of Golden May Editing

Developmental Editor: HEA Author Services

Line Editor: Empowered Writing

First Edition: January 2025

ISBN: 9781960239075 (paperback)

ISBN: 9781960239068 (ebook)

Published by Pandora Pierce LLC

www.pandorapierce.com

TABLE OF CONTENTS

Chapter 1 - Nyssa	07
Chapter 2 - Roan	15
Chapter 3 - Nyssa	24
Chapter 4 - Roan	34
Chapter 5 - Nyssa	44

Chapter 6 - Nyssa	56
Chapter 7 - Roan	64
Chapter 8 - Nyssa	76
Chapter 9 - Nyssa	86
Chapter 10 - Roan	98
Chapter 11 - Roan	109
Chapter 12 - Nyssa	119
Chapter 13 - Nyssa	129
Chapter 14 - Roan	139
Chapter 15 - Nyssa	148
Chapter 16 - Nyssa	163
Chapter 17 - Roan	172
Chapter 18 - Roan	181
Chapter 19 - Nyssa	189

CHAPTER 20 - NYSSA	201
CHAPTER 21 - ROAN	212
CHAPTER 22 - ROAN	220
CHAPTER 23 - NYSSA	231
CHAPTER 24 - NYSSA	241
CHAPTER 25 - ROAN	252
CHAPTER 26 - ROAN	261
CHAPTER 27 - ROAN	271
CHAPTER 28 - NYSSA	281
CHAPTER 29 - NYSSA	289
CHAPTER 30 - ROAN	301
CHAPTER 31 - NYSSA	314
EPILOGUE - NYSSA	323

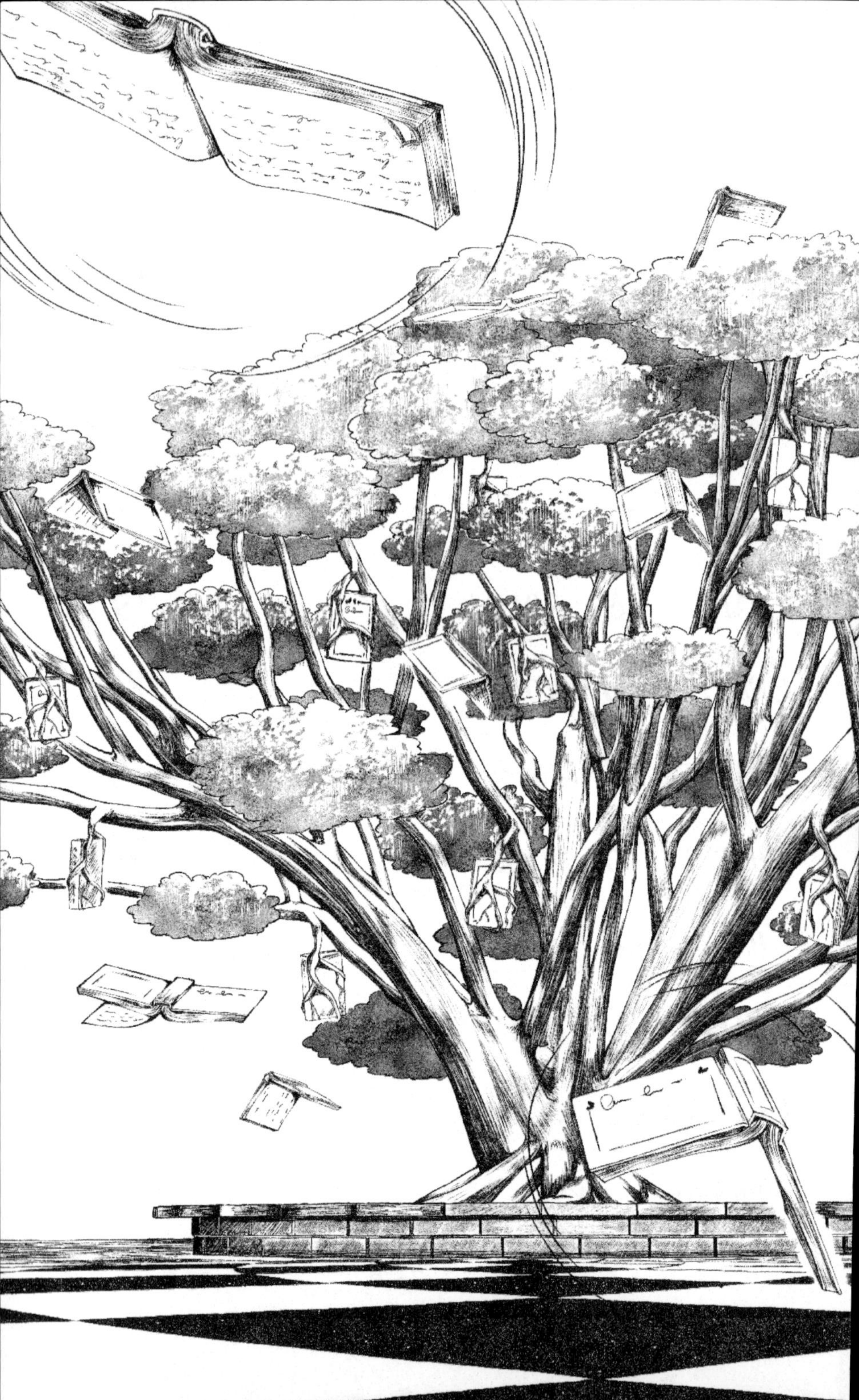

Chapter 1
Nyssa

Standing at the top of a rolling ladder gave me the perfect view of the magical library below. Dozens of books hung from the great book tree's branches like apples waiting to be plucked. One of them disconnected and flew off, flapping its cover like wings until it nestled onto a bookshelf. The stacks groaned, growing larger to accommodate the new book.

Magical libraries were constantly changing and it was a joy watching them grow. I shelved the last romance novel in my arms, running my hand lovingly over the bookshelf. The wood was warm beneath my fingers, alive with the library's magic. I loved working here, but another library needed me more than this one. Much more.

The very first library I ever visited, the one where I fell in love with reading, was in dire need of repair. It hadn't gotten the story gods' blessing in years and would lose its magic entirely if it missed a few more. Unfortunately, the month-long Tales and Tomes Festival was already underway, so I'd never have time to renovate the library before the final ceremony. That's when the most popular magical libraries were blessed with enough magic to thrive for years to come.

But next year? That blessing would be all ours.

The Librarians' Guild had finally approved my proposal, awarding me part of the Tomekeeper's Endowment, but when they tried to investigate the property to see what I'd need to do to revitalize it, the door was locked. They'd almost shot down my proposal right there, but I'd convinced them to let me handle it all. If they gave me the funds, I could make the library a wonderful place again.

But to do that, I needed books. Lots of them.

I made my way downstairs to help the other librarians with the book sale that would be the start of my library renovation plan. The endowment only provided so much money, and since I wasn't positive what the library would all need yet, I didn't want to spend too much of it too early. Which made this book sale the perfect opportunity to restock on a budget, especially if I took advantage of the closeout sale we'd inevitably do at the end of the day.

I trailed my fingers over an old leatherbound book with gold engravings, casually placing it underneath an end table where nobody would ever look. Books were meant to be read by the public, not gathering dust in a private owner's home.

I kept my eye on the other librarians as I moved around the room, sliding books underneath chairs, benches, tables, or whatever I could find. I'd collect them all later and buy them for the Misty Mountain Library. Nobody could be upset by that.

As I made my way around the sale, I felt a man watching me with bright blue eyes almost hidden beneath his wispy red hair. A faint smile curled his lips, as if I amused him. Guilt coursed through me as I dropped the book in my hands on a table, talking to a patron as if nothing happened. I wasn't hiding books. Nope. Nothing to see here.

I started actually doing my job and helping people find what they were looking for, but my gaze kept drifting back to the man watching me. Everything about him screamed danger, from the sword strapped to his back to the way his muscled body moved. He was a fighter, trained in battle I assumed from the scars.

So what was he doing at a library book sale? And why was he staring at me with that amused smile on his face? My curiosity drew me closer.

"Hello, can I help you with anything?" I asked, peeking at the book he held. It was old, too faded for me to read the title from this angle.

"I'd like to buy this," he said.

"Let me see." I smiled, reaching for it. It was a book of roughly drawn maps of the minotaur's labyrinth. They all ended abruptly, as if the creators hadn't survived long enough to finish them. Based on the different paper textures and stains, these looked like the originals, not copies. Definitely too rare to let go of. "Are you sure you want this book? The maps aren't even finished." I glanced at his sword again. Maybe he was an adventurer or a bounty hunter. "We have plenty of other dungeon maps."

"This one is fine. Unless there's a problem?"

His eyes sparked, challenging me. Had he seen me hiding books? Or was I imagining things?

"I just think you'd prefer these," I said, leading him to the dungeon map wing. "They're not for sale though, so you'd have to check them out."

"Trying to get me to come back, huh?" His low suggestive tone sent a shiver down my spine.

"Just doing my job." I cleared my throat as I slipped the labyrinth map book back on the shelf, making a mental note to grab it later.

"Do you always do that?" he asked, moving in front of me with a wicked glint in his eye.

"Do what?"

"Deceive people," he whispered, leaning closer.

The scent of leather and steel washed over me as he stared me down, his eyes shimmering.

He took another step closer. "I've been watching you, hiding books under furniture like they don't matter. It made me curious. You're either a terrible librarian or..."

That snapped me out of the moment like a bucket of cold water.

"I am a *great* librarian." I took a step backward. "Tell me what you're looking for and I'll prove it."

"Okay." His grin widened, like he wanted to gobble me up. "I'm part of the adventurers' guild. I'm looking for obscure maps I couldn't find elsewhere."

"Could you be more specific?"

"Surprise me." He shrugged, drawing my attention to the snug black and red leather jacket he wore. "If you're as good a librarian as you say, I'm sure I'll be impressed."

His jacket was well-worn, but also well-maintained so the scratches and scrapes enhanced the look instead of detracting from it. He seemed practical, like he got the job done. Which meant he probably wouldn't want artistic maps. He'd be using these to actually explore, not just learn about the regions.

I went to the catalog and started searching for a new map somebody had donated a few weeks ago for the floating islands. I'd tried to look up more information about them, but there wasn't much to be found beyond the basics. Floating island, impossible to get to, ruled by the wind god, etc.

There. I snatched the book up, grinning at the beautiful fold-out maps inside. This would impress that cocky adventurer.

"What about this?" I handed the book to him casually as if this wasn't the coolest thing I'd seen in years. "Impressed?"

His eyebrows rose as his eyes fluttered back and forth, examining the map. "More than impressed, nobody's ever been able to map this." He glanced around the library, as if in awe, before his gaze landed back on me. "You really are a good librarian, sorry about earlier. I'll take them all."

"Damn right I'm a good—" I frowned. "You'll take what?"

"All the books you're selling." His grin was dangerous, daring me to say no. "If they're even half as good as this one, I'll be the hero of the guild."

I swallowed hard. I'd been so focused on impressing him, on proving that I was a good librarian, that I'd forgotten my mission of hiding the books. I was supposed to be saving them for the Misty Mountain Library, but now he wanted to buy the entire book sale!

"Are you sure?" I asked. "I don't think you realize how many books that is. It's at least a hundred, maybe two, and they're pricey."

He pulled out a large bag of coins. "I'll take them all."

My gaze drifted from the money to his smug expression, wondering which annoyed me more. To think he'd just come in here and try to buy a whole wing of the library! Who did he think he was?

"You can't just buy the library."

"Isn't that the point of a book sale?" His eyebrow rose as he tilted his head. "Or is there a reason you're deceiving everyone here?"

"I'm not"—I paused, taking a deep breath.

The other librarians would be overjoyed if I accepted this adventurer's request. The Librarian's Guild received money from the government, but we also relied heavily on donations. As far as money went, the amount he was offering was rare. He was exactly the type of wealthy new donor I could use at the Misty Mountain Library actually...

"Do you even have room for all these?" I asked. "You could donate that money to revive a wonderful library instead. I'd even help you out with any research you needed."

He picked up a book, casually flipping through the pages. "So, you'd be like my...personal assistant?"

"Librarian," I snapped. "Do we have a deal or not?"

"Ahem." A loud cough to the side made me jump as one of the librarians crept over, her eyes wide at the size of that adventurer's money bag. "Did I hear right? You want to buy every book in the sale?"

"Absolutely." The man's eyes didn't leave me as he nodded. "This kind librarian was telling me how grateful she was too."

Grateful my ass. What was with this guy? I ground my teeth, holding firm to my librarian training to never yell at a patron. No matter how infuriating they were being.

"That's amazing!" The librarian clapped her hands together. "We'll get everything gathered up for you as soon as we can."

"No problem," he said, "but please make sure you find every book. Even the ones tucked away in hard-to-reach places."

He winked at me. Actually winked at me. He'd practically told her I'd been hiding things and now he was what? Rubbing it in? I'd be damned if I let him take those books. He whispered something to the librarian, but he kept glancing at me, as if daring me to tell her that I didn't want to sell those books.

I clamped my lips shut, unwilling to give him the satisfaction. He'd toyed with me, watching me to use everything I did against me. His money would help the library though, so I couldn't exactly hate him. Even if it meant it would take longer to reopen *my* library.

"Today was fun," he said as he walked away. "We should do it again sometime."

"Wait!" I called out as the librarians started stacking all of the books in my arms. "What about your books?"

He turned back with a soft smile. "They seemed to mean a lot to you, so why don't you hold onto them for me? They're ours now."

"Ours?" I almost dropped the books in shock. "What does that even mean?"

Had he bought all these books...for me? Warmth spread through my chest as our eyes met. I couldn't just let him leave now, not without even getting his name.

"At least tell me your name," I said as another book was piled into my arms, "and maybe help me bring these books home?"

Home as in the Misty Mountain Library, but he didn't need to know that yet. A trick for a trick. Plus, maybe he was worth getting to know a bit better.

His grin widened. "My name's Roan and I'd love to help you."

"Are you sure? It's going to be a bit of an adventure getting there," I said, barely containing my own grin. "Unless that's a problem?"

His laugh filled the room, warm and comforting. "I've got all the time in the world, but we should probably borrow a cart."

I nodded, making preparations with the other librarians. My last day here had turned out differently than I'd expected, but was definitely memorable. Roan sure knew how to win a woman's heart: with piles and piles of books.

Chapter 2
Roan

"So, when you asked me to take these books home"—I paused, glancing at the overgrown mountain path we were about to climb—"you didn't mention the part about portaling to another city, stopping to pick up construction supplies, or climbing a mountain."

"I didn't?" Nyssa gave me a wide-eyed innocent look. "I could have sworn I mentioned something about an adventure. You *are* an adventurer, right?"

"Well, yeah, but this path doesn't really look safe. Are you sure this is the right way?"

Loose rocks and fallen branches littered the ground and water had eroded the unstable path further, cutting deep ruts in the earth. This was what happened to man-made paths when they were abandoned: nature took them back by force.

"It's definitely the right way," she said, covering up a laugh with her hand. "But you don't really have to come if you don't want to. I've been up this mountain many times. I'll be fine on my own."

The longer I stayed in town, the more likely somebody from the Mistfall Adventurers' Guild would see me here, but that was a risk I was willing to take to get to know Nyssa better. Besides, it had been almost ten years. I doubted anyone would even remember me.

"I've got time," I said with a smile. "That's a perk of the job. I get to travel the world, taking missions when I want to and relaxing when I don't. Besides, what kind of adventurer would I be if I left a librarian to haul all these books up a mountain by herself?"

"You're lucky, I've always got way too long of a to-do list." She laughed as she activated the magic on the cart to get it moving again.

"Remind me again, where are we taking these books?" I asked, glancing at a moss-covered stone sign. Nyssa brushed it off, revealing an arrow leading up and a name. "The Misty Mountain Library?"

I probably should have recognized the name from the years I'd spent at the local guild, but I hadn't really been into books at the time. I'd only started reading for fun after I left.

"Yup, I'm reopening the Misty Mountain Library." A smile lit up her face. "I don't care what anyone else says, it's a magical place. The best library you'll ever see. Or it will be once I'm done with it."

If it was as rundown as this path, then she'd have her work cut out for her. But I wasn't about to say that, not when she was bounding up the mountain full of excitement.

"Why do you love it so much?" I asked.

"It's a library. Why wouldn't I love it?" Her eyes softened as she glanced back at the cart full of books. "I used to spend a lot of time there as a child. It was the only place I really fit in and it's why I fell in love with reading. In a world full of magic, there's nothing quite like getting lost in a good book. Working there and sharing that experience with others has been my dream for years." She nudged my arm, grinning. "And you're helping me revitalize that dream."

Sunlight glowed against her auburn hair, warm and beautiful. Listening to her talk about something she loved was oddly soothing, like I was getting to share in her big moment.

"I like books too," I said, "but I've never read one that made me feel like I was getting lost in it. Maybe you can recommend a few after you reopen."

"Really?" She did a little happy dance, but almost tripped on a tree root jutting up from the path.

I reached for her elbow to steady her, feeling myself drawn to her excitement like a moth to a flame. I wanted something to be this passionate about too. Sure, I liked adventuring, but it had become kind of boring lately. Same old missions, same old places. I wanted something exciting and new that was worth spending years dreaming about.

"That was close, thanks." She rested her hand on my shoulder. "How am I ever going to repay you?"

Her voice was low and her eyes glinted with mischief, making me momentarily forget how to speak. Who was this woman and how had I gotten lucky enough to walk her home? My heart thudded in my chest so loud she could probably hear it. Wait. No. That was something else.

I pulled back, drawing my sword as I studied our surroundings. The thump thump noise drew closer, almost like the sound of a shovel breaking open the earth.

"What's wrong?" Nyssa asked, gaze searching the tree line on the opposite side. "What's that noise?"

"Not sure, but I'll handle it. You're safe with me."

She nodded, standing firm even as the noises surrounded us. Shapes moved between the trees, oddly formed like no creature I'd ever seen. I squinted. They looked like they had square heads and only one leg? No. They were made of wood, some kind of box attached to a stake.

Nyssa let out a breath, laughing quietly. "They're just the library's little lending boxes. They're placed along the path in case people can't make it all the way to the library."

I didn't loosen my grip on my sword as the little lending boxes hopped closer. Their paint was chipped and faded, doors either missing or hanging off their hinges, and there wasn't a single book inside any of them.

"Do they usually move on their own?" I asked calmly, trying not to judge this wonderful library of hers.

"Well, no, not that I remember, but imagine how useful that'll be when I need to restock them every few days." She held out her hand to one of the boxes. "Come here little library, we're not going to hurt you."

It hopped up and down frantically, flinging its door open and shut, making a horrible squeaking noise that anything else on this mountain would surely hear.

"Be careful," I said. "We don't know what else is out there."

Nyssa waved her hand at me like I was being ridiculous as the lending libraries crowded around her. I kept close, ready to fend them off if they got violent, but they seemed more curious than dangerous as they leaned toward us, tilting this way and that.

I'd never seen anything like them. The elder gods had shaped our world out of magic through the power of their storytelling, imbuing magic into everything from the air we breathed to the food we ate. It's what formed the land and made the waters flow. It was beautiful and so full of potential, but when that potential was wasted, the magic spoiled, becoming wild with the need to finish its story. Even the gods couldn't say what it would do then.

And those cute little broken-down libraries that Nyssa was fawning over reeked of wild magic.

"Is this what you're looking for?" Nyssa asked the lending libraries, moving closer to the cart full of books. "Do you want more books?"

They hopped up and down like excited puppies. Nyssa smiled, not even a little afraid of them. I shook my head as she searched for just the right book to give each little library. She really seemed to care about them, even though she'd just met them and had no idea what they were. I admired that. Not enough people truly cared about others in this world. Not unless they got something out of it.

Nyssa handed out books like they were treats, giving each library one or two as she walked around the cart to reach them all.

"You know they're just going to lose those, right?" I asked, pointing at the lack of doors. "They need better doors, something with a latch that won't fly open when they hop."

Nyssa raised an eyebrow at me. "Here I thought you didn't like them. Now you're offering to help?"

"Wait, when did I offer that?" I shook my head. "I'd need tools and spare parts and stuff."

"Then I guess it's a good thing we picked up all sorts of stuff in town." She laughed, patting one of the libraries on its little roof. "They'll just have to come with us to the library so we can fix them up later. For now, it's time to head out!"

All the little libraries hopped to attention, creating a single file line behind her as she marched ahead like the pied piper, leading her ragtag team of lending libraries up the mountain. I couldn't help but grin, hurrying to keep pace with her.

"You're kind of amazing," I said.

She glanced sideways at me. "I know."

Silent laughter shook her shoulders as we walked together, followed by the thumping sounds of the library stakes and the creaking of the wagon wheels. I sheathed my sword, hoping that if anything else was going to attack us, it would have done it by now. We weren't exactly inconspicuous.

The path ahead grew more twisted and unkempt the closer we got to the library. Broken lights hung from the tree branches, doing nothing to guide our way as dense fog blanketed the ground. The air felt thick, buzzing and snapping around me like it was dripping with magic. Wild magic.

"We're almost there." Nyssa's voice rose with excitement. "I've been waiting for this moment for so long. The last time I was here was right before it got hit by a wild magic storm. After that, my parents and I ended up moving, but the librarians swore the place would heal itself." She sighed, shaking her head. "A few years ago, I realized that not only had the library not healed itself, but the Librarian's Guild had transferred most of the books to other libraries, basically shutting the place down."

"That's awful," I said, walking a bit closer to her. "I'm glad we've got a few books with us then."

"Yeah, good thing you showed up." She glanced back at the cart and then me, a smile tugging at her lips. "Maybe—"

She stopped talking as we stepped out into a clearing, her eyes widening.

A ramshackle library rose up from the mist, giant holes in the roof badly patched and windows boarded over like it was completely abandoned. The lending libraries raced ahead as Nyssa stood there, transfixed. The stone exterior was cracked as vines claimed the surface as their own.

I'd hoped the library would be as beautiful and magical as she remembered, but that just wasn't how the world worked.

"I'm sorry," I said, reaching out to comfort her, but she didn't look upset. She was practically glowing. "Wait, you still love this place even with it looking like that?"

"Of course I do. I knew it would need some repairs, so this gives me the opportunity to make it even better." She glanced back at me and shrugged. "What else am I supposed to say? That I give up on my lifelong dream to work here? Not a chance."

"Your determination is impressive. I respect that." Maybe I should spend a few days helping her clean up the place. I could help fix the big things at least. "Do you need a volunteer by any chance?"

She grinned. "Well yeah, but aren't you busy?"

"I'm in between jobs right now."

I should probably stop by an adventurers' guild to pick up more missions, but I'd rather wait until I got out of town. No matter what guild I stopped at, the local guild master always seemed to have some big job for me. That's the last thing I wanted to have happen in Mistfall.

"Excellent, then welcome to the Misty Mountain Library." Nyssa opened the door with a grin. Noises filtered out like people talking followed by a roar that sounded like it came from the depths of the earth, shaking the windows.

Nyssa slammed the door shut, spinning around and pressing her back against it. "On second thought, I don't need any volunteers. I'm all good here. You can head back to the guild."

My body tensed, waiting for whatever made that roar to rush outside. "You really think I'm going to ignore that noise?" I gripped the hilt of my sword tight. "What's in there?"

"Oh that? It's nothing. Just an alarm system to scare people off since the library's supposed to be closed." Nyssa laughed awkwardly. "It's really fine. You should get going."

Her eyes were on the ground and her hand gripped the door handle tight behind her back.

"Are you sure? Handling things like this"—I nodded at the lending libraries—"is part of my job. I don't mind taking a look inside. And I won't charge you if that's what you're worried about."

I wasn't hurting for money since the jobs I took usually paid pretty well, but it didn't feel like that was the issue here.

"It's really nothing," she said, meeting my gaze firmly. "This is library business, nothing to do with the adventurers' guild."

That was true, but it felt wrong just leaving her here without looking inside. Being an adventurer didn't give me permission to force my way into places though and she did seem pretty sure of herself. Who was I to doubt her word?

"Okay," I said slowly. "Why don't I come back later for those book recommendations then?"

"That sounds like a great idea." She nodded, sagging against the door in relief. "Thanks again for everything."

"Anytime."

I forced myself to walk away against my better judgement. In all my years as an adventurer, nothing had made me more curious than that woman and what she was hiding behind her back. There was more to that library than she was saying and I was going to find out what it was.

"I'll see you soon," I promised.

Chapter 3
Nyssa

Sending Roan away might not have been the best idea ever, but he was basically a stranger and I didn't know how he'd react. I'd only just gotten this endowment and I wasn't about to lose it to...whatever I'd seen inside.

Creatures. Dozens of them. From tiny flying dragons to giant hulking things I hadn't gotten a good enough look at.

I leaned my head back against the door, staring at the sky. There were *dragons* in there. I'd heard stories about them, sure, but I'd never actually seen one. It was like how I knew bears were real, but I didn't expect to find one in a library. And now there were dozens of them, just flying around like it was normal. Not to mention the other...things I'd seen. Things my mind wasn't making much sense of yet.

The Librarian's Guild would want an investigation, and if that went badly, they might never let me reopen this library. Or let it be part of the Tales and Tomes Festival. Without the gods' blessing, the Misty Mountain Library would fade away as if it were never here. Eventually a new library would grow somewhere else and the cycle would start again.

I couldn't let that happen though. This library held too many memories for me, important ones that I wasn't ready to let go of so easily. The best thing I could do now was keep those creatures to myself. At least until I knew more.

Once my racing pulse settled a bit, I dared to open the door again, just a crack. I peeked inside, but there was nothing. No dragons, no creatures, nothing. I swung the door open wide as silence greeted me.

Did I imagine them?

I stepped inside cautiously, half expecting somebody to jump out and yell surprise like this was some strange initiation to becoming a librarian here. Except, nothing happened. Well, that was a letdown. I sighed, closing the door behind me.

"Hello?" I called out. "I'm the new librarian, Nyssa."

Shuffling sounds came from multiple directions followed by tiny dragons flying in circles around me. I froze, not moving a muscle as they landed on the bookshelves nearby, quirking their heads as they stared at me.

Each dragon was a different color from emerald green to sapphire blue to bright amethyst, like a treasure trove of brilliant gems decorating the shelves. Their small wings settled against their bodies as they pounced at each other, starting to play as if they'd forgotten all about me already.

I let out a breath, relieved that they hadn't attacked me on sight, but why were they here instead of out in the wild with their own kind? And why were they so tiny? I really wanted to know more, but they weren't the only creatures here and I had work to do.

"Don't mind me," I said as I strolled through the shelves, "I'm just looking at what repairs need to be done."

The stacks were clean, not a speck of dust on them like I expected. Which meant somebody had been cleaning them. I smiled faintly, loving the idea of people stopping by to take care of the place. So it hadn't been fully abandoned after all. People still cared about it, just like I did. Maybe reopening wouldn't be as hard as I thought.

Something else was missing besides dust though: the books. Almost every shelf was empty, except for a few random books all by themselves. My stomach sank. It would be harder than I thought to restock such a big library. How could the guild give up on the Misty Mountain Library like that? How could anyone take the books away?

I guess I couldn't blame them too much. The library *did* look pretty rundown with the broken windows and holes in the roof. At least somebody had patched them up to keep the weather out, but not before water damage warped the floor. That wouldn't be an easy fix.

Had a wild magic storm really done all this? I rubbed my temples, silently calculating how much money the Tomekeeper's Endowment was worth vs how much it would probably cost to rip up a floor and redo a roof.

Maybe the contractors would take pity on me since it was for a good cause. I'd hire local workers, people who might remember the library from back in the day when it was warm and bright.

As I studied the mess of a floor, a patch of beautiful purple flowers caught my eye.

"What the..."

I knelt down, looking at the hooded flowers closer. Wolfsbane? That shouldn't be growing in the library. It was poisonous for one thing and for another, it was growing right on top of the floor, no dirt required. My gaze moved on to another patch of flowers and then another, leading me through the winding stacks like a path through a maze.

Something small and fluffy ran at me. I yelped in surprise as a three-headed puppy nuzzled against my leg. Purple flowers blanketed the floor as the adorable dog rolled over, exposing his belly. I looked around, but nobody else seemed to be here.

He wiggled on the floor, tail wagging, eyes begging me to reach down and pet his stomach. It was impossible to resist.

"Fine, I'll pet you." I knelt down, smiling despite the odd situation. All six of the dog's eyes closed in bliss like I'd found just the right spot to scratch. "Now what are you doing here, hmmmm?"

I'd heard of wild magic tainted animals, but usually the magic made them a different color or gave them some kind of magical aspect like glowing eyes or scratches that forced you to tell the truth. I'd never heard of wild magic changing their entire shape before, especially not giving them three heads. That was basically a whole new animal at that point.

Wild magic altered the purpose and intention of normal magic, it didn't make entirely new creatures. At least, I didn't think it did. I'd have to do more research.

A tiny bit of drool dripped from one of the dog's mouths and hit the floor. Flowers sprouted from it like magic. I jerked away. That was new. I'd never seen a dog do that before. Just heard stories about...

"Cerberus?"

The dog leapt up, wagging his tail, and eagerly looking at me like he wanted to play.

"No, you can't be Cerberus. You're all tiny and cute and...fictional!"

What was going on? Dragons I could handle, they were real even if I'd never seen one before, but Cerberus? He was the guardian of a fictional Underworld, created by an author a long time ago. Stories didn't just come to life and drool on your floor.

I searched the area, hoping for anything that resembled an explanation. The little pup followed at my heels, jumping at the flowers once in a while to play. It was hard not to give in and play with him, but something was very, very wrong here.

A book covered in so many flowers I almost missed it lay open on the floor. I picked it up, reading the title. "*Taming the Beast?*"

I raised an eyebrow at tiny Cerberus as he ran around the book in circles. That story was about an underworld goddess adopting a puppy and it causing adorable chaos in the underworld. The dog on the cover looked eerily like the dog wagging his tail in front of me, but that was just a story...

"Oh Cerberus, what are you doing here?" I whispered to the dog. "Actually, Cerberus feels a little too infamous for a cute puppy like you. How about Cerbie?"

He woofed his approval, coming to me for more pets. Well, whatever was going on didn't seem too bad. It's not like the dog came out of that book. That would be ridiculous. I mean, wild magic storms did a lot of weird things, but they didn't bring books to life. They just didn't. I'd have heard of it by now.

I bit my lip, staring at the dragons and three-headed dog in front of me. It would be really cool if books could come to life though. Imagine the swarms of patrons eagerly visiting their favorite book characters. The library would never have to worry about magic levels again since everyone would be reading, filling the area with magic for the book tree to absorb like water. I shook my head, laughing at how crazy that sounded.

As the stacks opened up to a large reading area circling the great book tree, I froze, all thoughts of stories coming to life gone. The book tree was withered, a husk of its normal self, with no leaves or books gracing its branches.

I pressed my hand against my chest, feeling the pain of that tree in my very soul. Book trees were gifts given to us by the gods, shooting up from the ground like flowers poking out of the snow in spring. One minute they were tiny little libraries and the next, they were full-sized and ready to use.

This one was almost out of magic though, as if it hadn't been blessed in over a decade. It had only been a few years though, there was no way it should have been this drained. If I didn't do something soon, all the repairs in the world wouldn't matter. The book tree was what gave life to a library, without it, there'd be no point in fixing up the building.

Could I even wait until next year's festival to gain the gods' blessing?

I needed help, somebody who knew more about library magic. My old research partner from school was getting his doctorate in arcane relics. Maybe he'd have some ideas.

I pulled out my communication crystal, holding it up to the light to cast a rainbow. "Connect me to Oren." I pet Cerbie, trying to calm my nerves as an image of Oren sleeping on a pile of books, glasses crooked, appeared in the rainbow. "Wake up. I've got a job for you."

He jerked up, running his hands over his face to readjust his glasses. "Nyssa? You never contact me. Is something wrong?"

I moved closer to the withered book tree so it would show up in Oren's crystal. "I'm reopening the Misty Mountain Library, but it looks like the tree's magic has been drained."

"Drained?" His eyes widened as I got closer to the tree, but then he frowned. "Something's wrong with our connection. It looks like the tree's...walking?"

I jerked my gaze from the crystal to a giant forest golem standing beside the tree. I tilted my head back to take all twenty feet of it in, watching it move with muscles made of corded vines holding the dirt, moss, and rocks together. One huge step swallowed the distance between us as I scrambled out of its way.

Cerbie ran circles around the golem, tail wagging with joy. It took another step, moving right past me as if it didn't even see me there. Red flowers sprouted from its shoulders, blooming brightly under the light. They reminded me of a book I'd loved as a child about a gentle giant. No, it couldn't be...

"Nyssa? What's going on?" Oren's voice snapped me out of my stunned silence. "Is that a golem?" Excitement colored his voice. He'd always loved mystical creatures, but hadn't seen any up close. Not like this.

"What do you know about...books coming to life?" I gazed at the impossible golem in front of me. "Specifically, can characters from books ever become real?"

"Of course not," Oren scoffed. "Unless..."

I'd seen that look in his eyes many times as he opened a book and got lost in his research for days on end. He always came up with an answer for everything I asked him, no matter how long it took him. This time would be no different.

Unfortunately, our conversation had drawn the golem's attention. It turned slowly, gazing around the library with wide glowing eyes. It leaned down, close enough for me to smell the damp earth and sweet flowers in its body.

"Gotta go, Oren," I stammered, before dropping the crystal. "Um, hello, Mr. Golem?"

"Not my human," it said, its voice rumbling like an earthquake. "Where is my human?"

Its voice was slow, drawn out, and something about its face, how its head tilted curiously and its eyes shimmered, reinforced my theory about it being *the* gentle giant, the one who'd saved a misfit child from harm and made both their dreams come true. I couldn't help but smile, remembering all the times I'd read that story, all the times I'd wished a golem of my own would find me.

"Nice to meet you," I said. "My name's Nyssa. Can you tell me why you're here?"

"Why I'm here?" It straightened, body groaning as the rocks and vines shifted. "Here is my home."

It's home? Golems lived in the wild, not in cramped buildings where they couldn't connect to nature.

"I'm sorry, but this is a library, not a magical refuge." I worried my lip, not wanting to hurt its feelings. "Do you know where you lived before? Was it outside the library or maybe...inside a book?"

A book fell off the mostly barren shelves nearby, making me jump. Then the shelves seemed to quiver as more books fell. One by one they hit the ground, making me cringe.

"What's wrong?" I asked, hoping the golem would stop whatever it was doing, but it just tilted its head, staring off in the distance.

Actually, it was staring at somebody walking toward us. A man, shrouded in darkness. Black horns curled over the man's head and his fingers were tipped in claws, black as the night like they'd been dipped in ink that crept up his arm to his very toned biceps.

"Get out," he said softly, but the words held weight, as if he fully expected me to follow orders. "We don't need a new librarian. It's time for you to leave."

I swallowed hard. He obviously wasn't human, but this was my library and I refused to be intimidated. Was he a character from a story like the golem? Or was he something else?

Before I could ask, the golem picked me up, my feet dangling in the air like a child too short for their chair.

My stomach lurched, but its large hand held me securely, carrying me outside. It set me down far more gently than I expected, but then slammed the door in my face.

My heartbeat thundered in my ears as I sat outside. Did they just kick me out? Of my own library??

I stood up, grabbing the door handle firmly. There was no way they were getting rid of me that easily. I pulled on the handle, ready to give that demon a piece of my mind, but the door didn't budge. I leaned back, putting all my weight into it, but the door stayed shut.

"Fine," I said, "if that's how you want to play it, then I'll just find another way in. I'm the librarian. You can't keep me out."

Not for long at least. I'd get back inside and reopen that library. I'd spent too many years dreaming about it to let a few books that had come to life stop me.

Chapter 4
Roan

I'd been planning on avoiding the Mistfall Adventurers' Guild, but I didn't feel right skipping town while Nyssa was at the library all by herself. That noise, no matter what excuse she'd made, was not normal, and the best place to hear all the local gossip was at the guild.

So I'd check in, get the information I needed, and get out.

My hand hovered over the door handle, but I couldn't bring myself to open it. The training grounds out back sounded especially lively today and the light from inside the guild glowed warm and bright. I knew when I opened that door, adventurers would greet me, sit me down for a meal, and ask about all the cool missions I'd been on since the last time I was here.

My shoulders tightened, already feeling claustrophobic. When I was young, walking into a guild with my parents had been the best feeling in the world, being welcomed like heroes returning home. But now? It just reminded me of things better left buried. They'd left me at one of those guilds, just tucked me in and never came back.

Apparently adventuring with a child in tow just wasn't as fun.

I gritted my teeth and yanked the door open.

Laughter and general merriment greeted me, buzzing against my senses as if I was walking into a beehive. The guild I'd been abandoned at had let me stay, washing dishes and cleaning up after everyone, until I was old enough to take missions. After that I moved around a lot, only staying in one place when I found this guild.

It had been so warm and inviting, full of people I thought had really cared about me. So, I stayed for almost three years, the longest I'd ever let myself settle anywhere. It was a mistake though; one I had no intention of repeating. Getting close to people, caring about them, was just asking to get hurt.

A few adventurers stared longingly at the quest board in the back, as if they didn't know what job to pick next or couldn't handle any of the ones there. My decision was usually easy: grab the toughest mission on the board. No fuss, no muss. Until today. I needed information more than something to fight.

"Roan," an older man's voice I knew all too well called out. "Is that really you? It's been way too long, my boy."

"Hello, Master Carmine." I turned to greet the guild master, noting how gray his hair had turned since the last time I'd seen him. How long had it been? Five years? Ten? "How have you been?"

"Good, very good," he said, staring at me with papers in his hands like he'd stopped in the middle of doing something. His eyes looked a bit watery. "Do you have time for a meal?"

No, but I felt like a jerk saying it. This man had taken care of me for a few years, even if it was just so I'd train his daughter and make her a worthy successor. He still treated me like I was one of his own.

"Sure, food sounds great." I sat down at a nearby table as he joined me. I squirmed in my seat, feeling like a teenager all over again under his watchful gaze. "I'm not staying for long, just looking for information about a situation on the mountain."

That finally broke his stare. "Oh, of course, you're always busy on a mission. But let's eat first. I'll have the cook make your favorite and it'll be like old times."

Old times. My chest ached remembering all the meals we'd shared, all the times he'd cleaned my wounds up after a battle, and all the kind words he'd said to me. He really was a good guild master, even remembering how much I liked a hearty hunter's stew after all these years.

If only I hadn't just been a means to an end to train his daughter. I'd heard she was a bloodthirsty, kickass adventurer now, so I guess she really hadn't needed me anymore. But that wasn't my problem anymore. *She* wasn't my problem.

"So, how's Jade been?" I felt myself asking even though I shouldn't care. We were close in age, which was why the guild master had asked me to work with her in the first place, but it meant I'd gotten attached too. We'd felt more like siblings than coworkers and those family vibes had been my undoing. "She's not here, right?"

Master Carmine smiled. "No, she's on a mission. Did you forget what time of year it is?"

I frowned, trying to remember the missions in this area since a lot of them repeated on a cycle. Legend has it that all the monsters in the world were created by the gods as a way to test us, because nobody could be a hero without something to fight against. I wasn't sure if that was true or not, but repeat missions did make me wonder.

When I was in the area a few years ago around this time, I joined a team of adventurers fighting...

"Is the Ant Queen migrating again already?" I asked.

"I knew you'd remember." Master Carmine beamed as he motioned for the bartender to bring us drinks. "Jade's going to be so upset when she realizes she was off slaying ants while you stopped by."

I highly doubted that since we hadn't ended on the best of terms. She flat out told me that she was better than me in every way, so why should a lowly adventurer like me keep training her?

She was skilled, but not invincible, and those ants were a menace if left unchecked. After they devoured all the gold they could find underground, they'd surface and start looking for it in new places and they didn't care where it came from. The more gold they ate, the tougher their armor became, so merchants paid the guilds highly to deal with them before they caused too much damage.

The bartender handed me an amber beer, one of the guild's specialties. It was rich and strong, just the thing to ease my anxiety about being back here. I drank deeply, enjoying the malty flavor.

"So, what have you been up to?" Master Carmine asked quietly. "I've missed you, you know. You left so abruptly and I never got to properly say goodbye. Did you go look for your parents? I heard they're retired and running an inn now."

Oh, I'd found my parents all right, just to make sure they were still alive, but they didn't deserve a happy reunion. Not when they'd never come back for me. They were so skilled and could have easily found one kid no matter which guild I'd gone to. Even after I'd proved I wasn't a burden anymore, that I could take on anything, they hadn't checked in.

I drank deeper, holding my hand up for another hoping it would stop this ache in my chest. Time to shift the conversation to something less personal. All this reminiscing was starting to get to me.

"Well, I did just help a librarian carry some books up a very scary mountain."

A beautiful librarian full of passion. She'd been so fiercely protective of those books that I almost thought she was going to slap me when I offered to buy them. If I'd known she was bringing them to another library, I'd have bought even more for her. Restocked the whole place just to see that smile of hers.

"Wait," the guild master leaned closer, "are you talking about the Misty Mountain Library?"

I nodded, downing the rest of my drink before motioning for another. I didn't usually drink like this, but it was an easy distraction until our food came. As a waiter handed me another, I realized the guild hall had grown quiet. Everyone was staring at me.

"What's going on?" I asked, glancing from wary look to wary look.

It reminded me of the night I left. They'd all just stared at me, unwilling to tell Jade off for what she'd said. They hadn't respected me enough to stand up for me then and they didn't respect me enough to speak up now.

Master Carmine shook his head. "Ignore them. Tell me more about the librarian."

"Well, she's determined and beautiful," I leaned back in my chair, remembering her hair shimmering in the sunlight. "I've never seen anyone as passionate about a library as her and—"

"Not that," a woman's voice snapped. "What's she doing bringing books to that library?"

I turned to see Jade standing in the open doorway, glaring at me with her hands on her hips. She was leaner than I remembered, but well-toned, like she'd spent her time fighting and training until she was all muscle. Twin swords peaked over her shoulders and daggers lined her belt. Muck coated her clothing and brown braid too. Had she taken care of the ant queen already?

I'd never admit it out loud, but I was kind of proud that she could hold her own against monsters like that. It was nice seeing her hard work pay off, even if she was a total pain in my ass.

"Don't tell me you're helping monsters now." Jade stomped over to me. "I know you like to do your own thing, but seriously Roan? Deal with that bleeding heart of yours already."

"Calm down," the guild master said, "he just got here, so he doesn't know about the library yet."

"Know what?" I asked as my frustration started welling up. The vibe in here had changed the moment I mentioned Nyssa and the library. "Tell me what's going on."

Jade laughed. "Shouldn't you know already? You are the big bad S-rank adventurer. People speak your name like you're some kind of hero, but here you are, clueless. I could tell you, if you asked nicely. I'd even be willing to show you around, help you understand what mess you just stepped into."

I rolled my eyes. She'd been like that since we were kids, always trying to prove she was better than me. But I didn't have the time or the energy to deal with her, so I turned to the guild master. "If something's wrong with the library, I need to know. I left that librarian all alone."

"You should check on her," he said. "The library's...a little haunted, if you believe the stories."

"A little haunted?" I gripped the edge of the table, the wood digging into my palm. "Why haven't you dealt with it yet?"

"It's not that simple," Jade snapped, plopping down on a chair next to us. She threw her feet on the table, just like she did when we were kids, before the guild master swatted them down. "There's never anything out of the ordinary when we go there."

"But you still think it's haunted?"

"Well obviously," she said. "Why else would the board be covered in missions about it? The townsfolk have seen things and I believe them."

The board. I hadn't actually looked at it. I stood and walked over, gaze sweeping from mission to mission about the strange noises on the mountain, the lights and figures at the library, and about the shadows that seemed to come to life and chase people away. The town was terrified.

And I'd just left Nyssa there, all alone. I clenched my hands. She must have known about the rumors, about the so-called haunting, and had sent me away on purpose when she saw what was inside. With how much she loved that library, she'd probably try to make friends with the spirits.

Dammit.

"I've gotta go," I said, instinctively reaching for my sword.

Jade blocked my path. "Not so fast. What makes you think *you* can do something when none of us could? You're not better than me, not anymore."

"I never said I—"

"Just forget that library and leave town already," Jade snapped. "It's the only thing you're good at. We'll go check on the librarian for you and deal with anything that's there."

My jaw clenched. Nyssa might be in danger, so now was not the time for Jade to throw a tantrum. I glanced at Master Carmine for an assist, but he just avoided my gaze like he'd always done when we were younger. He preferred we deal with our issues ourselves.

The more comfortable I'd become in this guild, the worse her attitude had gotten, as if every kind word her father had for me was a step toward me taking over the guild instead of her. It wasn't my fault I was more skilled than her. It was literally the reason her father had hired me, to train her.

And despite his current silence, I'd always trusted his judgment. The way he'd phrased the haunting, saying *if* I believed the stories, sounded like he thought something else might be at play here.

If that was true, then I had to figure out what. Jade—and the other adventurers at this guild—were the kind of slice first, ask questions later adventurers. If I left it to them, they'd just burn the place down eventually and call it a day.

"I'm not leaving until I settle this," I said, trying to get to the quest board to take the missions, but Jade still stood in my way.

I didn't have time for this. If Nyssa was in danger, I had to get there. Had to help her. Abandoning people in need was not something I did. Ever.

"Move. Or I'll make you move," I said coldly. She was not my sister. This was not my guild. I owed them nothing.

Jade stepped closer, filling my personal space. "You think you're tough shit, but one day, everyone will see you for who you really are. A coward. Just run along and let the adults handle this."

My blood pounded in my ears, but I refused to take the bait. She was a shadow of the girl I'd trained, just violence and anger now. I stepped around her and ripped all the library missions off the board, slamming them down on the counter next to the guild's receptionist.

"I'm taking these missions," I said.

"All of them?" she squeaked out, gaze darting to Jade and the guild master.

"All of them."

Jade shook her head, laughing. "Okay, but don't come crying back to us when you can't find anything either. Or maybe, you will find something and the spirits will gobble you up."

Nyssa. I had to get to Nyssa. I gripped my sword hilt firmly as I displayed my adventuring credentials so the missions could be assigned to me.

"You're still a member of this guild," Master Carmine said. "If you need help, ask. I'll be ready."

"I'm fine on my own. Always have been, always will be."

The moment the receptionist was done, I was out the door, heading for the Misty Mountain Library, the pained look on the guild master's face echoing in my mind.

Chapter 5
Nyssa

I crossed my arms, staring down the toughest foe I'd ever met: the Misty Mountain Library's door. I'd been trying to open it again all day with no luck; the damn door just would not budge. I glanced up at the sky as the sun lowered beneath the tree line. It would be dark in a few hours and I really didn't want to climb down the mountain at night.

If I was going to do this, it had to be soon. I refused to leave without getting back inside to see what those creatures really were. They'd looked like characters from books, as if they were the spirits of the stories coming to life.

Like they were story spirits.

Wait. Maybe *I* wasn't the one who had to open the door...

I rushed over to the cart full of books with a wonderful new plan: tempt the "story spirits" into coming outside so I could slip inside behind them. It was clear that they'd been taking care of the few books that were left, dusting the shelves and doing what they could to maintain the library. Which meant they probably loved books. And what book-lover could stand to see a pile of books just lying on the ground uncared for?

I eyed the dirty cobblestone path in front of the library, already cringing at the idea of putting books on it, but it had to be done. For the library.

A few lending libraries leaned over the cart full of books, hopping with excitement as I started sorting through them. One of them nudged my arm like a puppy with a cold nose begging for pets, and I couldn't help but laugh.

"Fine, fine, you can each have one more," I said, "but that's it. I need the rest for my mission."

They jumped happily as I searched for which books to lure the story spirits out with. I should probably go for wholesome happy ones just in case they came to life like that golem. Better safe than sorry.

With my arms full of books, I made my way to the library's door, setting a single book on the path in front of it. Then I took a half step back and placed another book down, and then another, and another, creating a little trail of books. Hopefully it would lead the story spirits far enough away from the library that I could slip in without them stopping me.

Unless they were smart enough to realize this was a trap and continued to ignore me.

If that happened, I'd gather the books before dew ruined them overnight. If the story spirits really did love books, they'd want to do the same. They had to. At the very least, they'd probably be annoyed enough to stop me at some point.

So I kept going, placing book after book on the ground, leading a winding path away from the library.

"Nyssa?" a man's voice called out, making me jump and almost drop the last book. Roan walked into the open courtyard in front of the library, holding his hands in the air. "Sorry, didn't mean to scare you."

"Oh, hello!" I put on my best fake smile, standing between him and the trail of books I'd been making. "What are you doing back so soon?"

"I was, um, hoping to be your first patron?" He peered over my shoulder, the corner of his mouth quirking up. "But it looks like you might be busy..."

Heat burned my cheeks as I watched his eyes follow the curling trail of books to the library's door, like candy left out for a child to hunt down. I scuffed my boot in the dirt, avoiding his smirk. Just who did he think he was coming back the same day? It would take months for this library to be repaired enough for people to return, maybe longer.

"What are you really doing here?" I raised an eyebrow. "Please tell me it's not about those rumors going around town about this place."

"Can't a guy just want to read?" he asked, his smile growing.

He'd avoided the question, which meant he probably *had* heard the rumors. The town thought the library was haunted of all things.

Well, I had to admit, they had good reason to think that, but it didn't help my goals at all. If I hadn't recognized the golem as a character from a book I'd read, I wouldn't have believed they were story spirits either. And if I barely believed it, how could I convince anyone else?

I had to keep the library safe at all costs, which meant keeping the story spirits hidden until I came up with a plan.

Roan stepped closer, his eyebrows pinching together. "I also wanted to make sure you were okay. Are you?"

"I'm fine," I said, nodding. "But we won't be open for a while. You'll have to take a raincheck on those recommendations."

He tilted his head, glancing from me to the library. "Maybe I can help out then? I'm sure you could use a hand with something."

I sighed. "You're really not going to leave, are you?"

"Not until you tell me what's up with the books." He nodded at the very suspicious book trail. "They are half mine, remember."

Damn him and his over-the-top spending habits. He was right though. These were half his, so he had a right to know why they were littered all over.

"Okay, so here's the thing," I said slowly, "there's.... people that sort of took over the library while it was shut down. And they don't exactly want me there. They threw me out actually."

Calling them people was a stretch, but I didn't want to reinforce whatever rumors he might have heard. Especially if I could convince him to leave before he saw any of the story spirits.

"What people?" He reached for his sword. "Are they like the lending libraries, something spawned of wild magic?"

His gaze roved the area. "I knew I shouldn't have left you here like that, I'm sorry."

"No, no, no," I said, holding up my hands. "It's nothing like that. They're just people who love the library so much that they don't want anyone else to go inside."

He raised an eyebrow at me, but put his hand in his pocket. "Okay, and remind me again how these books are going to win them over?"

"Oh, they're not," I said, shaking my head. "But I bet I can slip inside while something comes out to get them."

"And what kind of *thing* do you think that will be?»

"I don't know, maybe a—" I snapped my mouth closed. I'd said some*thing* instead of someone. He was way too perceptive. "Guess we'll see."

It's not like I could keep it hidden from him forever, but if the story spirits didn't come out, then there was no point in bringing it up. He'd just go off on his merry way again and be none the wiser. No wild magic to see here, none at all.

"You're adorable, you know that, right?" He grinned, making his way over to an old stone bench I hadn't noticed. It was surrounded by trees, as if the forest was taking over the open courtyard. "Mind if I wait with you?"

He paused before sitting down, turning back to look at me. When his eyes met mine, I felt a small flutter in my stomach. He might be cocky, but he was also polite and cared about what I wanted. Maybe it wouldn't be so bad having him here. He was an adventurer, so the story spirits shouldn't freak him out *too* much.

"I guess I don't mind," I said, joining him in his secluded hiding spot. "This might take a while anyway."

He glanced sideways at me. "Looks like we're having a stakeout then."

Our knees brushed against each other, sending sparks through me. He reclined, arms resting on the back of the bench, mere inches from my shoulders. If I leaned back, I'd be encircled by him, protected by those strong muscles he'd probably spent most his life developing. Oh how I wanted to give into that urge, but I was too busy for romance. I had to focus.

Thankfully, we didn't have to wait long for the door to crack open a tiny bit, like somebody was peeking outside. It closed again, but that peek was everything. They were interested. This was going to work!

Roan chuckled warmly. "Look at you, you're like the cat that got the cream. They barely even opened the door yet."

"Oh, but they will. Just you wait." I leaned back without a care in the world. His hand flexed on the bench and I couldn't help but smirk. "Want to make a bet?"

"Only if I can set the stakes." He paused until I nodded. "If this plan of yours works, and you manage to get back inside the library, then I'll help you fix the place up, free of charge."

That sounded like quite the deal. I could think of lots of things for a strong guy like him to help with, especially with how many repairs it looked like the library needed. Turning down a chance at free labor would be foolish, but I had a feeling my side of this bet wouldn't be as enjoyable.

"And if they don't come get the books?" I asked, curling the edge of my shirt around my fingers. "What do you get out of this?"

He leaned closer, until my entire view was full of him and my breath caught in my chest.

"If you lose," his eyes sparkled dangerously as he lowered his voice, "then you post a job request at the local guild for somebody to help repair the library. I'll make sure to take it."

I blinked. "Wait, so no matter what, you'd be helping me with the library?" When he nodded, I grinned, leaning forward with laughter. "You're a terrible gambler. I win either way."

"That's how I like it." He winked, then turned around slowly at the sound of a creaking door. "I think somebody's coming."

I almost jumped up to see, but his hand clamped down on my leg and he put a finger to his lips. I froze. Of course, we didn't want to scare off whoever was opening that door. I forced myself to sit calmly as it opened.

After what felt like hours, a beautiful woman in a purple dress stepped outside, gathering the books in her delicate arms one by one. I hadn't seen her in the library last time, which meant there were even more story spirits than I'd thought. I had the sudden urge to run inside and see them for myself, but the woman was way too close. She'd catch us for sure.

As she hummed, dancing along the book path, Roan and I slowly inched off the bench. He held up three fingers, lowering one at a time until there were none left. Then we ran. Adrenaline surged through me as I flung the door open, finally victorious!

The sounds of metal slamming against the floor froze me in place. Dozens of tiny armored knights lined the shelves, swords held against their chests and pointed at the ceiling. Pint-sized dragons circled the shelves, as if they were the knights' backup.

"Hello," I said, smiling politely, "don't know if you remember me, but I'm Nyssa, the new librarian."

I held out my hand, then realized how foolish that was since they were only a few inches tall.

"On me, knights!" The voice was quiet, but seemed to come from the knight with the most intricate glowing armor. He shifted, pointing his sword at me. "We promised Lady Lisa that we wouldn't let them pass."

"Remind me who these guys are again," Roan said. "Something about people who loved the library so much they didn't want you here? No wild magic involved?"

I laughed awkwardly, drawing my outstretched hand back. "I might have left a few details out. There's a tiny bit of wild magic here, but nothing dangerous."

"Right, they're totally peaceful." He motioned at the knights, who looked like they were about to leap off the bookshelves at us, and ducked as a tiny dragon spewed fire at him. "Maybe we should go back outside."

"You definitely should," a woman said behind us, "especially after playing that trick on me."

A towering stack of books blocked her from view as she swayed, slowly walking inside. She must have picked up every book in the trail all at once! I rushed forward, grabbing half the stack from her.

"Sorry," I said. "I just wanted to talk, but nobody would let me in."

"Did you consider we didn't let you in for a reason?" She smiled as she set her books down on a nearby table, but it didn't reach her eyes.

I gripped the books in my own arms tight. Honestly, I hadn't let myself really think about why they wouldn't open the door, because if I did, then I'd have to accept that they didn't want me here, and I couldn't do that. I'd quit my job, moved out of my apartment, and traveled all the way here just to open this library. I was in too deep to give up now.

"But she's the librarian," Roan said as he took the books from my hands. He gave me a reassuring smile before setting them down next to the other stack. "I'm guessing you're Lady Lisa?"

"Lisa's fine." The woman waved her hand in the air. "But I'm the librarian. We don't need another."

"You're a librarian too?" I asked. "When did you get here?"

Was she another story spirit or had the Librarian's Guild hired somebody else without telling me? She looked real, but so did all the other creatures I'd seen here. The golem even smelled like damp earth. The story spirits were so lifelike it was hard to tell.

"I've been here for years." She crossed her arms, staring me down. "I didn't abandon the library."

Her implication was clear: *I* abandoned the library. I clutched my chest, feeling like the air was knocked out of me. After my family and I had moved away, I could have visited, but it was so far away and I'd been trying to fit in in our new town. That's what kids were supposed to do in new places, or so my parents had told me.

I'd spent the past few years working on getting back here, but now that I was finally back, they didn't want me. What was I supposed to do?

A firm hand gripped my shoulder. Roan. "Nyssa just wants to help the library. Won't you at least talk to her?"

He was right. They should at least take the time to get to know me before throwing me out. I was here to help them. I smiled at Roan, silently thanking him for that reminder.

"I am not leaving." I straightened my back, ready to fight for the library. "My job is to repair this library and reopen it. Isn't that what you want too? To see it back to normal?"

"Who says what's normal?" Lisa asked, but then frowned as the knights and dragons behind us lost interest in me and began fighting each other. "Sheesh, they couldn't even behave for five minutes. Golem, we need your help!"

Her voice called out into the depths of the library where I heard the rumbling footsteps of the gentle giant coming toward us.

"Not again." I groaned, searching for another option, before turning to Roan. "There's about to be a twenty-foot forest golem trying to kick us out. Any ideas?"

A grin stretched across his face. "I've got a few."

"Any peaceful ones?"

"A few less," he said, wincing. "My sword does absorb magic though, so we could try that."

Lisa frowned. "A magic-absorbing sword, huh? That could prove meddlesome."

Wild magic might have created them, but I didn't want to dispel them if I didn't have to. Not if they really came from inside books. That was a whole new and fascinating kind of magic that I wanted to explore, not get rid of.

"Can we talk about this?" I asked Lisa. "Are you the one running things here or is it somebody else?"

"Me and two others," she said as a dragon landed on her shoulder. Lisa tilted her head as she pet it. "But are you sure you want to meet them? What if they also think we'd be better off without you?"

"Then I'll accept that decision," I mumbled, "but only after stating my case fully."

And doing everything in my power to convince them I belonged here. This was my library too and I'd be damned if I let them chase me out of it.

Lisa nodded. "Okay, then follow me."

Roan held me back a moment. "Are you sure about this? What if she's leading you into a trap?"

That was a fair question, but I wasn't worried. The story spirits didn't feel dangerous. Even when the dragons were spitting fire, all the flames missed us. And when the knights were aiming at us, they never actually attacked. Plus, when the golem threw me out, he carried me with such care and set me on the ground so gently that I didn't get a single bruise.

They cared about the library. I could feel that, deep in my bones, and if they truly cared about this place, they wouldn't hurt me. I was a librarian.

"I trust them," I said, following Lisa deeper inside.

Roan sighed, but followed as well. We'd meet this leader together. Having him by my side, ready to defend me if anything happened, gave me the space to be confident. To trust in the library I loved so much.

We'd be fine.

Chapter 6
Nyssa

No matter how much I *wanted* to trust these story spirits, each step I took following Lisa filled me with dread. What kind of book character would be powerful enough to manage them? I doubted they'd put anyone in charge who couldn't handle that golem and the dragons. To do all that, they must be a great warrior or a sorcerer. Maybe even a god.

I shuddered. I'd read so many books about gods and magical beasts, but had never really considered what it would be like meeting them in person. How was I supposed to run a library filled with story spirits that would terrify half the visitors just by existing?

Roan moved closer to me, leaning in to whisper. "The moment you don't feel safe, let me know. I'll get you out of here no matter what."

I studied him carefully, from his sword to the confident way he held himself. "You really would wrangle all these stories for me, wouldn't you?"

"Without a second thought," he said, staring at me with an intensity I wasn't accustomed to. "But that's not like any story I've ever seen." He nodded at the golem. "That, Miss Librarian, is a giant."

I smiled and shook my head. "I'll explain later."

Roan looked like the kind of man who wouldn't let you down, who wouldn't stop until the job was done. So what exactly was he doing here? Did he have a mission I didn't know about? Or did he come back for...me?

"We're here," Lisa said as she paused outside a conference room. "Are you ready?"

That didn't really matter. I'd walk in there, ready or not. I had to. I took a deep breath, and after one last look at Roan, I strode inside the room, blinking as the evening sun shone through the few intact windows.

"You again," a familiar growly voice said from across the room. "I thought I told you to leave."

Oh no, not the demon who'd kicked me out earlier. Anyone but him. I was about to plead my case, but an adorable, fluffy red panda caught my eye. He was sitting on a chair like a human, drinking bubble tea of all things.

"He's so —"

"Don't say it," the demon commanded. "Mochi is not a pet. He's in charge here."

I bit my lip, trying not to laugh at a demon calling a cute red panda Mochi. This was not what I'd expected at all when I walked into this room. How was I even supposed to reason with a panda? Give him food and hope he liked me?

Mochi chittered adorably while Lisa took a chair beside him.

The demon rolled his eyes and joined them too. "Mochi wants you to sit down," he grumbled. "I'm apparently not allowed to throw you out yet."

Roan and I glanced at each other before he answered. "So, you can understand the panda?"

"Of course I can," the demon snapped. "Can't you?"

I leaned closer as Mochi chittered with Lisa about something, she nodded and smiled, but it all just sounded like panda talk to me. He took a sip of his tea, rocking back and forth in his chair like he was having a great time. Well, at least he seemed happy. That had to be good for me.

"No, but we can make this work," I said, sitting down across from them. "Hello, Mochi, my name's Nyssa. I'm a librarian sent here to revitalize the Misty Mountain Library. I'll repair anything that needs repairing and breathe new life into the grounds so we can reopen the doors to the public. Does that sound good to you?"

Mochi munched on a piece of boba, then squawked at us a few times.

"He wants to know why you're here now," Lisa translated. "It's been years since the old librarians abandoned this library, giving up after the wild magic storm. Nobody's come back here since."

"Well, everyone was waiting for the library to heal itself." I paused when the demon's glare hardened, "but that's not a good excuse. I had to wait for an endowment so I'd have the money to do the repairs."

The demon leaned back in his chair slightly. Phew. Saved myself there. Demons were a tough crowd.

"And you couldn't visit?" Lisa asked. "Not even once in those long years since you were here last?"

"How did you know I'd been here before?" I frowned. "Did I mention that?"

Mochi slurped the last of his tea and scurried off his chair to hop in Roan's lap. He stood up, paws on Roan's shoulders, inspecting him. Roan didn't move, didn't even flinch.

"Mochi wants to know what he's doing here," Lisa said. "We've had...bad experiences with other adventurers. Is he going to harm us?"

"No, of course not!" I stared at Roan. "Right?"

He held his hands up. "As long as nobody hurts us, I won't do a thing."

"See? All good," I said, wringing my hands. "Does that mean I can stay?"

The demon laughed. "You really think it's that easy? You just show up and think you can take over? Humans are the worst."

"You did abandon this library," Lisa said. "How do we know you won't do it again?"

Fair question, but it wasn't one I had an answer to. How could I prove myself when I didn't know what the future would hold? All I could do was reassure them that I wanted to be here. Desperately.

"You've already thrown me out once and it didn't stick," I said. "I'll just keep coming back, no matter what you do to me. I love this library and now that I'm back, I'm not leaving it again. I want to make it like it was before, full of magic and people reading. Isn't that what you want too?"

The three exchanged wary glances. Was I wrong? Did they want something else?

"People bring nothing but problems," the demon said, crossing his arms over his chest. "We're doing fine on our own. We don't need you."

"Look around, the library's crumbling," I said softly. "Without patrons, it'll never get the story gods' blessing again and it will fade away. I'm sure you don't want that."

Mochi hopped off Roan's lap, looking downcast. His chitters were quieter as he laid down by Lisa. She patted his head softly. "Sometimes fading away is less painful than being rejected. Can you promise people won't abandon the library again if you manage to get them back?"

"Well, no, but you can't seriously be considering just letting the library fade away. What happens to you then?"

The demon shrugged. "We'll go back in our books like we do each night to rest and it'll be like we were never here."

I gripped the edges of my chair, swallowing hard. They couldn't really be okay with that, could they? I'd just met them, but the idea of them disappearing already bothered me. They were part of the library. My library.

"No, I don't accept that," I said firmly. "I won't let you give up on this library so easily. You have nothing to lose by letting me try to renovate it. I've already got a few ideas to make it more popular too, but you need to let me try."

"Oh?" Lisa leaned forward. "What ideas are those?"

"Well, this library is kind of hard to get to," I said. "It took Roan and I almost an hour to climb the mountain, so that's one of the reasons people choose the library in town instead. If we can fix that, we'll be able to get more people here."

Lisa and the panda nodded, reassuring me that I was on the right track, even though the demon continued to glare.

"To help with that," I said, "we need to make this library more of a destination location. The place everyone wants to go to no matter how far away it is. Like it's an experience more than just a library."

Roan leaned closer to whisper. "A destination location? Have you seen this place?"

"I want to not only repair it," I continued, ignoring Roan's and the demon's doubts, "but improve it. Add some cozy touches and amenities that other, newer, libraries have. We can think on it together if you want."

Mochi rolled over, wiggling happily as Lisa smiled. "Mochi says he's willing to give you a chance. He'll bring the snacks."

Yes! One down, two to go.

The demon groaned. "Mochi, how could you give into her so easily?"

"Maybe because he loves this library," I said.

"Love means different things to different people." He glared at us. "We just want to live our lives in peace until the library is gone. That's why we're here. So, I vote no."

My stomach dropped. Demon or not, how could he want that? I turned to Lisa, smiling with as much warmth as I could muster.

"Well, I vote for her to stay," Lisa said. "She's got good ideas and I'm not ready to give up yet. At least let her try."

I would have jumped for joy if the demon wasn't gripping his chair so hard I thought he might break the arms of it. Was two votes enough? Or was it an all or nothing kind of thing?

The silence in the room had me at the edge of my seat as the demon dragged his answer out, toying with me. The sun dipped beneath the horizon, casting shadows over his face and making him even more intimidating until the sun globes turned on.

"Why don't you leave"—the demon paused ominously, making my stomach tighten—"for today. It's getting late and I've been outvoted, so you'll be welcomed back."

"No way," I said, jumping out of my chair to stare him down. "It took me a whole day to get back inside last time. I'm not leaving, not even for a night!"

Roan cleared his throat. "So, does that mean you're sleeping here?"

"You bet I am."

The demon's lips curled up a tiny bit, almost like he was impressed by my tenacity. Or it was my imagination and he was actually disgusted with me.

"Then I'm staying too," Roan said, keeping a watchful eye on the others. "Can't let you get in trouble by yourself."

Mochi trotted over to us, holding wrapped sandwiches and drinks in his little paws. He dropped them in front of us, tilting his head back and forth. I glanced at Lisa, and she nodded, so I carefully pet his head. His fur was soft, smoother than any animal's I'd ever touched. Almost silken.

He purred, nuzzling into my hand for a moment before walking back to Lisa.

"He didn't want you to be hungry," she said.

That was the most adorable thing I'd ever seen.

"Where did he get the food though?" I asked.

The demon shrugged. "He always has something."

Interesting. Maybe they could pull things from their books? I'd have to ask Oren, see what he thought. Maybe he'd found something about the tree's magic in his research by now too. I picked the food and drinks up, following Lisa outside to a spiral staircase.

"There's a caretaker's room upstairs you can use. Try not to have too much fun," she said with a wink.

"Thank you."

I'd managed to convince them to let me stay for today, but tomorrow was another story. Determination strengthened my legs as I climbed the spiral staircase. My dream was finally in reach. I was really doing this. I was really going to reopen the library I'd loved so much as a child.

Tomorrow was the first day of my new adventure as a Misty Mountain librarian.

Chapter 7

Roan

Wild magic buzzed in the air like static, needling at me to pay attention. The library might not be haunted, but there was definitely something off about it.

Nyssa seemed to really believe that we could trust these creatures, and despite my hesitation, they hadn't given me a reason *not* to. Yet. I wanted to trust her, to believe that her instincts were right, but I knew all too well how fast wild magic could turn on people.

"Sleep well, cuties," Lisa said as she opened the door to the caretaker's room. "See you in the morning."

"Cuties?" I whispered to Nyssa, who just shrugged and covered a yawn.

Empty bookshelves lined the walls with a small table in the corner and a bed with a bookshelf headboard in the middle of the room. A side door opened into a bathroom with a large round tub inside. I didn't see anything suspicious though, no wild magic creations at least.

"Seems safe," I said, walking inside.

Nyssa followed and fell backward onto the bed with a sigh. "It's been a long day. I can't believe I won them over."

"What are they?" I asked as I took the chair by the table. "They had to have been created from wild magic, but they feel different than anything I've seen before. Wild magic usually changes and warps things that are already there, like the lending libraries, but these creatures feel different. New."

She turned to look at me, her beautiful auburn hair splayed out on the bed. "I think they're books."

"What?"

"I mean I think they're characters that somehow came out of their books." She sat up, excitement filling her eyes. "I recognized a few of them from stories I've read."

"No," I said, shaking my head, "that's not how wild magic works."

Or at least, no wild magic I'd seen before. But wild magic was....well, wild, so I guess it could do anything. Would the guild believe me if I said the library wasn't actually haunted, but full of books that had come alive? I set my sword on the table, laughing at myself. No way. They'd think I'd lost it.

"Okay, then what do you think they are?" she asked as she nibbled the sandwiches the panda had given us.

I scratched my head, at a loss. She'd been able to talk with them, reason with them, and they even made valid points back. They were sentient, that's for sure, but beyond that, I had no idea.

"We should bring some researchers here," I said.

"I've already got somebody working on it," she said, "besides, there's no way I'm letting strangers in on this just yet."

I leaned forward, elbows on my knees. "Aren't I a stranger?"

Her eyes darted to mine, long lashes blinking slowly as the corners of her eyes crinkled.

"Less and less," she said. "I wouldn't mind hearing more about you though. What's the guild like?"

"Full of possibilities. It's honestly a dream job. I get to travel the world, taking interesting missions and meeting all sorts of people. Nothing ever ties me down."

That last part was my own personal rule and the main reason I'd become an adventurer in the first place, but whenever I told people about it, they tried to fix me. Like there was something wrong with not wanting attachments. For right now, it's what I needed. Because that demon was right about one thing: humans were the worst sometimes.

Nyssa frowned, finishing up the last of her sandwich and handing me the other. "Isn't that lonely?"

Personal questions already, huh? I usually preferred to avoid those, but that might be hard if this job took more than a day or two. Might as well give her a few details.

"It's not that lonely. I partner up with other adventurers when I need to and go out with people often. There's something about only having a short time to get to know people that makes you experience it all the more deeply."

"So you'll be leaving soon then?" she asked, fiddling with the sandwich wrapper.

That downcast look of hers tugged at my resolve. "Well, not right away. I did lose the bet, so I'll help you repair the library."

"Ah, right, that bet," she said with a small smile, "almost feels like you *wanted* to stay."

Keeping her safe while I figured out what was going on here was part of my job, so the bet was just a means to an end. I didn't want her to send me away again though, so I went with it.

"Just for a bit," I said with a shrug. "This library's full of interesting things."

"Interesting things, huh?" Her gaze lifted to mine as a slight rosy hue spread across her cheeks.

That blush was beautiful. She was beautiful. Staying to help repair the library was one thing, but getting close to her was entirely different, especially since we were stuck in this room together all night.

Wait.

I glanced at the bed that Nyssa sat on, then around the room. How had that not crossed my mind earlier? There was only one bed.

"Something wrong?" she asked.

"No, just thinking about where I'm going to sleep..."

Her eyes widened, then she laughed. "You can have the bed. You are the one who traveled all the way here after a mission."

"What makes you think that?"

"Well unless you got that dirty walking," she paused, motioning at my clothes with her hand, "I'm guessing you ran into some trouble."

More like I was in such a rush to get back here that I slipped in some mud on the way up the mountain, but I wasn't about to admit that. No way. I had a reputation to uphold.

"Nothing I couldn't handle," I said, standing to stretch to cover up my embarrassment. "Why don't I go get cleaned up and you can get some sleep? I'll take the floor. I've slept in far worse places."

"I won't argue with that," she said, falling back on the bed again with a sigh. "But the bed is more than big enough for two."

I froze at the entrance to the bathroom. Was she offering to share the bed with me? When I glanced back, she was smiling so innocently that she had to know what I was thinking.

Oh, she was trouble.

I forced myself into the bathroom instead of taking her up on that offer, no matter how much I wanted to. Fleeting romances and one-night stands felt pretty hollow after a while and Nyssa deserved better than that. I should focus on the job, not on whatever I might be feeling right now.

Speaking of, I should update the guild. I pulled a piece of paper out of my jacket, jotting down a quick note. "I got inside the library. No signs of a haunting. More details soon."

I held the note in the air until flames licked the edges, sending my message to the guild like ash on the wind. There. That should hold them off for a bit. Now time for that bath.

My jacket was caked with mud and my clothes were dusty from the long trek here. I'd been sleeping outside for the past few weeks so I was really excited to have an enchanted laundry basin. I dropped my clothes in, brushing my hand over the cleaning crystal. Bubbles engulfed my clothes, lifting them in the air and spinning them so I could relax and take a bath.

I stepped into the waist high tub as water seeped through the stones, fulfilling its purpose before I even had to ask. Magic really was a wonderful thing. Before I could settle down, ice cold water touched my skin. I yelped. It was freezing!

"Everything okay in there?" Nyssa called out.

"Yeah, just fine!"

I searched for the heating stone, but the rune was already glowing. My breath caught in my chest as the freezing water rose up to my knees. I would not jump out of this tub and have Nyssa hear me. I would not.

When shivers swept through me, I pressed the stone for cold water on a whim. Glorious heat swept through the water. The runes were backward. Figures this rundown library would have mismatched runes too. I'd have to watch out for that elsewhere.

Steam curled around me as the water rose up to my waist. I sank into it, sighing with contentment. The heat dug into my muscles, easing the aches and pains from travel. It was always nice to rest and relax after a mission. The tub even had an angled top so I could rest my head back comfortably. It almost made up for that freezing water. Almost.

Something wet pressed against my cheek followed by a pop. My eyes snapped open. Shimmering bubbles filled the room, swirling around me like playful sprites.

Their iridescent sheen reminded me of wild magic storms, which might be why the tub was messed up. Magitek used careful programming to bind magic to crystals and runes, but wild magic liked to tweak that, causing all sorts of mayhem.

The bubbles pulsed in the air, growing bigger and smaller like they were breathing. Music chimed whenever they touched and light glinted off them like rainbows. Maybe this would be like the rest of the library and play nice? It was kind of cool looking.

I ducked underwater, running my hands through my hair quickly to clean up, but in that short time, the bubbles had gotten closer. They pressed up against me, popping explosively when they touched my skin. It tingled like my arm after lying on it too long, but it didn't hurt.

"Are you sure you're okay?" Nyssa asked, her voice right outside the door.

The bubbles merged around me, strengthening and pushing against my skin like they were searching for dirt to clean. I couldn't move, couldn't do anything but sit here. I reached for my sword, but realized I'd left it in the bedroom. Blast it.

This was why I should always take my sword with me to the bath. People laughed at me for it, but now I had a good reason. Wild magic frickin bubbles.

"So um, on second thought," I called out slowly, "could you, uh, bring me my sword?"

"Your sword?"

"Yes, and hurry," I said as the bubbles grew and multiplied. Soon there wouldn't be room for both of us in here.

The door opened after a few moments and Nyssa walked in, biting her lip to stop from laughing when she saw me. She had my sword though, loosely grasped in her hands.

"Now what?" she asked, gracefully not saying anything about the bubbles.

I sank deeper into the bath, face on fire. "Pop them with the sword. It'll absorb their magic."

At that she did laugh, but she went around the room popping bubble after bubble, dancing and laughing like a nymph in a bubble forest. When she got to the ones on me, she slowed, holding my sword out to me.

"Here, you can do these," she said.

I tried to take the hilt, but the bubbles wouldn't budge. They'd gone from easily poppable to firm. I stopped struggling, admitting bubble defeat.

"You can do it," I said, "but don't ever tell anyone about this."

"Whatever you say, big guy."

Mirth danced in her eyes as she carefully sliced each bubble, starting at my shoulders and working her way down. The bubbles had been covering me up pretty well, but the more she popped, the more naked I was. Her amusement turned to something else. That pretty pink blush was back as her gaze slowly traveled the length of my body.

"Think that's enough?" she asked, holding the sword out to me. "Your hands are free now."

Free to do what with? All thoughts of bubbles left me as steam dampened the curls around her face. She'd run in here without a thought, ready to help me with whatever wild magic was around. And now she was kneeling right beside me, making sure I was okay. If these bubbles weren't locking me in place, I might have kissed her.

The edge of her mouth curled into a smile as she leaned closer. "Your sword, Roan."

"Right, sorry."

I took it from her, and like the bubbles, the moment popped. She was already off investigating the wash basin. I freed myself from the last of the bubbles, and after making sure her back was turned, got out of the tub. I quickly wrapped a towel around my waist before inspecting the laundry where bubbles were still forming. At least my clothes were clean and dry, dropped on the counter next to it.

"Guess that's the cause, huh?" She pointed at the bubble crystals that must have been warped by wild magic. "I'll find somebody to take a look at them tomorrow. I already contacted a contractor about the holes in the roof and the windows earlier today, so what's one more thing?"

Her face fell, as if the weight of all the repairs was too much. She wasn't backing down though, just adding another thing to her list. There must have been a really important reason why she loved this library so much. I hoped she'd succeed with her plans. People who truly cared about something deserved to do well.

"Let me know how I can help," I said.

"Guess we'll have to see what you're good at then, huh?" She smiled, holding my clothes out to me. "I might enjoy that."

Water dripped down my chest, making me all too aware of my lack of clothes. This felt so uneven, her fully clothed and me with just a towel. The heat in her eyes made me want to say something, do something, but I didn't want her to think there could be anything between us. Instead, I took my clothes, pulling my shirt over my head as she left the room.

The heat left with her and I shivered, rushing to put the rest of my clothes on and join her in the bedroom.

"The contractor wants us to pull down all the old patching." Her voice was muffled behind her hand as she covered a yawn. "So we should get some rest. It'll be a long day tomorrow."

I opened a closet, hoping there would be extra blankets and pillows in there. Sure enough, it was well stocked. I pulled some out to make a cozy bed on the floor, but Nyssa frowned at them.

"The bed really is big enough for two," she said, "and I don't bite."

My skin tightened as warmth spread over me. I might like it if she did. "I'm really fine on the floor."

"Suit yourself," she said as she crawled under the covers. "Feel free to change your mind though."

She yawned again, then snuggled even deeper under the covers. I stood there frozen, instantly regretting my choice to sleep on the floor. She looked so cozy and the idea of cuddling with her scrambled my thoughts.

"Sleep well," she said, her voice thick with sleep already.

I laid out the first blanket out on the floor in front of the door. This was for the best. I was an adventurer in the middle of a library full of wild magic. I should be focused and on guard, not thinking about getting into bed with a beautiful woman like Nyssa.

I plopped down onto the still far too hard floor and leaned a pillow against the wall. This was fine. I'd slept in much more uncomfortable places before.

Nyssa's breathing slowed as she fell asleep, her hand hanging outside the blankets a bit. The urge to tuck her in was almost overwhelming, but I forced myself to close my eyes and ignore my thoughts.

This was going to be a long night...

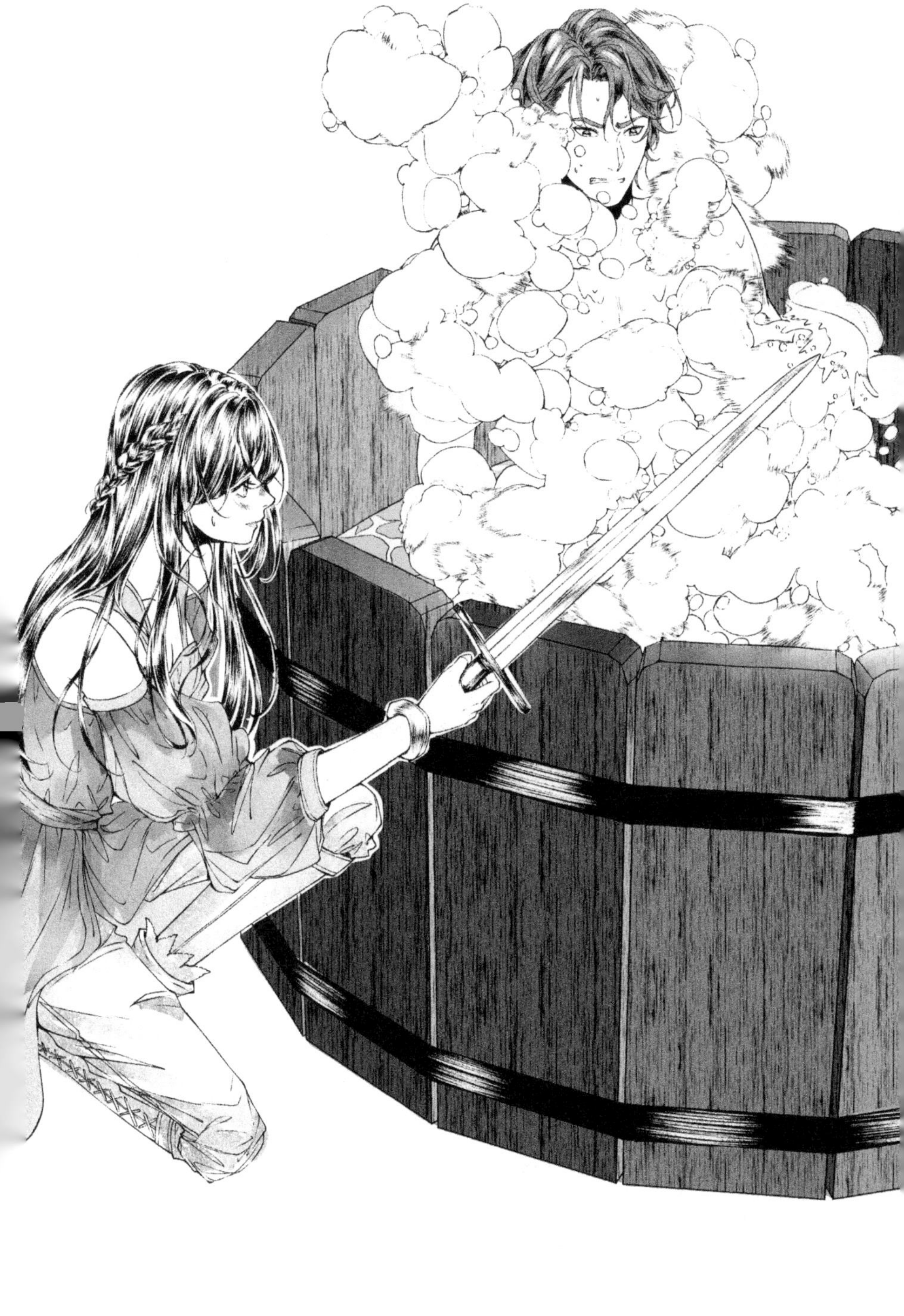

Chapter 8
Nyssa

The sounds of metal clinking pulled me from my dream, but my eyes were too heavy to open. I rolled over. Five more minutes.

Something pounced on my bed. I jerked awake as a slobbery dog tongue licked my face.

"Cerbie!" I said with a laugh, petting the three-headed puppy with vigor. "How'd you get in here?"

The room didn't look familiar. I rubbed the sleep from my eyes. I was in the library. Right. And the little knights climbing up the bedsheets as if they were a castle wall were totally normal. And so was the giant golem staring at me from outside the window even though we were on the second floor. Yup. It was all so normal that I didn't even blink an eye at the demon lounging next to a very fast asleep Roan.

Except, I somehow doubted an experienced adventurer would sleep that deeply.

"Uhhhh....Roan?" I called out as the knights finally made it to the top of the bed and started slapping each other on the backs like they'd won a great victory. "Roan!"

He jerked awake, stumbling to his feet. "I'm up, I'm up..."

"Ruining all my fun." The demon shook his head. "It took me a while to get those poppies from the golem for that sleeping spell, you know."

"You...you...," Roan's words were sluggish, "demon!"

I winced. Not his best insult, but it would have to do. Cerbie snuggled under the covers with me, heads resting on my lap. He was so adorable I couldn't help petting him, but I really didn't like the feel of all these eyes on me. Had the story spirits been watching us sleep?

One of the knights bowed to me. "Good morning, Lady Nyssa."

"Good morning," I said slowly. "Mind telling me what you're all doing here?"

The demon pushed off the wall. "I'm here to see what you're capable of, librarian. And they're here to escort you or something gallant like that."

He waved at the knights, who were bowing with a bit of a wobble because of the soft bed.

"Leave her alone," Roan said, shaking off the last of the sleep spell. "And don't use magic on me again."

Cerbie whined, heads looking between me and the demon.

"It's okay, Cerbie," I said, glaring at the frustrating demon. "We're all good, right? But if you're going to wake us up, you should at least tell us your name."

"Demon Lord is fine." His eyes hardened like I'd hit a nerve, so I wasn't going to ask about that Lord part. He sighed, petting Cerbie abruptly before turning to leave. "Follow me. You've got work to do."

Right, of course! I was supposed to be pulling all the patching down from the windows and roof to prepare for the contractors. They'd fit me in on short notice for a good cause, but I had to do as much as I could before they got here in a few days. They said they'd send over temporary sealant too.

"You're such a good boy," I said, petting Cerbie one last time before getting out of bed, trying not to jostle the knights. "Even the Demon Lord can't resist him."

Saying that felt so weird, like we were talking about a King. What story had he come out of? And were there more demons around?

"I'm sure he could resist if he wanted to." Roan stared after the Demon Lord, not moving to follow him. "I shouldn't have let them get past me. I'm sorry."

So much chaos and I'd only been awake a few minutes. I stretched my hands up toward the ceiling, then patted him on the shoulder. "It's fine. They were probably just curious about us. I'm sure they didn't mean any harm."

He frowned, scratching the back of his head. "I don't know about that. Why'd the demon spell me then?"

"They did say they'd had troubles with adventurers before," I said. "So maybe that has something to do with it?"

Recognition flickered in Roan's eyes and his lips parted slightly, like he'd just put something together. "That makes sense. I'll do better from now on."

Apparently, he wasn't going to share whatever he'd learned with me. It probably had to do with the rumors about this being a haunted library, but I knew those were false, so I let it go for the moment.

"Let me just get cleaned up quick and then we'll head downstairs," I said.

"Remember not to wash your clothes."

I clamped my lips together, resisting the urge to laugh at the image of him stuck in the bath covered in giant bubbles. That had been unexpectedly fun. "I've got extra outfits in the cart downstairs."

"I'll go grab them." Roan shooed the knights and Cerbie out the door ahead of him. "Be right back."

I hurried to get ready, gratefully accepting my bags when Roan came back, and then headed downstairs to start working. We had so much to get done, and I wanted to start off strong.

The library was already bursting with liveliness as the story spirits chatted and wandered around. Roan's back tensed, as if he was getting ready to go into battle. Ever since we woke up, he'd been on guard, like he didn't want to get caught unaware again. His dedication was admirable and it did make me feel safer, just in case something strange happened.

"Let's start with the windows," I said.

Wooden planks covered the damaged windows from the inside, but they weren't nailed on like I expected. I wedged my finger between them and the window, tugging to see if they'd come off easily, but the wood just creaked. It was like they'd grown out of the library's wall and looped over the window.

Libraries often repaired themselves, but not like this. This patch was sloppy, thrown on top of the library instead of blending in. Something else did this, probably because the library was too low on magic to heal, but figuring that out wasn't really important right now. We just needed to fix it and move on to the next item on the list.

"We're going to have to saw these off," I said. "Without damaging the walls too much, hopefully."

Roan nodded, sawing away at the planks while I held them steady. In no time at all, he had all the wood off the window and the sun was shining through brilliantly. I knocked out the broken panes of glass as well, making sure they landed safely outside to collect later, and put up a temporary seal on the window.

I stood back, admiring our work. "That wasn't so hard. Only six to go!"

Thundering steps crashed through the library as the golem raced toward us, eyes wide. It roared loud enough to make my bones tremble. Uh oh. What did we do to upset it this time? I thought we'd worked everything out, but apparently not.

"Hello, I was just—"

The golem roared as it swept me up in its giant hand. My stomach lurched as I swung through the air, a feeling that was all too familiar. It was going to throw me out just like last time! No way. Not again.

"Hey!" I shouted, slapping my hand against its vine and dirt shoulder. "The leaders and I made a deal. You can't throw me out. I'm just repairing the library like I told them I would!"

The golem ignored me, marching past the Demon Lord who was grinning from ear to ear.

"Mind helping?" I shouted at him.

"I think you're doing just fine on your own," he said, shoulders shaking with laughter.

Damn demons. I was trying to help and he knew it, so what was this golem's problem? It didn't charge over until *after* I'd pulled the first patch down. If the library hadn't made those, then maybe the golem had?

And if that was true, then it had also seen me tearing them down like they meant nothing at all. I sighed. No wonder it was upset. I needed a golem-human communications guide.

Roan raced after me, stabbing his sword into the golem's leg and using it like a climbing axe. The golem didn't seem to notice as it trudged on, opening the library doors wide. I'd get thrown out before Roan even reached me.

What should I do? In the book, the golem barely listened to anyone except the little girl it rescued. How did she get through to it? Think, think. That's right, she asked the golem for everything, phrasing things in a way that it felt like it was being useful. That it was needed by somebody.

"Golem!" I shouted. "I'm sorry about the patches. You did a wonderful job with them, really."

Its steps slowed as it knelt to leave the library. "Ruined my work."

"You're right," I said as Roan climbed up to join me. I shook my head, not wanting him to do anything just yet. "I'm sorry, golem. It's my fault, but I needed to take them down so we could make the library even better. Could you help me with that?"

Its glowing eyes shone bright. "How?"

Roan raised an eyebrow, as if asking the same thing.

I mouthed, "I don't know."

He sighed, tilting his head up. "You could help her reach the patches on the ceiling."

"That's right!" I nodded, grinning at Roan for the help. "Only a tall and sturdy golem could help me with that. There's no way I'd reach the ceiling otherwise and still feel safe. But with you helping me, I'd have nothing to worry about."

Its body shifted and groaned as it swung us back into the library, pausing to stare at the ceiling. "My patches are good."

"Yes, they're very good," I said. "But they were temporary to protect the library from the weather outside. Now they can get repaired fully, all thanks to your hard work."

"Really?" The golem's eyes glowed brighter as it headed back, open door forgotten. "No tricks?"

Sadness tinged its voice, reverberating through me as I remembered the times the golem had been tricked in its story. I should have been more careful, inspected the patches better before tearing them down. I could have asked who made them, but no, I'd been so eager to get the job done that I'd rushed in and yanked them down.

"I promise, no tricks." I patted around one of the poppies on its shoulder, inhaling the rather earthy scent of them.

I might be the librarian here, but it was in name only. These story spirits had been living here for years. If I ignored that, they'd keep throwing me out no matter what deals I made. Maybe I should try working *with* them instead.

"Why don't we use those planks for something else?" I asked. "Like a raised garden?"

At that, the flowers on its shoulders perked up. "Really? For me?"

"Yup, you can tend to it however you want. It'll make the library beautiful, so you'd really be helping me out."

"Golem's garden!" It shouted as it lunged forward, almost knocking Roan and I off our perch on its shoulder.

Roan wrapped his arm around me, clinging to the vines to keep us from falling. My heart pounded in my chest as my head spun from looking down. That would be a long fall.

"Thanks," I said, squeezing Roan's arm.

He tightened his grip, securing me to him and the golem. "Just try not to make it mad or excited or anything else until we're back on the ground, okay?

"Deal."

We rocked against the golem as it took long strides back into the middle of the library, Roan's arm was warm and comforting around me. He'd raced up this golem without a second's hesitation. I'd read about people like that, sure, but never thought somebody would do something like that for me in real life. My chest warmed, feeling a bit giddy over having my very own hero.

Once the golem's steps slowed, Roan helped me climb up by its neck. Above us was the largest hole in the roof, complete with golem-made patching over it. It really was pretty nice that the golem had done that, otherwise the library would have been flooded and even more warped over the years.

"Stay," the golem said. "I'll fix."

Then it reached its massive hand up to the ceiling, dim green light glowing around it. As it grew brighter, the wood patching curled away from the ceiling, twisting and coiling around the golem's hand before settling into its arm like bones inside a skeleton.

"That was awesome," I said, breathless.

The golem reached out his glowing hand to me. "New patch?"

Right. He must have seen me use the temporary patching before. I carefully scooted down its shoulder, landing softly in its palm. Roan followed me, both of us fitting on the golem's hand without a problem. My stomach flipped as we moved closer to the ceiling, high enough for me to assemble the temporary clear patch.

"All done," I said, gazing out at the library below, my arm on Roan's to stay balanced.

Even though it was warped and damaged, it was still the most beautiful library I'd ever seen. I could spot my favorite reading nook from here and the children's section that had held so much adventure for me. Was the golem's book still there, perfectly placed on the shelf? I should go read it again.

The Demon Lord looked small from up here, like all the world's problems melted away from another perspective.

"Beautiful," Roan whispered. "Absolutely beautiful."

"I know, right? This library is amazing."

He tucked a stray hair behind my ear, his hand brushing softly against my cheek. "I meant you."

My lips parted as I stared at him, hand still grasping his arm as my heart thundered in my chest. He thought I was beautiful?

"I mean yeah, the library is great," Roan said, dropping his hand as he laughed awkwardly. "You're doing really good work here!" His voice was overly enthusiastic, and a faint blush rose on his cheeks.

I bit my lip to stop the grin from spreading across my face. "Thank you. For that and for coming up here after me."

His smile felt warmer than the sun shining down from the hole in the roof. Maybe there was more here for me than fixing the library.

Chapter 9
Nyssa

I leaned back against the book tree's withered trunk with a sigh. We'd spent the entire day pulling down patches, but the view from high up on the golem had made one thing clear: this library was in dire need of more repairs than I could count.

From the windows and the roof to the floor and the bookshelves, it seemed like everything was at least a bit damaged. That's what happened after years of neglect, no matter how hard the story spirits tried to prevent it.

Would I have the money for all these repairs? Not to mention the money for improvements and books too? The Tomekeeper's Endowment could only cover so much.

If I couldn't manage all of those things perfectly, nobody would make the long trek here and this library would fade away so a new library could be born. As if it was that easy to replace something important. I wouldn't let all the wonderful memories I'd had here as a child fade away too. I'd visited other libraries, sure, but none of them felt like this one.

I'd met my first real friend in this library, learned to read, and got lost in so many wonderful stories. If I let that go, then nobody else would get to experience that like I did. They'd miss out on all the wonder the Misty Mountain Library had to offer and that would be such a monumental loss.

This library had helped me so much growing up, giving me a place to belong and feel welcome no matter what was going on in my life, so I wanted to help it in return. It deserved to be saved.

But what if I'd bitten off more than I could chew? Books were my thing, not damaged floors and withered book trees. Reading would help bring the magic back a bit since it recharged book trees over time, but I was only one person and could only read so much. This library needed serious help, maybe more than I could give it.

"You okay?" Roan asked as he eased himself onto the floor next to me. "You kind of lost your spark halfway through."

Lost my spark, huh? I pulled my knees to my chest, resting my head on them. "I'm fine, just a bit worried I won't be able to pull this off like I thought." Admitting that, even quietly, felt wrong. I gripped my knees tight. "No, it's really fine. I'll make it work."

"I think you mean we. *We'll* make it work." He stretched his arms out, sighing contentedly. "I'm here to help. Use me however you see fit."

I glanced at him sideways. "How good are you at replacing old wood floors?"

"Uhhh....I'm sure I could learn." He shrugged, an easy smile gracing his lips.

"Helpful," I said with a laugh, but fell silent when Cerbie started barking. "That's weird, the only time I've heard him bark was when I first came in."

Roan got to his feet, suddenly at full attention. "I'll check it out."

I hurried after him, hoping the contractors had shown up early. I hadn't had time to convince the story spirits that they'd have to hide when people were here, but I'd figure something out. Nobody would feel safe around a forest golem, let alone a Demon Lord! The inevitable fight was already giving me a bit of a headache.

A tall, lanky man stood in the doorway, telltale glasses and suspenders giving him away.

"Oren!" I called out, waving. "What are you doing here?"

And why did the story spirits let him in? They'd forced me to use tricks to back get inside, but him they just opened the doors for? Lucky duck.

"You know him?" Roan asked, sword in hand.

"Yeah, he's the researcher I told you about," I said, petting Cerbie to calm him down. "You're such a good guard dog!"

Cerbie preened under my hands, tail wagging fiercely.

Oren's eyes lit up. "Is that a three-headed dog?"

"Hello to you too," I said, "this is Cerbie."

Before Oren had even taken two steps toward us, he spotted the golem and changed directions, his curiosity getting the better of his manners once again. Roan frowned, looking at me like he had a million questions.

"Oren's the one looking into the book tree's depleted magic for me," I said. "I joined the guild at the same time as him and he's the best researcher I know. Once he's interested in something, he won't stop until he knows everything about it. Perfect guy for the job."

"So you trust him?" When I nodded, Roan sheathed his sword. "Good enough for me. Seems like he's going to be a handful, like you, walking straight up to wild magic without a care in the world."

"Hey now!"

Roan chuckled as he walked over to Oren. "My name's Roan. I'm an adventurer helping out."

Oren stuck his hand into a gap in the golem's vines and dirt, a gleeful smile on his face. "What story is he from?"

Roan glanced back at me, hand still outstretched in greeting.

"*The Gentle Giant*," I said, shrugging at Roan and whispering, "sorry, but he'll be useless until he inspects all the story spirits."

"Story spirits?" the Demon Lord asked, disdain in his voice. "Is that what you're calling us?"

I was hoping he'd gone back into his book to sleep for a while, but apparently, I wasn't so lucky. I honestly hadn't seen any of the books the story spirits had come out of, almost like they were hiding them. Which made sense since they were part of who they were, but I still wished I knew more about them.

The best way to overcome a difficult situation was to learn more about it. Even when that situation was a Demon Lord.

"Oren, meet the Demon Lord," I said. "And before you ask, I have no idea what story he's from. He won't even tell me his name."

The Demon Lord clicked his tongue against his teeth. "Is my name really that important?"

"Names have power," Oren said as he joined us, "so I'm guessing that's why you don't want us to know?"

Roan sighed. "Maybe he just doesn't have one. You know, like he's a side character?"

"What did you just call me?" the Demon Lord hissed, shadows swirling around him. "I am nobody's side character."

Roan and the Demon Lord looked like they were about to duke it out until Oren butted in to examine the shadows, turning this way and that as they followed him.

"Ohhhh, look at those shadows," Oren said, poking and prodding the Demon Lord. "How do you create them? Are you really a demon? What's that like?"

I winced. "Ummm...Oren? Maybe you shouldn't poke a Demon Lord."

"Right." He took a step back. "Sorry about that. I've been told I'm overeager sometimes."

The Demon Lord crossed his arms, but reigned in his shadows. "You humans seem to keep multiplying. Why?"

"Good question." Even if it was phrased horribly. I turned to Oren, tilting my head. "Why are you here?"

Oren readjusted his glasses. "I talked to a dryad that tends to magical libraries. She gave me a device that gauges the trees' magic levels so we can see where this library falls on the magic scale."

I hadn't expected him to come all the way here to look into it, but I was grateful. I could always count on his need to solve a puzzle.

"Come take a look then," I said, motioning to the middle of the library. "The tree might look withered, but it's still alive, I know that much."

Roan hung back, keeping his eye on the Demon Lord as I showed Oren the book tree. Roan didn't seem to trust the story spirits. I was happy he was being careful, but even the Demon Lord hadn't done anything to actually hurt us.

I didn't think any of the story spirits meant us harm, but if I couldn't convince Roan of that, how was I supposed to convince anyone else? I worried my lip, picturing patrons screaming and running for the hills after seeing the story spirits. What was I supposed to do with them when I reopened the library?

"Whoa," Oren said as we approached the tree, "that really doesn't look healthy."

Its dry, leafless branches reminded me of a tree from a horror novel. But it was still this library's book tree and I loved it, just as much as when it was bright and full of books. No matter what it looked like, it was the heart of this library.

Oren pulled a clear crystal from his pocket and held it up to the book tree. "The brighter green it shines, the more magic the tree has."

We waited a bit until faint light brightened the crystal, but instead of green, a kaleidoscope of colors burst out.

"And what's rainbow mean?" I asked, trying not to wince.

The shifting colors illuminated Oren's face, glinting off his glasses. "It means this tree isn't running on normal library magic. It's filled with wild magic instead!" His eyes widened as he examined it, moving the crystal this way and that. "But even that's running low."

"Is it fixable?" I asked softly, hating even bringing it up. "Or is it..."

I couldn't even bring myself to say it: dying.

Oren ran his hand over the bark. "It's alive, but it really needs a blessing from the story gods. Sooner rather than later."

Libraries received their blessings at the end of the month-long Tales and Tomes Festival as a final ceremony to close the celebration out and honor all the new books that were created.

"But the festival's already started." Panic gripped me like a vise. "And these repairs will take months, not weeks. Can't we find a way to keep it going until next year's festival? I'll read every day, all day, if that's what it takes."

Oren sighed, shaking his head. "Reading will help, but not enough to last until next year. It's like using old magic crystals. You can refill them as much as you want, but eventually, they just won't store magic like they used to and they'll need to be replaced. The blessing will make this tree new again. That's the only thing that will save it."

I sank onto the floor near the tree, feeling the urge to be near it, touching its bark. "There has to be another way."

"The dryads gave me something," Oren said, "but it's just a band-aid, not a fix. You'll still need to participate in the festival."

The festival wasn't something you just haphazardly joined. It was a huge event, full of people writing new books and celebrating old ones. It was a sacred month where everyone connected to the story gods more than any other time of the year. If I opened this library and nobody showed up, the story gods would take that as a sign.

But Oren wasn't giving me much choice. I had to make this work somehow. The library needed me to.

"Okay," I said, "please help however you can."

He rummaged through his pockets, patting down his clothes with a panicked look on his face.

"You did bring this magical fix with you, right?" I asked calmly. Oren was notorious for losing things or putting them in weird places. "Please tell me you have it."

"Of course I do." He dipped his hands into another pocket. His face lit up as he pulled out a bright green vial. "Here it is! The dryads said this was concentrated story magic, almost like nutrients for the tree so it can absorb more magic from reading."

"Oh, that's wonderful!" I eyed the vial as if it was filled with gold. "How does it work?"

He tipped it over, pouring it in a circle around the tree's roots with a shrug. "Like that? Now you really do need to read as much as you can. And make sure they're different books too, preferably ones you haven't read before, so your imagination is really sparking. The library will eat that reading magic right up."

I smiled, always loving the idea that me reading could help the library, but then my gaze fell on the mostly empty bookshelves.

"We don't have very many books yet," I said. "I was going to hold off on buying any until after we reopened. The repairs are going to take up my whole endowment I think."

Oren frowned. "What's the point of spending tons of money on repairs if you don't have enough books to draw in patrons? People don't come to libraries for the *looks*, they come for the *books*." He grinned. "But seriously, buy more books. Make everyone read them."

He was right. Books were too important to ignore and if reading new ones really would recharge the book tree faster, then I had to give it a try.

"Okay," I said. "I'll order a bunch of books and we'll have a read-a-thon to save the library!"

"That's the spirit!"

I held my hand up for a high-five, but ended up covering up a yawn instead. "Sorry, it's been another long day. And we have more work to do tomorrow." Wait. Two people in one bedroom was already pushing it, but three? "Umm...I'll sleep in the library and you can have the caretaker's room."

"No, don't worry about me," Oren said. "I'm more than happy to stay up all night talking to these story spirits. I couldn't sleep even if I tried."

"You sure?"

He was already wandering off, waving over his shoulder. "Mmmhmm."

Okay, well I guess that left me to keep the caretaker's room then. I paused, my hand on the railing of the spiral staircase. Was Roan going to join me again or would he be staying up with Oren? If I went to sleep without telling him, he might feel too awkward to use the room too.

What to do, what to do...

"Hey Roan?" I called out, waiting for him to head over. "I'm uh, heading to bed. Feel free to share the room again if you want."

He nodded. "Okay, that sounds good. I can protect you better that way."

"Focus on sleep. I'll be fine."

But it had felt nice having him there when I woke up surrounded by story spirits. He had this comforting aura about him, like he could take care of anything. That probably wasn't true, nobody was that perfect, but I liked the feeling anyway.

We walked up the stairs together the same as yesterday, but it felt different now. We'd worked so closely today that I was aware of every time his body brushed against mine or the way his eyes lit up when I caught his gaze.

I opened the door to the room, walking past the blankets he'd slept on. "Are you going to sleep there again? Or..."

Join me in the bed? Somehow the easy offer I'd made last night held more weight now. If we shared the bed, I had a feeling I wouldn't get a wink of sleep. But the floor couldn't have been comfortable, no matter what he said, and the bed really was pretty big.

"Or?" Roan asked, grinning wickedly. "I seem to remember you offering to share the bed?"

I raised an eyebrow. "And I seem to remember you declining that offer."

He laughed. "True, I really am fine on the floor."

"Okay, if you're sure..."

When he nodded, I went into the bathroom to get ready, grateful I still had another change of clothes for tomorrow. The contractors would be here soon and could hopefully fix the laundry crystals. Otherwise, we'd be going clothes shopping.

After a refreshing bath, I dried myself off and headed to the bedroom. Roan watched me closely as I passed by, his lips parted slightly.

I awkwardly picked up a book, flipping through the pages without actually reading them. "Oren said we should read to recharge the library's magic. So I'll be doing that for a bit."

I'd never shared a room with somebody long term before, so I wasn't sure what the protocol was. Did we have to go to sleep at the same time to turn the lights off? Or could I go to sleep while he was still up? Right, like that was a real possibility while he was moving to take his own bath, filling my mind with images of bubbles.

Each one I'd popped had revealed more of his well-toned body. That was some crafty wild magic. I almost wished it would happen again...

I slammed my book shut. No. That was ridiculous. I should just go to sleep. But even after crawling under the blankets, I couldn't stop picturing him. The sounds of water moving as he bathed filled my mind. He'd be done soon and then I could sleep. Right.

Ugh. This was hopeless. I got up, flinging the closet door open to grab some pillows. I stacked them along the middle of the bed, creating a wonderful pillow wall any fort-builder would be proud of.

There. Now Roan could share the bed with me and not feel awkward about it. And I could sleep in peace without the urge to cuddle up next to him.

Soft laughter drew my attention. "What's with the pillows?"

"They're for you. So you don't have to feel weird about sharing the bed."

My face felt hot, so I burrowed under the blankets, fully expecting him to take the floor still. I almost jumped when the bed creaked as he sat down.

"Are you sure?" he asked. "I honestly would feel more comfortable here." Comfortable? So he did want to share the bed? My pulse raced at the thought as he continued talking. "If the creatures come back again, they'll have to get through me to get to you."

Oh. So that's what he meant by more comfortable. He'd be a better guard if he shared the bed with me.

I dug my fingers into the mattress, not sure how to respond. "Let's get some sleep. We've got a lot of work to do tomorrow."

The bed shifted as he slipped under the blankets, with nothing but my silly pillow wall separating us.

Chapter 10

Roan

This bed was cozier than the ones in the inns I usually stayed at, soft and warm. There wasn't anyone talking in other rooms or the sounds of a busy dining room downstairs either. It was way better than roughing it outside too.

I shifted, my fingers brushing against Nyssa's arm resting on my chest. Her body felt nice and warm and her deep, even breathing almost made me doze off again. I hadn't woken up next to anyone in a while and it reminded me how much I craved it. I started to pull Nyssa closer—

Wait. My eyes snapped open, my heart beating frantically. The pillows she'd built into a nice respectful wall were strewn all over the bed and Nyssa was snuggled up against me like *I* was her pillow.

Her hair had fallen over her face in delicate strands, her eyelids fluttering like she was still deep in a dream. My mouth went dry. She was breathtaking, but this was the exact situation I hadn't wanted to happen. Getting close to her was just going to make leaving harder.

She nuzzled her head against my shoulder, letting out a soft mmmm noise that made my arms twitch with the desire to pull her even closer. My body seemed to have a will of its own, but it felt so good I almost didn't want to fight it. We were just cuddling, was that really so bad?

Man, she really destroyed that pillow wall. I smiled, spotting a few of them on the floor. She must be a restless sleeper, tossing and turning, but right now she looked so peaceful I didn't have the heart to move. She'd been working hard. The least I could do was lie here with her for a bit longer while she slept.

Her fingers curled into my chest like they were digging into the fabric of my heart. My skin tingled everywhere it touched hers. I took a deep breath to relax.

This was exactly why I shouldn't have shared a bed with her in the first place. She was too comfortable, lulling me into a false sense of security. I should get up now, go get ready for the day while she slept.

"G'morning," Nyssa mumbled, sleep making her voice raspy.

I froze. What was I supposed to say in this situation? Everything in me wanted to stay in bed with her all day, but I knew I had to move. Had to get away before these feelings started growing.

Flirt. That's what I'd do. She always snapped back when I did that.

"Good morning, gorgeous," I said in a low voice.

Her body tensed as her eyes slowly opened. "Why are you..." Her eyes widened and she jerked away from me. "I am so sorry! I didn't mean to do that."

"It's fine, we both needed the sleep." I forced a grin, already missing the warmth of her next to me. "I'd let you use me as a pillow any day."

She groaned, putting her head in her hands. "Never again. We're never talking about this again."

"Ouch, you wound me. But I can agree to that." I propped myself up on my elbow, leaning toward her. "But I can't promise I won't think about it."

A faint smile brushed her lips before she pushed me away. "Just get ready, will you? We've got a job to do."

"What's on the list today?" I asked, happy to have something else besides her adorable sleepy smile to focus on.

"Finishing up the patches, making the golem a garden, and"—she tilted her head at me—"fixing up the lending libraries?"

I'd almost forgotten about those little boxes that had followed us up here with their rickety doors and faded paint. She'd joked about me fixing them, but that meant interacting with the wild magic creatures one on one, helping them. What would the guild have to say about that?

That was a problem for future me. Right now, I was just a volunteer at a little library on a mountain.

"For you, I'll do that whole list and more," I said with a smile.

"Just the lending libraries is fine," she said as she went to get ready. "Oren will probably help you too."

Right. The other librarian who was researching the creatures for Nyssa. I could use that time to get more details on the creatures and how safe he really thought they were. Was he why we didn't wake up to an audience again?

I rustled through my pack, grabbing my last change of clothes.

"You ready?" Nyssa asked, poking her head outside the bathroom.

"Give me just a few more minutes."

After I finished up, we headed downstairs to see Oren having tea with the red panda in a circle of creatures all chatting animatedly. When the red panda saw us, it placed two more mugs on the table followed by rice balls and fresh fruit. If my stomach wasn't growling, I'd have asked where it kept getting all the food from.

It hadn't hurt us yet, so I was just going with it for now, but what was with the magic here? It felt wild, but it seemed stable. That was good enough for now.

"Thank you, Mochi," Nyssa said as she accepted a steaming mug of tea. "This is just what I needed."

The red panda chittered happily at her as it moved back and forth on its chair. Oren rubbed his eyes, looking like he might fall asleep right there if the creature librarian, Lisa, wasn't keeping his attention.

She sipped her tea, glancing at us. "So, how did you sleep?"

"Fine." I was not about to talk about my sleeping arrangements with a wild magic creature, no matter how human-like she acted. "Hey Oren, want to help me fix up the lending libraries outside?"

Nyssa's eyes widened. "You don't need to start right now. You can eat."

I could, but then I'd be having breakfast with a bunch of story spirits. No. Creatures. I had to keep calling them that otherwise I'd start treating them like normal people. One of us needed to stay objective just in case this all went sideways.

"It's fine," Oren said with a yawn. "The lending libraries showed me the way here, so I should thank them anyway."

Great. The tension in my shoulders eased as we made our way outside, but something tugged at my clothes. I glanced down to see the red panda holding out sandwiches.

"Mochi doesn't want you to be hungry," Lisa said, her kind eyes studying me. "He wants you to feel comfortable here."

The red panda was standing tall on two legs, holding out the food to me like an offering. It tilted its head this way and that, chittering as if asking me why I wasn't taking it. It was honestly too sweet to ignore.

I broke down and took the sandwiches. "Thank you."

Mochi spun in a circle, tail swishing back and forth as he raced back to Nyssa. She bent down to pet him, whispering something soothing to him that I couldn't quite make out.

I felt myself walking back toward them, but stopped. Nyssa had already proven to be too cozy and distracting, not to mention the whole warm vibe of this place and everyone eating together. Every time I'd given into something like that, my world had fallen apart.

It was better to keep my distance for now.

Eventually, I'd find a place I could settle down with people who genuinely cared about me, but for now, I had work to do and wild magic to investigate.

"So," Oren said, pausing as he held the door open for me, "I'm guessing you didn't just invite me out here to fix lending libraries."

"Why do you think that?"

His eyebrows raised skeptically. "Because you barely know me, you don't seem to like the story spirits, and Nyssa obviously wanted you to stay and eat with her. All of that points to you having a reason for asking me to talk alone."

"I'm really that easy to read, huh?" I said with a laugh, walking outside to find the lending libraries. They were slowly hopping around the empty book cart, their roofs drooping and their doors hanging open. "Hold on a minute."

I ducked back inside the library to grab a few books, remembering how the lending libraries got excited when Nyssa gave them each one. It would be much easier to talk to Oren if the lending libraries weren't depressed and causing problems. I'd just give them some books and ask them to sit still while we repaired them.

When I walked outside, they turned to me, racing over in big leaps like they were dogs who'd caught the scent of meat.

"Calm down," I said, holding a book in the air. "If I give you these books, will you sit still while we repair you? We've got new latches and paint to freshen you up."

Oren frowned as the lending libraries stood stock still. "Huh, I didn't expect that. You're really good with them."

"Just doing what Nyssa did."

If I treated them like puppies, it was much easier to ignore the fact that they were inanimate objects moving with a wild-magic fueled life of their own. Oren ushered them over to a picnic table while I grabbed the sandpaper, paint, hinges, and latches from the cart. This cart was starting to feel like one of those magical bags that never ran out of space and you could find anything in.

"So about these...story spirits," I said. "Do you think they're dangerous?"

I grabbed a piece of sandpaper and started sanding down the old rough paint on the lending libraries. They stayed true to their unspoken word and didn't move very much, which was nice. I could almost pretend they were normal.

Oren took a piece of sandpaper and joined me. "Well, I've only been here a day, but I don't think so. They seem like they're connected to the library somehow, none of them willing to leave it or do anything that might damage it. The way they talk about this place feels like they're talking about their best friend."

"And that means...?"

"That they wouldn't do anything that would risk harming the library," he said, moving to the next lending library. "If that's true, then they probably wouldn't do anything to hurt people inside it either."

"Probably?" I paused, sanding an extra rough spot smooth. "How can we be sure though? Nyssa is determined to stay here and get patrons back. I can't let that happen if it means putting people at risk."

I hadn't said that to anyone yet, but it was the truth. Sure, I'd turned a blind eye to the wild magic here for now, but I had to know if it was dangerous before anyone else got involved. The guild would knock me down to E-rank if I let a library full of people get attacked.

"What does Nyssa think about that?" Oren asked as he opened a bucket of paint. When I didn't answer, he looked up at me. "Wait, you did tell her, didn't you?"

"Not exactly, but I will."

Oren shook his head. "I don't know what's going on between you two, but she seems happy. Don't screw it up by keeping secrets."

"I think you've got the wrong idea about us," I said, brushing sawdust off one of the lending libraries. "She's happy because she's back in the library she loves and I'm just here helping out for a bit. I'll be gone once I'm sure this place isn't a danger to anyone."

"Okay." Oren raised an eyebrow. "I'll do more research. See if we can find a solid answer for you."

We worked in silence for a bit after that, sanding and eventually painting once the sawdust blew away. Oren was supposedly a great researcher, so if I let him handle the wild magic research, then I could keep focusing on the physical repairs. But my mind kept drifting back to Nyssa, wishing she'd walk out here and check on us or wondering what she was doing inside.

That woman was always doing something unexpected...

"So, how well do you know Nyssa?" I asked.

"Pretty well," Oren said, spreading a not so perfect line of paint across a lending library. "I was kind of a mess when I first joined the guild, always dropping things and miscategorizing books, so she ended up helping me out a lot. She's always been kind like that, helping anyone who needed it. We became friends after that, helping each other become the best librarians we could be." He smiled softly. "I'm glad she finally found her way back here. It was all she talked about for years. I had thought she was going through a breakup when she called me one night devastated, but she'd just heard how rundown this place was."

"Sounds like her," I said, remembering how excited she was on her way up the mountain the first day. "I really want to trust these creatures for her sake, but I also don't want anything to happen to her. You didn't see how the golem reacted when she tore down its patchwork. It was furious."

Or how the bubbles pinned me down in the bathtub, but I wasn't about to admit that one.

"If there's one thing I know about Nyssa." Oren raised his paintbrush. "It's that if she says she can do something, she's going to do it. She's not a foolish risk-taker. If she thought she couldn't handle the story spirits, she wouldn't be doing this. Give her a little faith."

That was true. She certainly didn't back down from a challenge.

I'd have asked more, but a chivalry of knights appeared at my feet. "How can we help, Sir Roan?"

"We're good here." I tried to ignore them, but they climbed up the picnic table. "Really, we've got this, but thank you."

"But sir, this is our library too," the commander said. "We must help in the restoration efforts!"

Oren grinned. "You can help me, if you want."

The knights whispered amongst themselves, glancing between Oren and me. I got the strange feeling that they wanted something from me by how they kept staring, but I continued painting as if they weren't there. Once that dried, I could add the new latches to keep the books in and we'd be done.

"We are warriors here to help another warrior," the commander said, bowing politely at Oren. "Sorry good sir, but we must decline."

"Well then, I guess I'll leave you to it," Oren said, lips pressed together to stop from laughing.

I rubbed my forehead. "Thank you, but I really don't need your help."

That seemed to encourage them even more as they hauled a latch up one of the lending libraries, stabbing into the wood with their swords.

"Hey, you're going to damage them even more." I picked up the knight commander. "Just go back inside and play with the dragons or something."

The tiny man's eyes widened. "Play? With dragons? You must have no idea what a dragon's capable of. They burn villages, kidnap princesses, and destroy whole fields of crops just for fun. We do not play with dragons here. We fight them!"

The rest of his men cheered, clanking their swords against their armored chests and scurrying up the other lending libraries, getting paint everywhere. A headache pounded behind my eyes.

I couldn't handle dealing with the lending libraries *and* these knights. Especially not when I saw the telltale signs of dragon fire out of the corner of my eye. The last thing we needed was a dragon fight scorching the lending libraries.

"Sorry, but this is for your own good," I said as I picked the knights up one by one, putting them inside the libraries where the books would go. I attached the new latches and locked them in. "There, peace and quiet. Now what were we talking about, Oren?"

His mouth dropped open. "Are you sure that's okay?"

"They've got air holes."

And they were wild magic creations, not real knights. They came from a book and were just figments of that story. Wild magic playing tricks on people.

Right?

The knights pounded on the glass like they were in jail, but they were perfectly safe, the dragons weren't coming over here, and the lending libraries were happily bouncing after their new paint jobs. All in all, it was the best I could hope for.

Chapter 11
Roan

I finished screwing in the last of the new latches, the sun gleaming off the warm bronze. The lending library swung its door open and closed without a single squeak before bouncing back and forth.

"Okay, okay," I said, patting it on the roof. "You're all set now."

Wait. When did I start talking to them as if they were people? I jerked my hand back. It was far too easy to get comfortable here.

"We're finally done!" Oren wiped his brow, accidentally streaking paint across his forehead, before collapsing on the picnic table. "Phew, that took all morning. I'm ready for lunch."

"Lunch sounds good."

Nyssa walked outside, grinning. "They look amazing!"

As she oohed and ahhed over each lending library, I felt a bit of pride swell in my chest. They really did look good.

But then her eyes widened. "Uhhh, Roan? Why are there knights inside these libraries?"

Oops. I'd forgotten to let them out. I winced, then put on my best smile.

"They were...repairing the lending libraries from the inside," I said, giving them a knowing look as Nyssa unlatched the lending libraries. "We couldn't have finished so fast without them."

The commander was a bit red in the face, but he readjusted his armor and nodded. "Right, we did our duty well."

I let out a breath, grateful he'd played along, but Nyssa didn't seem convinced. She stared at me, arms crossed and eyebrow raised.

"Fine," I said, "they were causing a ruckus. You should have seen them! Just ask Oren."

Oren laughed, holding his hands up. "Leave me out of this."

"Riiiight." Nyssa smiled just a bit as she carefully removed the knights from their little prisons. "Run along and stay away from the big scary adventurer for a while."

"Yes, my lady. Thank you," the commander said with a bow.

I rolled my eyes. "It wasn't that bad, I promise."

"Try and behave." She shook her head, walking back inside.

As I sealed the paint and put away the tools we'd used, noises pulled my attention to the path leading up the mountain. The sounds of wagon wheels and people talking was unmistakable.

"There's people coming up the path," I told Oren. Who would be visiting? And what would the creatures do when they saw even more people barging into their territory? "Take the lending libraries to the woods out back and hide. I'll head inside to wrangle the rest of the creatures in case they make their way inside."

"Leave that to Nyssa," he said, "she'll find some way to keep them out. She's the librarian after all."

"Right, stay safe."

The library was aflutter with creatures helping Nyssa with the patching. She sat on the golem's shoulders with several creatures while others marched around the area picking up after her.

I leaned back, cupping my hand around my mouth. "Nyssa!"

She glanced down. "Roan? Need something else freed from a make-shift prison?"

"No, listen. There's people coming up the path. You need to go talk to them before they burst in here and see... all this."

Her eyes widened, but her voice stayed calm. "Golem, could you please put me down for a minute? I need to go figure a few things out."

"Okay," it rasped, taking Nyssa in its hand and lowering her to the floor painstakingly slowly.

I felt myself bouncing just like those lending libraries earlier, glancing from the door to Nyssa anxiously. Come on, come on. If she didn't hurry, the creatures would see whoever was outside, and I might not be able to stop what came next.

There had to be a reason so many townsfolk had posted missions about spooky things on this mountain, like shadows chasing them through the woods or a witch who lured you into danger with her song. The creatures hadn't been too keen on Nyssa walking in the first time. What's to say they wouldn't react badly again?

When Nyssa's feet touched the ground, I raced her to the door. "Oren's out back with the lending libraries. What do you want me to do here?"

"Hide them," she said, eyebrows pinched together. "They won't like it, but we can't let anyone see them. Not until I figure out a way to explain them to the Librarians' Guild."

"That *sounds* like a good plan," I said, staring at the 20-foot forest golem, "but how am I supposed to hide and control that?"

"With creativity and perseverance?"

I groaned as she walked outside just in time to greet the guests.

"Hello, I'm Nyssa, the Misty Mountain librarian." Her voice was muffled through the door, but I could hear pride in it.

"Oh hello," a man's voice said. "We're the contractors you hired. We finished our last job early, so thought we'd head up here."

"That's great! Let's take a look around outside first."

Good, that would buy me some time to hide everyone in here while she distracted those contractors. First things first: what room would be big enough to hide everyone together so I could keep an eye on them?

Hmmm....the special collection exhibit should work. It was empty right now and had sliding doors to separate it from the rest of the library. Nothing needed to be repaired there either, but it was a bit small for all of us.

"Listen up everyone," I said, trying to cast my voice loud enough for them to hear, but not loud enough to draw unwanted attention. "The contractors are here a little early to fix the windows and the roof, but we need to get out of their way so they can work. Follow me to the special collection exhibit."

For some reason, I half expected them to actually follow my lead. But that was a big fail. The golem pulled down the last remaining patch Nyssa had been working on while the dragons swooped over the shelves in a race. The Demon Lord was thankfully nowhere to be seen, but that still left the knights who were currently scaling the stacks to shoot arrows at the dragons, and the three-headed dog.

The contractors would definitely run away screaming if they walked in here.

"Nyssa really needs your help," I said. "They're going to put in all new windows and make it so the rain doesn't come in anymore. Isn't that what you want too?"

A dragon shot by my face doing a barrel roll. Great. Just great.

Lisa covered a laugh behind her teacup. "Do you possibly need some assistance?"

This whole day was trying my nerves. I was supposed to get rid of wild magic, but here I was, hiding these creatures away instead. If this were any other mission, I'd have dispelled them and called it a day.

So why wasn't I doing that now? Because of Nyssa? No, it was something else, something needling the back of my mind. This library wasn't normal and neither was the wild magic inside it. If wild magic was doing something new, the guild deserved to understand it better and I was the best suited to learn.

"Yes, I'd appreciate your help, Lisa," I ground out to her amusement. "Can't you just go back inside your books or something?"

She shook her head. "No, dear, a few of us always need to be awake to guard the library. Do you really think we'd leave that all up to you? We have a duty."

I stared at her for a moment, wondering just what kind of duty they thought they had and who had told them that. But before I could think on that more, the red panda leapt off his chair and raced across the room, running straight up the golem's arm. Mochi shot up to its shoulder, chittering and squawking louder than I'd ever heard it. Everyone in the room stood with rapt attention, hanging on every noise the panda made. I didn't know what it was saying, but even I felt the power in it.

Mochi wanted them to help me.

These creatures really didn't seem that bad. They didn't act like they were made from wild magic; they weren't hurting anyone or causing chaos. It was like the wild magic had brought them to life, but lost its edge after their creation.

The story spirits ambled into the special collection exhibit, quietly letting me close the doors without incident. My back itched though, knowing they weren't going to stay this cooperative all day. The longer we were cooped up, the more likely they'd try to do something to the contractors. I'd have to be ready for anything.

There wouldn't be another mission posted to the guild on my watch. Not about haunted libraries at least.

I pulled a chair in front of the sliding doors and sat down, guarding the exit from the inside. Just in time too, as the sounds of people clamoring around filled the library.

The creatures huddled in the small room, the golem squished in a corner with dragons using it as a roost. Lisa pulled out a book and started reading, an amused smile on her face like she was waiting for this all to fail miserably. Or maybe that was me.

Minutes ticked by as hammers pounded away outside. Mochi shuffled over, offering me a cookie.

"No thanks," I said, too focused on keeping an eye on everyone to eat.

The knights had already given up on being quiet and were wrestling on the table while the dragons leaned down, eyes full of playful curiosity. As long as the golem didn't join in, I could handle them.

The three-headed dog trotted over, dropping a ball in my lap.

"Sorry, I'm in the middle of something," I said, setting the ball down carefully so he wouldn't chase it. "Maybe later."

He whined, his heads drooping as he curled up in the corner. My heart ached seeing him like that, especially when Lisa clicked her tongue and went over to pet him, whispering soothing things to him. The dog perked up, wagging his tail, but one head still stared at me with puppy dog eyes.

Was I the monster here because I wouldn't interact with these creatures? No, I would not let a wild magic animal make me feel guilty. No matter how much it might *look* like an adorable dog.

Two knights ran over, fired up about something. Okay, they were definitely about to escape, now was my time.

"Sir Roan, settle a bet for us," one of them said. "Which is better: a broadsword or a rapier?"

I slumped back in my chair. "That's what you're asking about?"

"It's important!" he shouted. "This fool thinks a rapier makes him look dashing, but a broadsword always gets the job done."

I pinched the bridge of my nose and closed my eyes. "They each have their own merits. A rapier is best when you need agility against an unarmed foe and the broadsword is best when you need power against an armed opponent. Now please, try to keep it down."

"Ohhh, he could be onto something," one of the knights said with a bow. "Thank you, Sir Roan."

Then they were off, rejoining their group.

Lisa joined me, sitting on the arm of my chair. "You know they respect you, right? They just want you to see them as warriors like they see you."

"They're pint-sized wild magic creatures."

"So?" She raised an eyebrow. "I didn't take you for a man who judged people by their size."

"That's not what I—" I sighed. "What do you want?"

"These creatures, as you call them," she said with a disapproving look, "are just living their lives, however they can. We're all striving for something more though, reaching for the thing that will make us feel whole. We're part of stories that haven't finished yet, we're incomplete. Maybe you can empathize with that?"

Empathize with them?

"But you're made of wild magic."

"Again I say, so what?" She patted my shoulder. "You should really be more open-minded. Are you the expert on wild magic? What's to say it can't be good?"

She had a point. The wild magic I'd seen had all been chaotic, but did that really mean all wild magic was? Maybe it had fulfilled its purpose by bringing those creatures—no, story spirits—to life. Maybe they were something new now, a whole different kind of magic. Library magic.

The three-headed dog shifted in the corner, still staring at me with those sad eyes. I really could have thrown the ball for him once. It wouldn't have hurt anything.

"Fine, I see your point." I leaned down to grab the dog's ball. "Come here Cerbie, do you still want to play?"

The dog leapt up, eyes bright and tongues wagging. Instead of going for the ball, he leapt into my chair, knocking me back. I laughed quietly as he licked my face, pressing against me like he was the happiest dog ever. I petted him for a while until he curled up in my lap, obviously not realizing how big he was for a lap dog.

But it was fine. Cerbie was happy and at the moment, that made me happy too. He was a good dog.

Maybe Lisa was right and I didn't know everything about wild magic. Maybe these story spirits weren't going to do something unpredictable and cause a magical mess. And maybe everything would be okay after all.

That felt like wishful thinking, but I'd never wanted to be wrong more.

Chapter 12
Nyssa

The lower the sun dropped in the sky, the more anxious the contractors got. They'd gone from laughing about the stories of the haunted library to flinching every time they heard a noise. Which had been far too frequently. Thankfully the two teenage apprentices had gone up to work on the roof, where they couldn't hear anything strange.

Like metal clashing or pandas chittering or even a golem's deep and mournful sigh.

Nope, they couldn't hear any of that if they were outside. Which only left their boss, William, who'd opted to work on the interior, within dangerous earshot.

"Thanks again for coming all the way up here," I said with a smile as he climbed down from a ladder. "I don't know what I would have done without you."

The roof looked like it was pretty much fixed. They hadn't touched the windows yet, but new ones were lined up against the walls. There was no way they'd all get put in today though, so we'd need at least one more day of this ridiculous game of hide and seek.

"Just doing my job," William said, but his gaze flitted around the library like he kept expecting to see something amiss. "Are you sure you want to work here? There's another library in town that doesn't have..." He shook his head. "Nevermind, not my business." He walked outside and shouted up to the two teenagers on the roof. "Let's call it a day for now."

The kids climbed down, one of them grinning. "Afraid of being here after dark?"

"Think a monster's going to get us?" the other asked, moving his hands like a ghost floating through the air.

"Course not." William frowned at the sky. "Just don't want to get stuck on the mountain path, that's all. Now get moving or I'll leave you both here."

If only they knew the kinds of things that happened here at night. Would they be terrified or excited? There had to be a way we could introduce people to the story spirits without scaring them.

The kids laughed as they went inside and gathered up their tools. This would all be over soon and we could relax for a bit after a job well done.

"When will you be back?" I asked.

"Day after tomorrow? The boys have off for a—" A bright yellow ball rolled across the floor, stopping at

William's feet. He bent down to pick it up. "What's this? Do you have a dog?"

Before I could even think of a lie, Cerbie raced into the room, tail wagging and eyes bright. When he saw the ball in William's hands, he leapt toward the contractor, tongues hanging out just waiting for him to throw the ball.

It was like time stood still for a moment, as all eyes fell to Cerbie and his very obvious three heads.

"I can explain," I said in a calming voice. "This is—"

"The hellhound!" William shouted, dropping the ball like it was on fire.

The boys' eyes were wide. "They say it steals your soul if you look it in the eyes."

"No, he's not like that at all," I said, walking over to Cerbie to pet him. "He's a good dog, I swear. He just looks a little different."

"Run," William shouted, pushing the boys outside. "Don't look back, just run."

Their faces were white as sheets as they fled the library, as if their souls really were on the line.

"Wait!" I called out after William. "What about the windows?"

They were already halfway across the courtyard, with no sign of turning around. I stood there, gaping at them. How could anyone see Cerbie and think *terrifying hellhound*? When I looked in his adorable eyes, all I saw was love.

"You're a good boy." I scratched behind his ears as he leaned into my hand. "You're not a monster."

Cerbie licked my hands, all three heads eager for attention. I smiled, laughing as he almost knocked me over.

"Sorry," Roan said, racing out of the supposedly closed off library wing. "He got away from me."

"Got away from you?" I snapped. "You were supposed to be hiding them, but it sounded like you were having a party in there! It took everything I had to explain the sounds away, but now?" I sighed, standing up as Cerbie played with his ball. "There's no way those contractors will come back, and they'll probably warn everyone else away too."

"That's not entirely my fault," Roan said. "You try and keep dozens of story spirits quiet for hours locked up in a room together. It was hopeless from the start."

He was right. I should have planned better, should have known what time the contractors were coming and found a better way to hide the story spirits. Rushing never led to good results, but I'd been too worried about the library to slow down and think. Now the whole town would probably hear about Cerbie and the haunted library.

I felt myself smiling just a bit, mumbling, "Cerbie and the Haunted Library. Sounds like a good book."

Cerbie nudged the ball at Roan, staring at him with big puppy dog eyes.

"Don't look at me like that. Not again." Roan ran his hand over his face, shoulders slumped. "We can't play fetch right now."

Wait. That ball hadn't rolled out of the room on its own and Cerbie hadn't been chasing it for no reason.

"Roan," I said slowly, "did you, maybe, throw that ball for Cerbie?"

He shook his head. "No way. Why would I do that?"

I leaned down to pet Cerbie again, making my own puppy dog eyes at Roan.

"Not you too," he groaned. "Okay fine, I did throw it, but the knights were the ones who pried the door open. How was I supposed to know they were claustrophobic? And the golem, man does it not like being told to be quiet."

Roan started rambling about all the story spirits and how they were such a handful today, but all I heard was that he'd actually gotten to know them. He'd talked to them, played with them, and even worried about them. I knew I should be upset about the contractors leaving, but I couldn't help but smile.

Roan was bonding with the story spirits. And if he could do that, then other people could too. This could still work, if I just figured out why everyone was so afraid.

"What's that look for?" Roan asked. "I thought you'd be mad, but you look weirdly giddy instead."

I smiled as I wrapped my arms around his strong shoulders, hugging him close. "Thank you."

"You're welcome?" He stood there, frozen for a moment, but then his arms encircled me. "You're kind of weird, you know that, right?"

His breath tickled my ear as he leaned down, holding me tight. Then he pulled away, looking everywhere but at me.

"Well, what's the plan now?" he asked. "Whatever the story spirits did, the town's terrified."

"You're right." I glanced over at the other story spirits who were sheepishly hiding in the room still. "You can come out now. I've got a few questions for you."

The golem trudged out with the tiny dragons resting on its shoulders, followed by Lisa, the knights, and Mochi. With their gazes pinned to their feet, they looked like naughty children who'd been caught stealing the pie from somebody's window.

"The townsfolk seem terrified of you and I want to know why." I crossed my arms. "So, who wants to go first?"

Mochi wandered over, chittering quickly about something. He put a sandwich on the ground, then ran across the room and put a cupcake, and then a cookie down, spreading them out all over the room like we were on a treasure hunt.

I glanced at Roan, hoping he'd know what the heck that meant, but he just shook his head as Mochi continued to chitter.

When Mochi was done, he stood in front of us, head tilted like he was waiting for an answer.

"Umm...," I glanced desperately at Lisa. "Translation?"

"When we first appeared," she said as Mochi handed her a cup of tea and she sat down like she was about to tell a really good story, "Mochi ran into a little girl lost in the woods outside. He gave her some food so she wouldn't be hungry and helped her find her parents again. After that, he started leaving food all over the mountain in case anyone else got lost too."

"That sounds nice," I said slowly, "so why were they afraid?"

Her lips twitched. "Well, nobody expects to find cookies and cupcakes in the woods. The villagers decided a witch was leaving them, sending her familiar out to steal children with its treats."

I sighed. "And then?"

"Mochi left even more of them," she said with a laugh. "He really is thoughtful."

Roan joined Lisa at the table, grinning. "Okay, so what about Cerbie? Why do they think he's going to steal their souls?"

"Oh, that's a good one," Lisa said, leaning forward. "The dragons were playing outside one night with Cerbie and the Demon Lord, using their flames to make Cerbie's shadow giant. The Demon Lord thought it would be fun to have his shadow run through the woods barking at people. You know, to let them know we were here."

I groaned. "Of course he did."

He wasn't out today, so I'd have to ask for an explanation later. It sounded like he'd scared the townsfolk on purpose whereas Mochi had done it on accident.

"And you?" I asked. "Have you scared anyone since you've gotten here?"

"Absolutely," she said with a grin. "It was just too fun not to join in. Our own little game at the library."

"Why?" Roan asked as he threw Cerbie's ball down the stacks. "What was the point of making everyone afraid of you? Didn't you want visitors?"

Her eyes turned dark as she ran her finger along the edge of her teacup. "At first, but then we realized they would never understand us. All they saw was a golem about to crush them or an army of knights that couldn't possibly exist at that size or a demon out to destroy them. Trying to win them over didn't get us anywhere, so we switched to scaring them away instead. Better to be alone by choice than unwanted."

The knight commander patted her hand. "We tried our best, but they just didn't understand us. Lady Lisa was so sad. We had to do something."

"So you terrified them?" I sank into the chair by Roan, feeling a little hopeless. "I get it, but it really didn't help matters. Now the whole town thinks the library is haunted. How are we ever going to get patrons back now?"

Lisa shrugged and sipped her tea, avoiding my gaze as the other story spirits deflated a bit. The knights stopped climbing on things, Cerbie dropped his ball, and the dragons drooped on the golem. This obviously wasn't a topic they liked talking about, no matter how fun they'd made scaring people away seem.

If the hauntings were a defense mechanism, a way to protect themselves from rejection, then I couldn't blame them. They did what they felt like they had to do. But something was nagging at me.

"Why didn't you just tell them you were from books?" I asked. "I'm sure at least a few people would have thought it was awesome and patrons would have flooded the library to meet you. That's what you wanted, right?"

Lisa's gaze finally met mine. "You have no idea what we want. We're here for the library, not for the townsfolk."

"Okay, but still, why scare people instead of explaining?"

None of them answered me. I glanced at Roan, who just shrugged. He didn't know what was going on any more than

I did. But, the *why* didn't matter as much as what they'd do in the future.

"Fine, you don't need to explain," I said, "but you do need to stop."

Lisa frowned. "Stop?"

"Scaring people," I said. "I'll do everything I can to reopen this library and that includes making sure people know that you're characters from stories, not monsters in the night. But I can't do that if you keep playing this little haunting game of yours."

Mochi jumped up on the table, chittering. He moved from story spirit to story spirit, putting a paw on them as if they could communicate somehow, then stood in front of me.

"Mochi agrees with you," Lisa said. "We'll try it your way for now."

"Thank the gods." I smiled, petting Mochi for a moment. "So, tell me more about the hauntings."

Lisa's lips stretched into a wicked grin. "Okay, so people have this weird aversion to women singing creepy songs in the woods, right? So, I'd go out and sit in a tree, singing every morning when the fog was thickest."

I sat there, listening to the haunting tales of these wonderful story spirits terrorizing the town and couldn't help but feel bad for them. They'd been all alone out here, using devious tricks to scare people away. It was like they were so afraid of being rejected that they didn't even try anymore.

My heart ached for them. If I'd just come here sooner, I could have helped them. Maybe they wouldn't have had to scare anyone at all. Maybe...

Roan reached over and took my hand in his, rubbing his thumb against my knuckles. He didn't say anything, but the gesture filled me with warmth. I wasn't in this alone. None of us were.

We were going to change this library's story together.

Chapter 13
Nyssa

The story spirits had been quiet since the contractors left yesterday, hiding in their own little areas of the library. I wasn't sure how to help them, but I did know one thing that needed to be taken care of: these damn windows.

The library had to look its best if we expected patrons to come back, but I had no clue how to put new windows in.

I was a librarian though. When in doubt, look it up in a book.

Except, this library barely had any of those and certainly none on window repairs. I sighed, investigating what else the contractors had left. A roll of extra sturdy MagiHold tape and some sealant. Maybe it was as easy as putting the double-sided tape up and popping the window in? Couldn't hurt to try...

"Need help?" Roan asked as I dragged a bulky window into place. I tripped on a warped floor board, but he reached out to steady me and the window. "Hey now, be careful. Maybe you should take a break?"

Curse that warped floor and these windows and the contractors too afraid of a puppy dog to do their jobs.

"We don't have time for breaks," I said, dragging the window again. "The library isn't going to fix itself and we're already behind. We need to be ready for the festival. Otherwise..."

Otherwise, the Misty Mountain Library would fade away. My chest tightened as I glanced back at the great book tree, which was only a little bit healthier than when I first came here. If I didn't work harder, I'd lose this beautiful library for good.

Roan nodded and hefted the window up as if it weighed nothing, putting it into place as I taped it in, sealing it. Some of the tension left my body. He would help me at least. I wasn't alone.

Together we put in two more windows before Lisa came over.

"Somebody's coming," she said, nodding at a speck in the sky. "They'll be here soon."

Somebody was flying toward us on a winged horse with a huge crate hanging underneath it. Maybe it was the new books I ordered?

"Go, I'll keep working on these," Roan said as he grabbed another window.

I smiled, grateful for his help, and flung the doors open as the mail courier swooped down, carefully setting the box on the ground. The beautiful black pegasus neighed as it flapped its wings. I shifted from foot to foot, almost dancing as I withheld the urge to pet it.

"Hello, ma'am," the courier said with a kind smile and a wave. "I've got your order from Arcadia Books. Please sign here."

I took the tablet from him and signed, frowning at how big the box was. "Isn't that too heavy to fly with?"

"Weight-reduction magic. It's the only way to fly!" He unhooked the box, floating it to the door.

I leapt in front of him before he opened it. "Uh, it's fine right here."

"Are you sure, ma'am?" he asked with a frown. "It's no trouble to take it inside. I'd even help you unpack it if you'd like."

He was so nice, exactly the type of person I wanted at this library. But not while the memory of those contractors screaming as they ran away still echoed fresh in my mind.

I smiled. "It's fine. We're in the middle of some remodels and I wouldn't want you to get hurt. You should stop back once we're open again."

"I'll do that, thanks." He gazed at the library fondly. "I fly over this mountain a lot and always wondered about this place. Glad to see it's reopening." As the box of books settled on the ground, he hopped back on his pegasus. "Thank you for your business and I hope to deliver here again soon."

The pegasus leaping into the sky was a beautiful sight. I blocked the sun with my hand and followed them until they were a tiny dot and my eyes were watering. Seeing him excited for the library to reopen gave me hope that there were more people like us, more readers eager to browse these shelves again.

Now to find some help carrying all these books inside. The golem was crouched over by the new garden area we'd been working on. Raised flower beds surrounded the library, making use of the old patches we'd pulled down so the golem didn't have to feel bad. Flowers already sprouted from them as the golem spent every minute tending to them, rocking back and forth on its heels like some kind of dance.

"How's the gardening going?" I asked as I wandered over. "Do you like the new raised beds?"

A deep rumble sounded through his body. "Love."

I couldn't help but smile watching such a big golem shift dirt around with its fingertip to avoid disturbing the plants. Bright red flowers had been the first to sprout, poppies like the ones on the golem's shoulders, but it looked like there were other kinds of plants too.

"I can't wait to see them all in bloom," I said. "Do you mind helping me carry a box of books inside?"

The vines in the golem's body shifted as it stood up, lumbering over to the library's front door. I had to run to keep pace with its long strides and the box was already inside and open by the time I got there.

"Thank you!"

The golem nodded, then trudged back outside to its happy place. I'd felt like a monster after seeing how upset the golem was about me tearing those patches down, so I was really glad it liked the gardens.

I pulled out a few books, admiring their vibrant covers. Each one was like a precious gem in a treasure chest. I sorted them into piles based on genre, stacking them on a nearby table, but there were a few I didn't recognize. More than a few actually and there were multiple copies of them too.

"I think they mixed up our order," I mumbled, searching through the box to see what else was wrong.

Lisa joined me. "I might have...altered your order a bit."

"You did what?"

"I'm a librarian here too, you know." She gave me an innocent smile and a shrug. "So I added a few books you overlooked."

I sighed. "We're on a tight budget, you can't just add things like that without talking to me."

"And you shouldn't have ordered anything without talking to *me*."

We stared at each other for a while before I broke down. "Fine, I'm sorry. Please tell me about the books you added."

And they better be worth it otherwise I'd be sending them right back to the store.

Lisa ran her fingers lightly over a cover. "I thought you might want to get to know us better by reading the books we all came from. Maybe the patrons would like that too."

"Your books?" My mouth dropped open.

I'd asked them about their books when I first came here, but they were cagey about it and I'd never seen them on the shelves. So I'd focused on the repairs instead, but I could have looked into it more. I'd known a few of their stories already and the rest...I just hadn't had time for yet.

Was I a terrible librarian? There were books that had literally come to life right in front of me and I hadn't even read their stories yet.

"Thank you, Lisa," I said, with as much sincerity as I could. "I really appreciate you helping me with this. I'd love to read your stories."

"I thought you might," she said. "We don't like anyone touching our original books, but these duplicates are fine."

Ah, so that's why I hadn't seen their books anywhere: they'd been protecting the ones they came out of. That made sense. It made me happy that she wanted to share her story with me now though. Like I'd earned her respect as a librarian.

Roan wandered over, looking at the books over my shoulder. "Still sure you don't want to take a break? Maybe read some books?"

"Tempting, so very tempting." I trailed my finger along their pristine spines, wanting nothing more than to crack them open and be the first to read them. "But we still have work to do."

"Taking time for yourself is important." He gazed at the story spirits peeking over at us. "I think it would be good for everyone."

He was right. I'd been pushing forward on my to-do list, but the story spirits weren't acting normal. They said they had scared people for fun, but seeing those contractors run away from them in terror had obviously taken a toll. If I wanted to repair this library, keeping their spirits up was part of that. Plus, reading would help the book tree regain some magic.

Maybe a break really was exactly what we needed.

"Hey everyone," I called out, holding some of the books up, "let's get together and read each other's stories. We can recharge the library's magic and get to know each other better. Who's in?"

At first nobody really moved, but then I heard clanging metal as the knights marched over, the unmistakable chitter of Mochi, and even the flapping of dragon wings as they joined us.

Warmth blossomed in my chest seeing everyone grabbing different books, discussing who they wanted to read about most.

This was why I loved the library so much, why I had to bring people back to it.

No matter who you were or what problems you were having, books could bind us together and give two complete strangers common ground. They were magical and created such wonderful moments. It's what made this library such a bright spot in my childhood. Even Oren pulled himself out of his research text to grab a book.

"What book are you going to read?" Roan asked as he sorted through a few, picking up the one about Cerbie.

"There's so many options, I'm not sure," I said, looking over all the books Lisa had kindly added to my list, pausing on one with a beautiful woman in a purple dress on the cover. "This one. It's about time I got to know Lisa better."

She was a librarian, just like me, and I had to start acting like that. I wasn't alone in any of this.

I dragged various chairs underneath the book tree in a circle so we could all read together, as close to the tree as possible. When everyone was settled in, I relaxed into a cozy chair and read the back of Lisa's book. It was a story about a dream library that you could only reach when you were sleeping and a woman in a coma who became its librarian.

Would she wake up and forget all about the library she'd come to love? Or would she stay asleep forever and make other people's dreams come true?

Neither of those sounded like the right ending for Lisa, so I was curious to see what actually happened. The excitement of starting a new book swept over me as I opened it to chapter 1, a chapter full of possibilities.

If only I had a blanket and some tea, this would be perfect.

Roan scooted a chair close to mine. "Mind if I join you?"

"Not at all," I said, motioning for him to sit down. "I hope you like Cerbie's book."

"I'd like anything we read together like this," he said, grinning at me.

My face flushed.

He not only enjoyed reading, but he wanted to read *with* me?

Maybe we could make reading a night time ritual, in the name of saving the library of course. More reading would help it recharge and maybe make falling asleep in the same bed a bit less awkward too...

A dragon's roar followed by the clashing of metal made me spin around, catching the knights warring with the dragons again. If they weren't careful, they'd set the new books on fire! A few dragons had even picked knights up, flying them high over the shelves. They better not drop them.

"Hey, knock it off," I said, marching over. I loomed over their tiny three-inch selves. "Why do you keep fighting with the dragons?"

"They started it," the knight commander said. "They're always dive bombing us or shooting fire at us or plucking us up like we're toys!" He motioned at the knights dangling from dragon claws above us. "Just look at poor Bob and Mikey."

Bob and Mikey? I'd expected more knightly names if I was honest, but that wasn't the point.

"Dragons, put the knights down and come over here," I said firmly. They completely ignored me. "Come on, don't make me get the golem."

The image of a giant trying to swat flies came to mind. Probably not the best idea, but the dragons landed anyway, dropping the knights unceremoniously on the ground.

"Now, I need you all to start getting along," I said. "We can't make this library a success if you keep making it a warzone."

One of the dragons rolled over, glancing at me with a tongue lolling out of its mouth. Another pounced on a knight, who stabbed at it in return. Hmmmm....the dragons reminded me of cats wanting to play. Could all those attacks the knights mentioned just be the dragons wanting attention?

"Hey Lisa? What's the dragons' book about?"

She smiled at me behind her tea cup. "Dragon hatchlings that destroy everything until people play with them."

"Couldn't have told me that sooner, huh?" I sighed, pinching the bridge of my nose.

"You never asked."

That was fair. I'd have to do a lot better if I was going to manage these story spirits.

"Okay knights," I said in an official-sounding voice, "I command you to play with the dragons. No slaying, just playing."

They groaned, but the dragons leapt into the air with excitement while I went back to my nice cozy chair to read. We had a mission: read as many books as possible to give the library more magic.

Mochi wandered over to hand me a cup of hot cocoa that melted my heart. "Thank you, Mochi."

He chittered and bounded back to Lisa, snuggling up on her lap to read with her.

"You're good with them," Roan said. "I think you're doing a great job, honestly. You're a fantastic librarian."

"Thank you," I muttered, diving into my book so he wouldn't see how much that made me grin.

Roan thought I was a good librarian. Things were all coming together. Maybe we could actually pull this off if we worked as a team.

A few dragons settled on my lap, their warmth sinking into my body. This was the life. A good book, a kind man, cozy drinks, and warm dragons. I couldn't ask for more.

Chapter 14
Roan

Sunlight warmed my skin as I finished my morning workout and washed up in the stream nearby. We'd spent the past few days working hard on the library repairs and reading every chance we got. Things were really starting to come together and it felt good to make progress.

Cerbie was waiting for me at the edge of the water, practically vibrating with excitement as he nudged a ball my way.

I picked it up with a grin. "I've got something better today. Come on."

Cerbie woofed and followed me back to the library, bounding along the path like a puppy full of too much energy. I'd been playing fetch with him every morning to calm him down, but throwing balls for a three-headed dog was more difficult than I expected.

If I threw a single ball, Cerbie's heads would either fight over it or the middle one would snatch it up and the others would be sad. If I threw three balls, they'd inevitably end up in different places and Cerbie wouldn't know which one to chase after. He'd literally fallen over a few times trying to run after too many at once.

So today I had a new plan. I'd made a toy just for him, one perfect for a three-headed dog. I reached under the bench where I'd hidden it earlier and held it out to the dog like a grand prize.

"What do you think, Cerbie?"

His tail wagged faster and faster as he sniffed the new toy, which was really three of his old toys put together. I'd strung rope between three balls so none of them could roll away and each of Cerbie's heads could carry one. I really should have thought of it sooner.

I threw the toy as far as I could, watching it sail through the air as Cerbie raced after it. He jumped, catching the toy midair. Instead of each head getting one, the greedy middle head came back with all three balls in his mouth like a squirrel gathering nuts.

"Cerbie, that's not how it works," I said, but couldn't stop laughing. "Let's try again."

We kept playing until the sun was clear over the trees and Nyssa poked her head outside.

"Time for breakfast," she said, smiling warmly. "Looks like he enjoyed the new toy, huh?"

Cerbie barreled into her, showing the toy off proudly. She laughed and knelt to pet him, but her gaze was on me. Something about the way she was looking at me warmed me more than my workout had. It felt nice being here, helping her. Almost too nice.

"He loved it, yeah. Let's go eat." I motioned for her to lead the way to the table at the back of the library where we'd been eating our meals lately.

A fluffy stack of pancakes was waiting for us, warm and melty with chocolate chips. Nyssa plated a few for both of us.

"I hope you like pancakes," she said.

The smell of maple syrup and melted butter washed over me as I sat down. "You made these? I didn't know you could cook."

Or that there was a kitchen here. Mochi had been providing most of our meals since we got to the library, so it hadn't really come up.

She smiled softly. "Yes, I can cook. But this is the only breakfast food I'm good at."

And she made them for me. I couldn't stop the smile spreading across my face as I took my first bite. Hold on...

"Are there apples inside?"

She nodded. "Little pieces of apple give pancakes a nice texture, don't they? It's how my mom taught me to make them."

I took another bite, practically groaning over how delicious the apples were. What a thoughtful addition. It felt like she was sharing part of her past with me too. Working out, playing with Cerbie, and then having a wonderful meal with Nyssa was how I wanted to spend every morning.

Wait.

Every morning? Had I really gotten that comfortable here?

I paused with my fork halfway to my mouth, watching the syrup drip down. This was supposed to be a short visit where I helped repair the library and had some fun, but now I had routines and...feelings.

Sleeping in the same bed as Nyssa definitely wasn't helping. I'd only been doing it to keep her safe, but each night we moved a litttttle bit closer and I'd wake up feeling like I must still be dreaming. There was no other explanation for me suddenly playing house with a beautiful woman like her.

It was all a bit *unsettling*. I was used to being on my own. It made me happy to travel, to see the world, finding new people and completing missions.

Staying in one place for too long just didn't work for me. So what was I still doing here?

"Everything okay?" Nyssa asked. "Don't tell me I burned them or something?"

I shoved the pancakes in my mouth, shaking my head. What could I even say to her to begin to explain what I was feeling?

I'd used our bet as an excuse to stay here for a while, but that was wearing thin. The story spirits obviously weren't dangerous creatures and the guild would see that if I talked to Master Carmine about it. Jade would probably argue, but I'd find a way to deal with her somehow.

Because even if Nyssa did appreciate me being here, it was probably just because she needed help repairing the library, which anyone could have helped with really. I'd just been here at the right time. She needed me, but that didn't mean she *wanted* me.

I had to end this, for both our sakes. Once we fixed up the library, it was time to move on. "Nyssa—"

"Hey!" Oren shouted, hurrying over with a big goofy grin on his face. "The book tree has new buds."

"New buds?" Nyssa jumped up, racing after him to inspect the tree. "Roan, come look at this!"

My jaw clenched with words left unsaid, but I finished my last bite of pancakes before following her. The book tree looked greener than before with half a dozen buds on it, and Nyssa's smile was so bright it was hard to look at.

"What's up with you?" Oren asked. "Trouble sleeping?"

"Just tired, yeah," I lied. I actually hadn't slept this well in years. It was like Nyssa was a sleep sorceress or something, pulling me into a cozy dreamland every night. I had to escape before it was too late.

"The book tree's really healing!" Nyssa let out a breath and rested her forehead against the tree's bark. "The library's going to be okay."

Which meant there was really no reason left for me to stay. The roof was solid, the new windows were all in, and the golem was even slowly straightening the floorboards. If I could just convince the guild that the missions I'd taken weren't necessary, then this library would be all set.

I gently touched the tree's bark, only inches from Nyssa's cheek. My gut twisted as I felt the magic thrumming through it, weak but definitely growing stronger. There was nothing left for me to do here.

Leaving would be best for both of us, so why was I having such a hard time telling her that? I never hesitated when it was time to go back out on the road. I loved new adventures and all the new places I'd get to see. People needed my help, so I couldn't just stay in one place and let my skills go to waste.

But something about this just felt wrong.

Did I...want to stay?

I rubbed my hand over my chest, suddenly feeling like something was lodged there. If I didn't tell her soon, I might stay here for another week and then another. And then it would be even more painful to leave.

"I have to go," I said abruptly. "The library's all fixed up, so the bet's over. I'm going to go pack up."

Nyssa froze. "What?"

My mouth went dry. I cleared my throat, avoiding the surprised look on her face. "The library's healing wonderfully and you're doing amazing as the librarian. I'm really glad I could help you with your dream, but I've got to get back to the other people who need my help too."

I forced myself to turn away from her, to walk up the stairs to the room we'd been sharing, and pack my things up as if nothing was wrong. I was an adventurer. Moving on was what I did.

Nyssa stood at the bottom of the stairs, blocking my path.

"Are you really leaving? Just like that?" Her expression looked panicked and a little angry as her hand gripped the railing. "You don't even want to see your hard work pay off? See all the patrons return for the festival?"

That was the problem: I did want that. She'd worked *so hard*. She deserved to flourish alongside this library. I wanted to see the joy on her face when that first patron walked through the door and commented on how nice the library looked. Or when somebody pet Cerbie instead of running away in terror.

I wanted it all.

But wanting something that badly was the most dangerous emotion I'd ever felt.

Hope only led to disappointment.

As she stood at the bottom of those stairs, all I saw was my childhood self, waiting and waiting for my parents to come back, but they never did. That hope each time the door opened was torture and I wouldn't put myself in that position again.

One way or another, we would disappoint each other. I'd rather we left as friends, able to be proud of the library's success.

"I'm sorry," I said, swallowing my emotions. "I know you'll make the festival amazing and the story spirits will help you. You don't need me anymore and this was always a temporary arrangement."

She dropped her gaze, moving aside slightly to let me pass. Each step felt heavier, like my feet were turning to stone, but it had to be done.

"I might not *need* you," she said softly, "but what if I *want* you?"

My eyes widened as I turned back, her words the exact opposite of what my thoughts had been earlier. Nyssa met my gaze, walking brazenly toward me. She...wanted me to stay?

What was I supposed to say to that? Sorry, but I didn't want to?

My pulse raced. I couldn't lie to her, but I couldn't stay either. I hadn't been this torn since I left the guild. I cared about her and about this library, but I'd cared about the guild master and Jade too, like family. I knew how this would end up if I stayed.

"Sorry to interrupt...whatever this is," the Demon Lord said with no concern in his voice at all, "but adventurers are coming up the mountain."

It took a second for his words to sink in, but once they did, my hand flew to my sword.

"What?" I cursed, racing outside.

If they were here, it had to be for the haunted library missions. I'd taken them all to avoid that though. Unless those contractors had posted a new one. They were probably here to dispel the so-called spirits.

"What should we do?" Nyssa asked, glancing at the shadows oozing off the Demon Lord like they wanted to devour somebody. "Feels like this could get out of hand real quick."

She was right. The Demon Lord was the last story spirit I'd want the guild to meet, not the first.

"Go back in your book," I told him. "Let me handle this."

He scoffed. "Like I'd trust you. You're an adventurer too."

"And I'm higher ranked than almost anyone who'd come here," I said, trying to reassure Nyssa. "It'll be fine. They know me, so if I explain the situation, I'm sure they'll understand."

Nyssa's eyebrows pinched together. "Are you sure?"

"Yes." That was going to be my plan anyway, so this was just accelerating that. As long as they were reasonable adventurers, we should be fine.

Nyssa nodded. "Okay, we'll let you deal with them. You can think of it like your last mission before you leave."

The sarcasm in her voice stung like nettles. I hadn't meant to upset her, but now wasn't the time for that. Because the adventurer walking up the path with those telltale twin swords on her back wasn't a friend and was definitely not reasonable.

Jade.

Chapter 15
Nyssa

Four adventurers sauntered into the courtyard, three men and a woman. They were joking and laughing about something I couldn't quite hear, but their gazes were taking everything in, like they expected to be ambushed at any time. The woman's eyes hardened as she spotted Roan.

Roan.

I hadn't even had time to process what he'd said about leaving before this group showed up, but now wasn't the time to ask him about his feelings.

"That woman seems like she knows you...?"

"Unfortunately." Roan sighed. "Jade's the guild master's daughter. She's got a terrible attitude and resents that I'm higher ranked than her, so she likes to show off when I'm around." He glanced at me apologetically. "I'll explain everything and get rid of her."

Great. So not only was Roan leaving, but the library was in the middle of their battle of egos. A few minutes ago, it had felt like everything was going right for us. We'd been having a nice meal and the tree was healing, all good things.

But now? I'd just be grateful if the story spirits could stay hidden long enough for Roan to send the guild away.

"Come on," I said, dragging the Demon Lord inside while Roan walked into the courtyard to greet the adventurers. "Didn't Lisa mention you guys usually hide from adventurers?"

He scowled. "Just because a little knight got captured *one time* she expects us to be cowards."

I raised an eyebrow at him. "A knight got captured?"

"In a jar like a bug, yeah." He shrugged. "The library handled it, don't worry. It just sent him back to his book."

The library handled it? Wait...

"Does that mean the library controls you? And knows what's going on?"

He gave me one of his classic are-you-an-idiot looks before staring out the window. Right. Of course the library didn't control them. It was magical, sure, but it was still just a building. If magical libraries could do something like that, every librarian would know about it.

The adventurers stopped in the courtyard where Roan stood waiting. Jade looked at the library with such disdain that I wanted to send her away myself, but one of the other adventurers smiled warmly and waved at Roan. So at least some of them were on good terms then. Two others followed behind, but they seemed like extra muscle more than anything else.

"Sorry, but we're not open yet," Roan said. "You should come back later."

The nice adventurer's smile widened. "Come on, you know that's not why we're here. Show us this haunted library of yours."

"Yes," Jade said, "please show us the incredibly dangerous spirits you've let roam the mountain without a care for anyone's safety."

Since when did being scary equal being incredibly dangerous? And why did it sound like Jade was blaming that all on Roan?

Oren joined me, raising an eyebrow at the group of people outside. "Who's she?"

I held a finger to my lips, not wanting to miss anything outside as Roan started talking again.

"I didn't —"

"Didn't what?" Jade cut in before Roan could finish. "Didn't do your damn job like everyone expected you to? You're supposed to be some kind of hero, an S-rank adventurer who can solve anything." Her voice was overly dramatic. "I can't believe my father thinks you'd make a better guild master than me."

Oh, so that's what this was really about. The way she glared at him was full of anger, but also something else. Something that looked a lot like pain. There was more going on here than I knew, but I still didn't like her tone. How dare she march up here with her muscle and talk to him like that? He was just trying to help us.

"Whoa now," the Demon Lord teased, "I thought you wanted us to stay hidden."

Without realizing it, I'd moved closer to the door, as if I'd wanted to go defend Roan's honor or something. My cheeks flushed. Roan was perfectly capable of defending himself, he didn't need me interrupting them. But it just wasn't right.

"You're looking a little red," the Demon Lord mocked. "Want me to teach them all a lesson?"

"Quiet," I whispered back.

Oren paced in front of the window, then stopped and gave me an apologetic look. "Sorry, but I'm going out there. They're too emotional to deal with this."

"Oren!" I reached out for his arm, but he was too quick and already out the door. He strode up to the woman with a wave, apparently not caring how her eyes narrowed or how she reached for her sword.

"Hello, my name's Oren and I'm a researcher here." He held out his hand.

She ignored it and glared at Roan. "So, you brought more innocent people here, huh? Figures."

Oh this was not going to end well. I almost joined them, but I felt the other story spirits gathering around us. If I left them alone, they might do something drastic themselves. For now, I'd stay inside and trust Roan and Oren to handle this.

"Look, this is all a big misunderstanding," Oren said calmly, "the books come to life. They're story spirits, not ghosts."

Roan nodded. "He's right. If there was wild magic here, it's stable now. There's nothing to dispel."

Jade stared at Oren like he'd grown another head. "Books? You really think books came to life and scared people away? The townsfolk aren't that stupid and neither am I. You have no idea how frightened each person was after fleeing the mountain. No idea what they experienced. They attacked children, Roan. Children."

Children? I glanced at the Demon Lord, but he just shrugged again. "We just scared them, that's all."

That somehow didn't feel as reassuring coming from him than when Lisa said it. That didn't matter right now though because if we couldn't convince these adventurers that they weren't ghosts, then we'd have a real problem on our hands.

As Jade and Roan glared at each other silently, neither willing to budge an inch, shadows swirled around me. The Demon Lord looked like he was about to go give Jade a piece of his mind.

"Oh no." I pushed him back. "We're supposed to be proving this isn't a haunted library, so no adding fuel to the fire."

He glared at me, shadows curling around him like a cloak. "I'll do what needs to be done to protect this library. Just because you think that means inviting people in doesn't mean I do."

I sighed. If he really wanted to go out there and fight, I couldn't stop him. I had no idea how the library had put him or anyone else back in their books in the past, but the better question was why wasn't it doing it now? He'd said the story spirits usually hid inside their books, but that hadn't happened when the contractors came or now.

"Why are you here instead of hiding?" I asked the Demon Lord. "Why confront them at all?"

"Because you gave the library hope," he said, "and now it wants people back, even if that means rotten adventurers at its doors. This is your fault, so don't even try and stop me."

Wait, what did he mean by the library *wanted* people back? Was the library....no, I didn't have time for crazy thoughts like that. Libraries didn't have feelings, no matter how magical they were. I had to do something about these adventurers right now.

If we were going to reopen, we needed people to feel safe. To be excited about the story spirits instead of fearful. Which meant we had to prove that the story spirits weren't ghosts.

"Wait!" I grabbed the Demon Lord's arm before he could storm outside just like Oren had. "We need a plan. Whatever the adventurers are here to do, we have to prove them wrong."

As we stood there, staring at each other, the other story spirits peeked out from behind the stacks. Mochi wandered over, patting the Demon Lord's leg. He looked down, having a silent conversation with the panda, before ripping his arm away from me.

"Fine, what do you have in mind?" he asked.

I glanced outside as Roan and Jade started yelling at each other about something, with Roan standing between her and the library. It looked like they were about to come to blows. Cerbie raced over from wherever he'd been playing outside, growling and snapping at the adventurers. I'd never seen him look so fierce before, defending Roan.

Apparently, the adventurers thought so too as they all drew their swords. I had to do something before this got out of hand. Something that would give everyone what they wanted...

"What would happen if those adventurers tried to dispel you like a ghost?" I asked. "Like if you let them burn sage or chant or whatever they're planning on doing?"

"Absolutely nothing," the Demon Lord said. "We aren't ghosts."

"Then let's get out there and prove that." I grinned, looking around the library at all the story spirits. "If none of their techniques work, then they'll have to accept you're not ghosts. Are you with me?"

Mochi chittered, his fluffy tail swooshing back and forth. The dragons raced outside without a second thought as the knights charged after them. That just left...

"Demon Lord?"

"I really can't scare them away?" he asked, sighing when I shook my head. "You're really annoying, you know that right?"

"I know," I said, barely containing my laughter. "But you'll come outside anyway, right?"

I didn't wait for him to answer, assuming he would. We were running out of time. The adventurers had formed a circle, their backs to each other and swords out, as the dragons flew overhead, thankfully not breathing fire. Yet.

"Hello," I said, interrupting everyone. "I'm Nyssa, the Misty Mountain Librarian. Mind telling me what you're doing here?"

Jade barely looked at me, her gaze locked on the story spirits. "I'm Jade. We're here to help with your haunted library problem."

"As Oren already explained, these creatures are story spirits, not ghosts." I smiled warmly as a dragon landed on my shoulder and Cerbie came over to stand between me and Roan. "They're made with library magic so they're part of the library. You cannot dispel them."

"I can't, huh?" Jade scoffed. "Just watch me, lady. They might have fooled you, but I know they're dangerous and I'm going to dispel them."

Exactly what I'd been hoping she'd say. She could try her heart out for all I cared as long as she admitted they weren't ghosts in the end.

"Be my guest," I said, shaking my head at Oren who looked like he wanted to protest. I pulled Roan aside to whisper. "We've got a plan, just play along."

His gaze met mine, holding it for a moment. Then he nodded. "I trust you."

My stomach fluttered at that look, like he fully believed I could handle this situation without even telling him my plan. After this was over, I'd find a way to talk to him about leaving. See if it was what he really wanted or if something else was going on.

The adventurers lined up candles in a large circle, lighting them as they chanted ominously. As Jade bent to light her candle, one of the dragons flew over and beat her to it. She gaped as the dragon's flames melted the candle in half, making one of the other adventurers laugh.

"Focus," Jade said. "Don't let the spirits distract you."

"Good luck with that." Oren laughed as he knelt to replace the candle. "Distractions aren't always bad, you know."

She glared at him. "When I want advice, I'll ask for it."

"Oh calm down, Jade," Roan said. "You're always so quick to judge."

That set them off arguing again like children. Roan hadn't really told me much about his past, but I'd bet she was related somehow. Only relatives argued like that.

While they bickered, Mochi curled up next to the candles as if sitting by a fireplace, handing out mini marshmallows to the little knights. They gathered sticks, spearing them with vigor as they proceeded to roast the marshmallows over the candles. The sweet scent of toasted sugar filled the air, making my stomach growl.

"You can't do that!" Jade said, trying to shoo them off. "Those are sacred candles, not some backwoods campfire."

I knelt down by Mochi and the others, ignoring her entirely.

"Do you have any chocolate or graham crackers?" I asked Mochi, who chittered and pulled them out of thin air. "Ohhh, thank you!"

The panda munched on a marshmallow, getting white fluff all over its fur. I laughed softly as two knights solemnly handed me a normal-sized marshmallow that came up to their shoulders and a sharpened stick.

"Your spear, my lady," the knight said with a bow.

"I said you can't do that!" Jade's eyes widened, complete bewilderment on her face.

Apparently she wasn't used to people doing the opposite of what she said, so I probably shouldn't push her too far.

"Sorry, you can keep trying to dispel them," I said, turning my marshmallow over once it was golden on one side. "We're not stopping you."

The knights completely ignored her too, daring to offer one of the roasted marshmallows to a dragon flying by. My heart swelled. It was the first time I'd seen them getting along, even if it was just to tick off these adventurers.

Roan laughed. "You heard her, keep trying. I dare you."

Jade's face reddened. "Get the salt."

The two bulky adventurers behind her pulled salt out of their packs, using it to draw a large circle around us. When the circle was complete, it glowed bright white for a moment. Was it actually going to contain the story spirits?

I glanced around nervously, but then the Demon Lord bent down to pick up some salt, sprinkling it on my marshmallow before taking a big bite. Jade's mouth dropped open as Mochi followed suit, salting everyone's marshmallows with the spelled salt. The panda handed me another marshmallow too since mine had been so rudely devoured.

Jade blinked, apparently at a loss for words, but Oren just laughed as he finished toasting his own marshmallow.

"They're pretty tasty," he said, holding the sweet treat out to her. "Wanna try one?"

Roan burst out laughing, but tried to stop when Jade cuffed the back of his head. "Sorry, but you should see the look on your face right now. Nyssa, Oren, and the story spirits make this library a wonderful place. If you'd stop hating me for a second, maybe you'd see that.

"You're part of the library too, you know." I stood up, shoulder bumping against his. "An important part."

His eyes widened, but Jade cursed loudly before Roan could say anything.

"Get the damn sealing books," she shouted, "we'll bind them to the pages."

Okay, that one sounded less fun and a lot more dangerous. The story spirits came from books, so binding them might actually work. The Demon Lord's shadows swirled again and the knights had completely forgotten about their marshmallows, letting them burn to a crisp over the candles.

"Wait a minute," I started, but Jade grinned.

"Scared?" she asked. "I knew I'd find something that worked. I should have tried the books right away."

Roan stepped forward. "Come on, you know they're not ghosts. They passed your tests already. Ghosts wouldn't be able to eat salt or hang out having fun inside a protective barrier. Let it go already, because honestly, we both know why you're really here."

I frowned. Was this because of what Roan said earlier, about how Jade always tried to outdo him? Or maybe about the whole guild master thing?

"Maybe he's right," one of the other adventurers said. "Let's just head back. There's nothing dangerous here."

Jade shook her head. "No way. These spirits might have tricked Roan and all of you, but I won't let them trick me. I'm better than that."

Roan snorted. "Right, of course you are."

"Roan," I said, "maybe we should—"

"Just get out of here, Jade," Roan snapped. "Your issue is with me, not them. If you leave, so will I. Then you won't have any reason to show off, right? You can just let the library live in peace."

No! What was he doing? Was he really that eager to leave…or was he trying to protect us?

Jade shook her head. "Oh Roan, you never know when to quit, do you?"

Then she took one of the books from the adventurers behind her and started chanting, holding it in front of the dragons. Their bodies flickered just enough for fear to clamp around my heart as they flapped their wings harder than usual, as if something was trying to drag them back.

Jade was really going to seal the story spirits.

One of the dragons cried out, a horrible sound that tugged at my heart. I had to help them, but I didn't know how. I tried to knock the book out of her hand, but the two muscle-bound adventurers moved to stand between us.

The Demon Lord growled. "Enough."

His shadows latched onto the shadows of the adventurers. They couldn't move, couldn't run, couldn't finish their ridiculous chant that was absorbing the dragons into that book. I let out a breath. Good.

Jade struggled to move, frozen by her own shadow. Sweat dripped down her face as fury and betrayal distorted her features. We were supposed to be making peace, not deepening their hatred.

This had to stop. It wouldn't help anyone.

"Stop!" I shouted. "Just stop. This isn't the way to solve anything."

But both sides were too upset to listen. I glanced at Roan, who was also pinned in place by his shadow. Really? The Demon Lord didn't trust him either? What was I supposed to do now?

I turned frantically toward the library, not knowing what I expected to see, but I was at a loss. Help us. Somebody had to help us. Maybe Lisa could deal with them. Nobody ever said no to her.

"Please," I pleaded softly. With who, I wasn't sure. "Save them. Don't let them get captured like the knight did."

After a long moment of silence, the story spirits glowed and disappeared. Jade and her group almost fell over, free from the Demon Lord's shadow binding.

I blinked. Did the library do that? Or did...I do that?

"What just happened?" Jade asked.

Roan glanced at me, but when I shrugged, he turned back to her. "That was us saving your ungrateful ass. Now leave and don't come back."

"Where did they all go?" Oren asked, rolling his shoulders as if making sure he had full control. "They're okay, right?"

I nodded, trying to think of anything rational to say that wouldn't make them even more scared of the library. I didn't have the power to return story spirits to their books and if it wasn't me, then it had been something else. Something these adventurers would probably deem too dangerous to survive.

For now, I had to cover it up and act like everything was normal so they'd leave. Then I could figure out the truth.

"They're back in their own books," I said with more confidence than I felt. "No way was I going to let you steal them from the library. They're not ghosts, they're the souls of precious stories. You have to at least believe that, right?"

The adventurers looked unconvinced.

"We'll be back," Jade said, glancing at Roan. "I won't ignore a mission and let the town down. And we're bringing that one with us." She nodded at Oren. "He can explain everything to the guild master."

Oren's eyes widened. "Wait, what? I'm just a researcher, not the librarian here. Why don't you ask Nyssa?"

Jade raised an eyebrow at him. "Are you saying you don't want to come with me? Pity. Here I thought we might have some fun."

He gulped, looking at me with frantic eyes like I should save him. But I had something else on my mind right now, something we needed to look into right away.

"Sorry, Oren, but could you handle this?" I asked. "I'll make it up to you."

He sighed. "Fine, I'll do what I can."

Jade smiled, slapping him on the back. "Good, now we can go."

That was going to bite us in the ass later, but right now, all I could think about was the library.

I'd asked for help and that's what I got.

My mind reeled as I looked back at the library. The big main entrance, door slightly ajar. The windows, open wide as if the entirety of the building was listening in.

I knew that didn't make any sense, but it felt right as that warm feeling I'd had ever since I stepped foot inside finally clicked.

The library had heard me. And it reacted.

Was the library...sentient?

Chapter 16
Nyssa

I'd been staring at the library for the past few minutes while Roan apologized. It wasn't his fault the adventurers had shown up, but it was his fault for egging Jade on. She'd probably cause more problems later, but my thoughts were on something else entirely.

Was the library *alive*? Or was my imagination just playing tricks on me?

Magical libraries were part of the fabric of our society, but this had never happened before, at least not as far as I knew. Still, it felt like it *was* aware of what was going on around it, and it was capable of action.

Sentience.

I had to test my theory and figure out the truth.

"Weren't you leaving?" I asked, sounding a little blunter than I'd meant to. "For your job I mean, weren't you going off to do other missions?"

I had to know, because if he was going to walk away, he shouldn't get to know the library's best kept secret. Or laugh at me if I was wrong about the whole thing. Not that I thought he'd actually do that. Ugh. This was all such a mess. Why was he thinking about leaving *now* when we were on the verge of something amazing?

For the library...and between us.

I thought we'd been getting closer lately, but maybe that was all my imagination too. Getting lost in a romance novel was a lot easier than trying to experience your own.

Roan paced next to me, still not answering my question. I pulled my gaze away from the library to look at him, and when our gazes met, he stopped in his tracks.

"Nyssa..."

The way he said my name, soft and intimate, made me want to tell him everything racing through my mind even if he was leaving. I wanted to know his opinion on it, see what he'd come up with for how to figure out if the library was alive or not. I could ask it directly, sure, but how would it answer?

Wait.

The story spirits seemed to know what the library was thinking. All those times they said things like the library was abandoned or it didn't trust people made more sense now. They acted like the library was a friend, like they were its protectors.

Had the library summoned them because it was...lonely?

Books had been my best friends for a few years too, but this was different. If the library had actually pulled characters out of their books for company, then it wasn't just sentient. It had feelings, hopes, maybe even dreams.

How could I let a library like that fade away?

I had to know what was real and what wasn't before I let my mind wander anymore.

"Here's the deal, Roan. The library needs me, so if you're leaving, I'd really prefer you just leave now." I took a cautious step closer. "But if you want to stay, if you want to keep helping the library, you're more than welcome to."

The corner of his lips quirked up in a smile. "It almost sounds like you want me to stay."

"That's not what I said at all." I rolled my eyes, but felt myself smiling back. "I just don't want to get the story spirits' hopes up if you're going to leave soon. A clean break is better, before they get more attached to you."

Before *I* got more attached.

He stared at me for a bit too long. I glanced away, turning back to the library as if it would somehow show me if it was alive or not if I looked hard enough. But this time, my gaze kept flicking back to Roan.

Would he leave? Or would he stay with me?

"Okay, I'll stay for a while longer," he said, "until we can make sure the library is safe. Jade won't let this go and that's my fault, so you shouldn't have to pay the price for our issues."

The tightness in my chest loosened and I felt like I could breathe easier. He was going to stay. Not forever, of course, but long enough to help the library and for me to figure out what I actually felt about him.

That would have to be good enough for now.

"Then we've got a new mission." I grinned, excitement charging every step I took toward the library. "We're going to figure out if the library is sentient or not."

"Sentient?" Roan asked, disbelief in his voice. "Where'd that come from?"

"You'll see." I rested my hand on the door, feeling magic flowing through it.

This library had comforted me and filled my childhood with adventures. If it was sentient, if it knew what was happening, then that changed everything. I hadn't just been a kid having fun at the library. I'd been a kid spending time with a friend...

"If you're alive," I whispered, "please, please find a way to let me know."

The door creaked open, sending a shiver through me. This was so insane, but exciting at the same time. After I'd been thrown out the first day, this door had stayed shut with almost unnatural force. Nothing I'd done had budged it, almost like the library itself had refused to let me in. But now? It welcomed me with open doors.

I stepped inside slowly with a new reverence for the place. Roan followed me, silent but curious as his gaze swept the area.

"Library?" I called out, not sure what to actually call it. Maybe using its proper name would be better. "Misty Mountain Library?"

Roan's lips twitched.

"Do you have a better idea?" I asked him.

His gaze fell on a pile of books next to one of the reading chairs. "Even if it's sentient, it might not be able to talk like you and me. Try asking for a book instead."

Asking for a book, huh? When I was younger, books used to fly through the air like beautiful birds, flapping from the book tree to the shelves like it was the most natural thing in the world. Had the library been directing them even back then?

I walked over to the great book tree, reaching my hand out to touch its bark. Magic thrummed under my fingers, warm and inviting. If anything was the soul of this library, it was the tree, so I should talk to it here.

My throat felt tight. What if I asked it something and nothing happened? I could be wrong about the whole thing and make a fool of myself. Roan stood behind me, resting his hand on my shoulder. I drew from his strength, his confidence filling me. This was my library and I had to know the truth.

"Library," my voice was barely above a whisper. I cleared my throat and tried again. "I'm looking for a good romance novel. Do you have any suggestions?"

I closed my eyes, too anxious to even look, but the sounds of the book tree's branches swaying made me open them again. One of the branches brushed against my shoulder where Roan's hand was. That had to be the wind. Right?

A book flapped through the air, hovering in front of me like a curious bird waiting to see if I had any seed. I reached out for it and the book settled into my hands, no longer moving. The cover was vibrant and eye-catching, the title *Divine Duelist* scrolled across the top. It was a romance novel about magical card game players mixed up with mythological gods.

The library had sent me a romance novel. Just like I'd asked.

"You're really alive," I said, happy tears filling my eyes. "I'm so happy to meet you."

Roan's grip on my shoulder loosened as he moved to examine the tree. "Well, I'll be damned. It really can understand you. Is that because you're the librarian or does it listen to everyone?" He tilted his head. "Library, could you find me a good action-adventure story?"

He'd accepted my theory so quickly. No arguing, no mocking. Nothing but trust. My heart swelled as I blinked back tears of relief. His trust reassured me as stoutly as his sword protected me. He'd probably seen all sorts of magical things as an adventurer, so if it made sense to him, then I couldn't be *that* crazy.

Another book that looked like it was about one thousand pages flapped through the air, dipping low every once in a while since it was so large, before dropping in front of Roan like a rock.

"That is so cool." Roan grinned as he took a seat, flipping through the book.

I ran my hands across one of the book tree's leaves. "Thank you."

The branch curled around my hand, magic tickling my senses.

The library was *alive*.

No matter how many times I thought that, it still felt monumental, like one of the world's great secrets had been entrusted to me.

"I have so many questions," I said, not sure where to even start. "Is there a better way to communicate with you? Writing maybe?"

"I can help with that," Lisa called out from behind us. She smiled, giving me a knowing look. "We thought you might want to talk in person."

My mouth dropped open. "Then you really can communicate with the library! Why'd you kept it a secret all this time?"

"It's all very new," she said, taking a seat beside the tree, "and I didn't want to put the library at risk if the wrong people found out. Who knows what they'd think of a library that could think."

A library that could think. What a beautiful concept.

Roan nodded. "That was a good idea. I've never heard of another library being alive like this one and people always get weird when new or strange things happen. Just look at how they're treating you guys."

"Exactly," Lisa said, pouring herself a cup of cold tea that Mochi must have left out. "So we decided to be cautious and keep it to ourselves."

I frowned at the book tree. "Why tell me then? And why now?"

"Honestly?" Lisa sighed. "We pushed you away at first because we didn't trust you. You could have gotten our hopes up, torn the place apart trying to improve it, and then lost interest and left. That would have crushed what little spirit the library had left and we wanted its last months or years to be happy. We had no hope of it coming back to life. But the harder you worked, and the more joy you brought to this place, the more we thought it might be possible."

I blinked away more tears, feeling far more emotional than I'd expected. These story spirits believed in me enough for the library to reveal its greatest secret.

"Is every magical library alive?" I asked.

My question hung in the air, heavy and full of implications. If every library was alive, we had to rethink the whole concept of magical libraries and their librarians. We should be more like caretakers than anything else, making sure they were happy and healthy and loved. Definitely loved.

Lisa lifted her shoulder in a half shrug. "I don't know. I don't think a library has ever been able to communicate before, not like this one. So if they are sentient, nobody knew about it." She sipped her tea, frowning at it like she just realized it was cold. "The wild magic storm changed everything here by allowing the library to summon us. Through us, it found new ways of communicating. It's grown bold and intelligent."

The library was learning.

Excitement danced through my body. I wished Oren was here to hear all this so he could get to researching right away.

This library had taken care of me as a child, welcomed me into its shelves, and showed me wonderful books. I'd felt its soul even then, but when I grew older, I'd brushed it off as a childhood fantasy.

But now?

Now I would do everything I could to protect it. To repay it for all the years it had taken care of me.

"What do you need me to do?" I asked.

Lisa smiled. "Prepare for the Tales and Tomes festival. We need it to be the most amazing festival anyone's seen in years to ensure we get the gods' blessing. Your passion has inspired us all, so we'll help as much as we can." She gazed up at the great book tree, wonder filling her eyes. "If this library hadn't gotten lonely, I wouldn't even be here. I owe it everything and more. It gave me life. It *chose* me."

It felt like it had chosen me too. Like I'd been working toward this my entire life.

"Then we'll start preparing for a festival," I said confidently.

The Tales and Tomes festival was the biggest story festival of the year. Celebrations lasted for an entire month, filled with new writers penning stories and wonderful readers sharing their favorites. Passion for books was the heart of the festival and magical libraries were at its core.

Every library around the world could participate, but people expected them to go all out if they did. The popular libraries were full to the brim every year for the final celebration, but smaller libraries often struggled to have enough people to make it worth it.

We'd have to outshine every library around if we were going to get enough patrons to make this festival a success. With all of us working as a team, we'd make this festival one that nobody would ever forget.

Because the Misty Mountain Library was counting on us.

Chapter 17

Roan

The stars shone brightly, glittering in the night sky like diamonds as I laid on the grass watching them. I'd wanted to give Nyssa some privacy to talk with the story spirits and the library, plus, it really was a beautiful night out. Owls hooted hellos to each other while the thrum of insects created a melody in the background.

Stargazing was always so calming. I did it as often as possible, enjoying the familiar sight no matter where I traveled. The constellations might change, but the vibes were the same. Peaceful and quiet, as if this view was just for me and nature.

It was especially helpful when I had some tough thoughts to work out. I'd been all set to leave, to start a new adventure, when Jade showed up and made herself a problem. How could I leave now when I had no idea what she was planning?

The library deserved better than her sniffing around, even if she meant well. She was too focused on being the best that she often missed what was right in front of her. I guess we all missed this one though.

I couldn't believe the library was alive. How many magical libraries had I visited over the years? How many times had I felt that comforting aura and just assumed it was because the building was full of good books and good people?

After all this time as an adventurer, the world was still full of surprises.

The library's warm glow spilled out as the door opened and Nyssa walked outside with a fluffy blanket in her arms.

"Thought you might be getting cold out here," she said, unfurling the blanket on the grass next to me. "Mind if I join you?"

"Of course not," I said, shifting onto the blanket. It offered a warm barrier against the increasingly damp grass.

Nyssa settled on the blanket beside me, her shoulder brushing against mine. I felt myself drawn to the way her skin glowed softly in the moonlight and the way she studied the sky with a little smile on her face. Suddenly, I had something even more beautiful than the stars to look at and that scared me.

"So about Jade," I said, "she's not going to give up easily."

She sighed. "Yeah, I figured. We need a plan."

"I've been thinking a lot about that, actually. Adventurers work on jobs that people post at the guild. If we can convince the people who posted those jobs to take them back or mark them as complete, then she won't have any reason to act against the library anymore."

Her eyes widened. "Is it really that simple?"

"In theory, yes," I said with a laugh, "but in practice? Probably not. I'm not sure how we'll convince anyone the library isn't haunted, but it's worth a shot."

Nyssa nodded. "Once people meet the story spirits, I'm sure they'll have a change of heart. Thanks for the good idea." She shifted onto her elbows, looking down at me. "You know, I can handle that part on my own if you still wanted to leave."

"No, I said I'd stay until the library was safe. It wouldn't feel right leaving in the middle of all this."

She frowned. "I know you said that, but you're not obligated to help us. You said so yourself: adventurers take missions people post at the guild. I didn't post any missions and that little bet of ours is already done, so you really don't owe me anything. You can leave and I won't blame you. I've got a plan now and the story spirits will help me." She smiled warmly. "We'll be okay."

My hands clenched as an uncomfortable feeling swept over me.

"But Jade being here is my fault," I said slowly. "I'll stay until she's taken care of."

"She's apparently been here before, so she would come again with or without you. It's not your fault." Her long hair drifted in the breeze, tickling my arm. "You don't work for the library, so I can handle it from here."

Everything she was saying made sense, but my chest ached more and more with each word. She really didn't need me. I'd always known that, but hearing it spoken so assuredly was painful. I could give my missions to Master

Carmine and let Nyssa know which townsfolk to talk to about them. She was surrounded by people who would help her and she'd never give up on her dreams, so I knew she'd succeed.

I could leave tomorrow and she'd be fine.

She frowned again, her gaze falling on the blanket as she fiddled with it. "I'm not saying you have to leave, just that you can if you want to. You seemed pretty set on it earlier." Her gaze flicked up for a moment, meeting mine. "I thought you were happy here, but then you suddenly wanted to leave, which is fine, I'm just curious about why?"

I gazed at the stars, shining brilliantly above us. If I was going to leave, I might as well tell her the truth. She deserved that much.

"It started with Cerbie," I said, feeling a little foolish. "I realized I'd gotten into a routine with him and that freaked me out."

"Routines freak you out?"

"Pretty much, yeah," I said. "I rarely stay anywhere long enough to build habits. Once you do that, you're attached to people or places, and it hurts a lot more when you have to leave."

"That's...fair," she said, nodding. "But it also sounds lonely."

"Better to be alone than to have people disappoint you all the time."

Her eyes widened as she reached out to touch my arm. "Do you really believe that? It kind of sounds like you're afraid of getting hurt, but you don't strike me as the type of guy who gives in to fears like that."

I stiffened, pulling away from her. That wasn't a fear, it was a fact. People always disappointed me if I gave them the chance.

My parents. Jade. The guild. Everyone I'd ever gotten close to.

"It's just how the life of an adventurer is," I said, "constantly on the move and all. My parents were the same way, always moving around even when I was a kid. Until one day they left me at a guild and told me to adventure on my own from now on. That I was old enough to get by."

"That's horrible," Nyssa said softly. "I'm sorry that happened to you. If it were me, I'd want a home even more after something like that."

Home. That was a word I didn't really understand, but something I was craving more and more. Being here had shown me a glimpse of what a home could be like, what it should feel like, and it was beautiful.

"I'll settle down eventually," I said, forcing a smile on my face. "Just not right now. I haven't found anywhere I'd feel comfortable calling home yet anyway."

My gaze drifted to the library, to the warm glow of the lights shining in the windows and the sound of the story spirits having a good time. Cerbie woofed in the background, making me wish he was out here with us.

"How can you find a place you feel comfortable if you keep running away?" Nyssa asked, her eyes kinder than her words sounded. "It doesn't have to be here, of course, but you should find somewhere that makes you happy and try staying there for a while. See what you feel after that."

"Not worth the risk."

"If that's not worth the risk, then what is?" she asked, her eyebrows pinched together. "You travel all over, fighting and doing missions, but none of that really matters if you aren't happy. If you don't let people see how amazing you really are, then you're taking all those risks for nothing. What are you really getting out of it? Gold? Reputation? Is that what makes you happy?" She shook her head. "I somehow doubt that, because I've seen how happy being here has made you. That's what you should be risking everything on. Find people that make you happy and don't let them go. Don't abandon them before giving them a real chance."

Her words were like a shock of cold water being splashed in my face. Abandon them? Was that really what I'd been doing up until now? No, I was happy with how my life was and I certainly wasn't the one doing the abandoning.

I didn't need friends or family. I was fine on my own.

Or at least, I thought I was. Before I spent time here. Maybe I didn't want to give anyone the chance to leave me again, so I actually did prefer abandoning them first. What kind of person did that make me?

Nyssa laid back down on the blanket, staring up at the stars while my thoughts raced. Eventually, she nudged me.

"See how those stars look like a nest with a really bright one in the center?" She pointed up at the sky. "That's the Phoenix Nest constellation and just like the phoenix can start over whenever it needs to, so can you. Just because you've always done something one way, doesn't mean you always have to. And just because you might see a new way now doesn't mean the old way was wrong. It's just different."

"The Phoenix Nest, huh?" I followed where she was pointing. "I was always told that was the Dragon's Lair and that bright star in the middle was the treasure."

She rolled her eyes. "Of course an adventurer would be taught about treasure instead of rebirth."

I laughed and the tension in the air eased a bit. A breeze drifted over us and Nyssa shivered. I scooted closer, until our sides were touching and her muscles, tense from shivering, relaxed. She smiled as the back of her hand brushed against mine, fingers reaching out as if she wanted to hold my hand.

We continued pointing out other constellations like the Book of Creation and the Forge of the Gods. I made a few up on the fly too, just to see how she'd react. She smiled and pushed me, getting a bit closer with each movement. Soon she'd be in my lap if this kept up. Oh how I wanted this to keep up.

I finally shifted my hand, lacing my fingers through hers. Her breath hitched as she turned to look at me, her gaze falling on our interlocked hands.

"Maybe we should head inside and warm up," she said abruptly, extracting her fingers from mine. "I didn't mean to keep you out here so long. You're probably leaving in the morning, right?"

My whole body felt cold, already missing her warmth as she sat up. Did I do something wrong? Maybe she was taking a page from my book and not wanting to get close to somebody who was going to leave.

"Honestly? I don't know anymore."

"Oh?" She shifted, putting her hand on the ground on the other side of my waist so she was leaning over me. "You know you can stay here, right? If you want to. It doesn't have to be forever, but you can try the whole getting close to people thing if you want. Make some friends, play fetch with Cerbie a few more times. Whatever makes you happy."

That almost sounded too good to be true. Maybe I should try it, just for a bit.

Behind her, the sky lit up as shooting stars fell to the earth. It was beautiful, backdropping Nyssa in an otherworldly glow like she was a goddess. My goddess.

"Turn around," I said, pointing up at the sky.

Her mouth dropped open as her eyes lit up in wonder. This was my idea of a perfect night, just watching the stars with a beautiful woman on a serene mountaintop that even the gods had shown favor on. These shooting stars blessed us.

She grinned down at me. "Make a wish."

"What?"

"You're supposed to wish on a shooting star," she said, shaking her head like she couldn't believe I didn't know that. "Maybe it'll come true."

She was so full of hope and dreams, always seeing the best in every situation. Her passion was infectious, making me want to try new things too. But most of all...I wanted her.

And for once, I wasn't going to run away from that. No, I'd stay here, protect the library, and give myself time to figure out all these feelings between us. I closed my eyes, wishing for the one thing I was most afraid of wishing for: to be wanted.

To be loved.

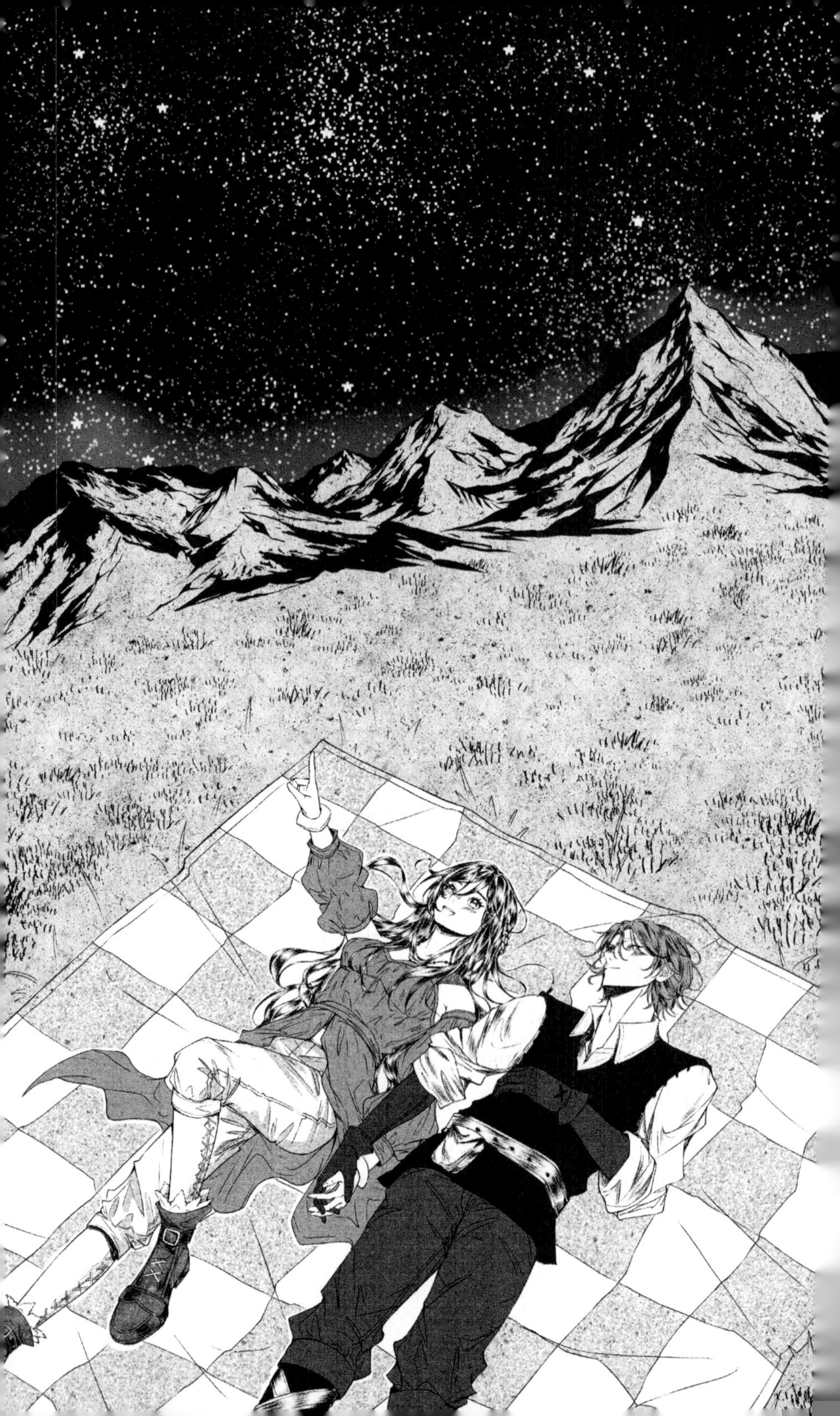

Chapter 18
Roan

It had taken a few days for us to track down everyone who'd submitted a mission about the haunted library to the guild and convince any of them to meet the story spirits, but we finally did it. A determined old apothecary named Mabel who just wanted to gather her herbs again strode up the mountain behind us, walking stick and half muttered curses included.

"If these herbs weren't so damn useful," she said, huffing as she tried to catch her breath, "I'd never come up here. The climb is just too rough on these old bones."

I glanced at Nyssa. "That's a good point. Maybe we can figure something out for you. Make the climb easier?"

The apothecary barked out a laugh. "If you could do that, I'd convince the whole town to visit that creepy library of yours."

"Hey now—" Nyssa shook her head, abandoning her objection. "I mean, that sounds like a deal!"

Her hand brushed against mine as she glanced back, her eyes questioning. It was like she thought I had all the answers when I was just doing my best not to stumble over my words with her the past few days. We'd been so busy that we hadn't had time to really talk since that night, but something felt different between us.

I was more aware of her now than ever before and noticed her every move. It felt like once I'd considered the possibility of sticking around, the floodgates to my emotions had broken open. I had to be more careful now than ever. Be sure that if I took her hand, if I kissed those beautiful lips of hers, that I meant it. That I was here to stay.

She deserved nothing less.

"Are we here to flirt or to collect herbs?" Mabel asked harshly, but her eyes were twinkling. "Young love, so wonderful and annoying."

"Young love?" I jerked away with an awkward laugh. "We're not dating or anything."

Nyssa's lips quirked up. "I didn't realize you felt so strongly about that. It must be horrible having people think you fancy a librarian of all things."

"No, that's not what I —"

She laughed. "I know, I was just teasing."

"Careful, or I'll start teasing you too," I grumbled.

"Promises, promises," she whispered, a devious look in her eyes.

The back of my neck warmed. When had we gone from innocent flirting to flirting with implications attached? But the idea of teasing her did sound tempting. Oh the fun we could have...

Mabel muttered a few more curses as the path got steeper and her breath grew ragged. This honestly was a pretty harsh hike so it made sense that not many people had visited the library even before the wild magic storm damaged it.

"Maybe we should take a break?" I asked.

Mabel shook her head. "It's just up ahead."

So we kept going forward as we moved around rocks and over tree roots, careful none of us fell. The way Nyssa kept glancing back at me, as if she was checking on me too, warmed my heart. Nobody had really ever watched out for me before, or worried if I'd fall on a rugged path. It was nice, those little backward glances.

"Ah, there it is!" Mabel shouted, springing forward with far more pep in her step than before. "The blazebloom has grown beautifully here."

The plant she'd so eagerly rushed to had red leaves and soft orange flowers. I'd seen it somewhere before, but I couldn't quite place it.

"These are for burn ointments, right?" Nyssa asked, kneeling beside the older woman to help her pick the red leaves. "I studied some of the plants on the mountain when we heard an apothecary came up here a lot."

When had she managed to do that? Nyssa always went the extra mile, getting to know at least a little about everything we did. It was a useful trait to have, especially for a librarian who always needed to look things up for people. It was actually good for adventurers too.

"Yes," the apothecary said, "it can also relieve anxiety and makes for a wonderful steak seasoning."

"Steak seasoning?" I asked. Now that was my kind of herb.

As I knelt to join them, a tiny blue dragon head peeked out from the plant in front of me, almost making me fall over.

"What are you doing?" I whispered. "You're supposed to wait at the library until after we're done here."

The dragon tilted its head, as if it didn't understand me. They'd been responding to Nyssa lately though, so I knew they did. Well, whatever, as long as it didn't scare the apothecary, I guess it wasn't that big of a deal. It nibbled on the red-leafed plant contentedly, so I left it be.

"What other plants do you gather up here?" I asked the apothecary.

"Starlight moss, wind root, and all sorts of things," she said, groaning as she shifted to another plant. "The mountain is a treasure trove of mystical plants and my stores are so low since it's been harder and harder to gather them. Those damn spirits kept chasing me off, even when I hired bodyguards."

She harrumphed, then shouted and fell on her backside as blue flames shot over my shoulder. Nyssa gasped as the dragon from before flew over us, dipping and spinning like it was drunk. Its flames turned purple, then green, before it finally fell to the ground, rolling on its back like a dog.

"The spirits are here!" Mabel shouted. "Those flames! That always happens when I come here. They've almost burned the forest down, forcing me to run away."

Nyssa rushed to pick the dragon up, chastising it as she did so and bowed to the apothecary. "Sorry about that.

These little dragons are a bit excitable, but they don't mean any harm."

The dragon belched a bright pink flame that made the old woman quiver. I sighed as a few more dragons munched on the blazebloom, rubbing against its leaves, rolling in them, and honestly looking kind of intoxicated by them.

Wait...they looked like cats when they found a patch of catnip.

I laughed, finally remembering where I'd seen these plants before. Nyssa and the apothecary frowned at me, but I just shook my head.

"Sorry," I said, "but these plants actually go by another name. You might use them medicinally, but dragons use them recreationally."

"What?" Nyssa asked.

"It's like catnip to them," I said, crumbling a leaf up so the smoky aroma filled the air for the little dragons. Their eyes widened with excitement. "See? It's dragonnip. I saw some dragons high on it one time and let me tell you, they're much less terrifying when they're small like this."

Mabel studied them, her keen eyes focused on the little creatures like they were a plant she was analyzing under a microscope. She nudged one with her walking stick and it just rolled over, cooing at her and wiggling its body around on the ground. A small smile touched her lips.

"I see," she said, nodding, "I guess I was wrong then. These are just dragons looking for a good time and I was interrupting them. But why are they so small?"

Nyssa let out a breath. "They're characters from inside a book, brought to life by library magic. I'm not sure why they're so small though." She tapped her chin, staring at them. "I should ask the knights."

"The knights?" Mabel asked. "There are knights too?"

"There are all sorts of story spirits," Nyssa said, grinning like she just hooked a big fish. "When you visit the Misty Mountain Library, the books literally come alive before your eyes. You can talk to all sorts of characters, learn more about their stories, and have fun like you never thought you could."

That's the pitch we'd been working on the past few days and it worked just as good as we'd hoped. The apothecary hung on her every word, nodding and smiling as she started to casually play with the dragons.

"But what do they want?" Mabel asked as she leaned down to pet one.

And that was my cue. I pulled a book from my bag titled *Dragons Just Wanna Have Fun.*

"Here's a copy of the book they come from," I said, handing it to her.

Nyssa smiled, nodding at her to give it a try. "We've already checked it out in your name, so feel free to take it home and read it. You can bring it back to the library whenever you have a chance. I hope it helps you understand them better."

Mabel stared at the cover, glancing between the decorative dragon art and the actual dragons in front of her before finally cracking it open.

"Every young dragon knew that there was a time to be serious and a time to be silly," Mabel read solemnly, glancing up at us. "Really? They just want to have fun?"

"As much as possible." Nyssa grinned as a dragon landed clumsily on her shoulder.

The other dragons circled Mabel, as if summoned by her reading. Some curled up by her feet while others stayed in the air, but they were all focused on the book, giving it far more attention than I thought dragons high on dragonnip could do.

But then one of them fell from the sky in a plume of violet fire while the others did the dragon equivalent of giggling. Yup, they were still enjoying the nip.

Mabel smiled, looking like a weight had been lifted from her shoulders as the fear of this mountain drifted away.

"Okay," the old apothecary said softly, "I'll rescind my mission with the guild."

"Really?" Nyssa practically jumped with joy. "Thank you!"

"On one condition." Mabel held up a finger, staring at us both with utter seriousness. "You must find a way to make this wretched climb easier on these poor old bones of mine. Otherwise, I'll never be able to return this book."

"Deal," Nyssa said with no hesitation.

I raised an eyebrow, but chose not to comment. This was her library, her mission to fulfill. Maybe we could build portals, buy self-driving carriages, or find the secrets to cloud transportation. Actually, this was right up my alley as an adventurer. There were so many wonders hidden out in the world if you were brave enough to look for them.

Maybe we could even search for the solution together and have our own private adventure...

"Okay, enough lollygagging," Mabel said. "We've got three more herbs to collect before the sun goes down and these dragons aren't going to calm down anytime soon."

Nyssa nodded, but looked back at me. "Think they're okay on their own?"

The little dragons were shooting multicolored fire now, lighting up the sky like a fireworks show as they dipped and twirled through the air. Honestly, I'd stay and watch them all day if I could. Maybe we should plant some of this closer to the library. Wait, no, they'd probably burn the library down if we did that. Better to have their fun far enough away that they couldn't cause any damage.

"I think they're fine," I said. "Mabel did say they've been doing this for a while, so they probably come here a lot."

"True..."

Nyssa leaned moved closer, watching the silly little dragons for another minute before tugging me after the apothecary. Every day with her was a wonder, a new adventure without even leaving the mountain. Maybe staying in one spot had its own perks if the place was full of people like Nyssa and these dragons.

The library really was a magical place and we were one step closer to revitalizing it.

Chapter 19
Nyssa

We'd managed to get three haunted library missions taken down at the guild, but there were still a few more and we were running out of time before the final ceremony of the festival. Especially since we had to officially sign the library up for the event and decorate for it too. Before we did any of that though, I had to make sure we actually could host the festival. There were a few library essentials I hadn't seen anywhere yet.

"Hey, Lisa?" I asked as I joined her at the table. "Does this library have a book well? And statues of the gods and all that?"

She flipped a page in the book she was reading, eyes widening. After reading a bit more, she set the book down with a satisfied smile.

"Sorry," she said. "I was at a really good part. But yes, of course we have statues and a book well. What kind of library do you take us for?"

One that hadn't gotten the story gods' blessing in years and was about to disappear, but I wasn't about to say that. I thought I remembered them from when I was a kid, so maybe the statues were just hidden away somewhere for safekeeping, not destroyed or given to a more popular library.

The well should have been noticeable though since it couldn't exactly get up and walk away. A book well was our connection to the story gods, the one place where we could talk to them and actually get a response. Every year, hundreds of writers tossed their books into it like pennies in a wishing well, hoping the gods would be pleased with their stories. It was vital for the festival.

"Okay....but where are they then?" I asked.

Lisa took a slow sip of her tea before answering. "We moved the statues into storage when the roof started caving in. The well is where it always was, in the lobby."

"In the lobby?" I walked back over there, studying the wide-open space yet again, but all I saw was a large potted plant, some cozy chairs, and a few bookshelves. "There's no well here."

"Look closer," Lisa called out from her seat at the table.

I frowned, not really sure what to look closer at since there wasn't much here. The potted plant actually looked a little wilted though so I went to get it some water.

And that's when it hit me.

The plant's pot was made of wood that came up from the floor, as if the library itself had grown it. Which meant it wasn't a pot...

"No way," I whispered, poking around in the dirt a bit. Sure enough, there was a wooden cover holding all the dirt up. "You're using the book well as a planter??"

Either she was too far away to hear me or she was too engrossed in her book, but either way, that was just plain wrong. The book well was our connection to the gods, not some corner store flower pot. It was supposed to be filled with the magical water of hopes and dreams, not dirt and rocks!

My hands itched to rip that plant out and toss it outside where it belonged, but I took a deep breath and thought about it for a minute. The golem was the only one who cared about plants enough to do this and I'd already upset it once when I'd torn its window patches down without asking.

Maybe if I asked the golem to transplant this, it would be okay.

I wandered outside to where the golem was pulling weeds from its body and smashing them underfoot.

"Weeds," it muttered, "always weeds."

I'd never thought about if golems grew weeds like normal dirt did, but now I'd never unsee it. The golem carefully yanked weeds from around the poppies on its shoulders, smiling once the last one was gone and the flowers basked under the sunlight, tilting their petals up.

"Hello." I waved to the golem. "How's your garden going?"

"Beautiful," it rumbled, motioning at the very full flower beds.

Honestly, they really were beautiful. Each flower bed held a different assortment of plants, like a living mosaic of greenery. Some of the flowers glowed like they were filled with magic, making them even more eye-catching. The floral scent filling the air was rather comforting too, making me want to sit and gaze at them all day.

We should add some chairs outside for people to read and enjoy the flowers at the same time. I bet the golem would like that.

"Do you know anything about the plants in the book well?" I asked.

The golem leaned down, like he was going to whisper something to me. "Library was sad. Nobody visited the well."

Its voice was loud in my ear, but I just smiled and nodded. "So you planted something inside it to make it more appealing?"

"Yes." Its eyes glowed bright as it smiled. "Plan worked."

I mean, I guess that was technically true since people stopped to water it and check on it sometimes, but it couldn't stay there. Not when we had a festival to run.

"That was thoughtful of you," I said, patting its large rocky hand. "I bet the library was happy. Weren't you, Misty?"

"Misty?" The golem asked, then lit up when the library's windows opened and closed like it was saying yes. "Ohhhhhh, Misty!"

I grinned, loving how excited the golem got about everything. "Yeah, I thought it could use a name now that we know it's sentient. Misty Mountain Library felt a bit too formal."

The golem nodded, lumbering over to the library to pat its walls. This really was the most magical place I'd ever been. I wouldn't trade it for anything, which meant I had to keep moving forward.

"You know, that plant would look amazing out here with the rest of your garden," I said. "Do you mind if we move it so we can get the book well ready for the festival?"

The golem shook its head. "Don't mind."

Well that was far easier than I'd expected. I was glad I'd taken the time to ask instead of just doing what I thought was best like last time.

"Can you dig a hole for it out here?" I asked, heading back inside after the golem nodded.

The plant's roots weren't grounded in anything, so it was pretty easy to pick up and carry outside. A trail of dirt followed me that I'd have to clean up later though. Once it was safely replanted outside, I removed the well cover, carefully setting it aside so I didn't get more dirt everywhere.

My stomach sank as I stared down the dark, very empty, well.

The water was completely gone!

But that didn't make sense. Magical libraries grew on top of underground water caverns so the tree and well would always be taken care of. I'd never seen a book well without water brimming at its surface. Was that part of the damage from the magic storm? Or a downside of not getting the story gods' blessing for years?

Either way, we couldn't host the Tales and Tomes Festival with a bone-dry book well.

I sank to the floor, leaning my back against the well.

"I'm sorry, Misty. I should have checked that right away."

The library didn't respond, at least not in any way I noticed. Maybe it really was sad about the well like the golem had said, which made me sad too. I just wanted to revive this place, but every time I turned around, something else needed fixing.

I sighed as my thoughts spun. How was I supposed to fix the well?

If only we hadn't scared the contractors away. They were one group we hadn't been able to get a hold of yet, but I had a feeling they wouldn't be so easy to win over. Not after they'd literally fled the mountain in terror.

So it was up to me. To fix a well.

I groaned, rubbing my hand over my face. I was a librarian, not a...well fixer?

"Need some help?" Lisa asked as she joined me, frowning at the piles of dirt everywhere. "You've got dirt on your face, you know."

My hands were covered in dirt, darkening my skin like ink. I used the edge of my shirt to wipe the smudges off my face, hoping I got them, then looked at Lisa expectantly.

"Better." She nodded, then rested her hand against the well. "This has been a sore spot for years. I think we need to dig the well deeper."

"Can't the library do that?"

She paused, staring at the great book tree. "Yes, but I'm not sure if it wants to. Digging the well deeper means we're capable of hosting the festival and I'm not sure it's ready for that yet."

Roan walked in with a towel around his neck like he'd just been working out. "Being abandoned isn't easy to forget about. Maybe the library is still worried it'll happen again."

Of course it was, how could it not be? Us being here for a few weeks didn't make the past few years disappear. I glanced at Roan, who's eyes were downcast. Was his pain still just as prevalent?

"You know," I said softly, "the library and you have a few things in common. Maybe you could talk to it?"

His eyes widened. "You want me to talk to the library?"

"Yeah, but call it Misty. It likes that." I smiled as the books quivered in excitement nearby. "See? Let us handle the well, you handle the library."

Lisa nodded. "Agreed."

Roan walked over to me, holding out his hand to help me up. "Are you sure about this? What if I screw it up?"

"Just be honest," I said, running my thumb over the back of his hand. "You'll do fine."

We stood like that for a few moments, just holding hands and staring at each other, before he nodded.

"Just don't blame me if the well gets even dryer," he said with a little half smile.

"Deal." I squeezed his hand one more time before letting it go. "Now, how do we dig a deeper well?"

I leaned over the edge, not sure how far down it actually was.

"We don't." Lisa gave me one of those looks like I was missing something obvious. "We let Roan talk to the library like you said. Once it's ready, it'll dig the well deeper itself.

And if it's never ready, then we'll respect that decision and stop all this festival talk."

I wanted to argue with her, to tell her that there was no way I'd give up on the festival, but watching Roan awkwardly lean up against a bookshelf and try communicating with Misty tugged at my heart. Everyone here was trying so hard to understand each other and make this place better.

"Okay," I said with a nod. "But I believe Roan can turn this around."

Lisa smiled. "So do I."

So instead of jumping into the well with a shovel, we watched Roan chat with the library. He picked up a book, flipping through the pages as he talked in a voice too soft to make the words out, but it was comforting and warm.

What was he telling Misty?

I wanted to go over and listen too, but this felt like a moment just for the two of them. The library deserved to have more people on its side than just me and this was the perfect chance for them to get to know each other better. I could always talk to Roan about it later.

"You look jealous," Lisa said, amusement coloring her voice. "That's how I felt when you first showed up."

My gaze jerked to her. "Really? Why?"

"The library is my best friend, my only friend if I'm being honest," she said, tracing her finger along the edge of the well. "I was worried that it would think real people were more important than us story spirits and it would forget about me eventually. Like one day...I just wouldn't come out of my book anymore and that would be that."

"That would never happen," I said vehemently, grabbing her hand. "You're a Misty Mountain librarian, just like me. You're too important to disappear and Misty knows that. Besides, the library isn't your only friend. I'm your friend too."

Silence stretched between us as she studied me. Had I said something wrong? Maybe we weren't actually becoming friends like I thought. I dropped her hand and smiled at her even as my face warmed.

"You matter to people, that's all I meant." I cleared my throat, turning around to watch Roan laughing as books flew around him excitedly. "Looks like things are going well over there."

Suddenly, Lisa's arms were around my shoulders, pulling me into a hug. "I'd gladly be your friend. Thank you."

The sound of rushing water drowned out anything I might have said in return, pulling all of our attention to the well. Shimmering water flooded it, surging toward the surface beautifully. Magic thrummed under my fingers as I leaned over to see my reflection in the water.

I had a big stupid grin on my face. We were really going to save the library.

"Hey Roan," I shouted, "come over here!"

Lisa trailed her fingertips through the water, smiling. "I knew the library didn't want to be reborn anywhere else. It just needed a little kindness and warmth. Just like all of us."

Roan leaned over the well next to me. "I didn't think that would work. All I did was tell the library about my past and how good coming here felt."

I gazed at our reflections in the water. His red hair bright next to my dark hair. His strength next to my bookishness. We were an odd pair, but we looked good together. Happy.

"It does feel nice having you here," I said softly. "I'm sure the library feels the same way."

His eyes widened, but a small smile touched his lips. He shifted closer, his hip brushing up against mine. I froze, not wanting to ruin the moment, but he was giving so many mixed signals lately.

When we'd been stargazing, it had seemed like he liked me. Like he wanted more than just friendship. But after that? It was like he was a deer in an open meadow, startling at every little noise I made. I'd been starting to think I made the whole flirtation up, but I'd caught him staring at me a few times, like he was trying to puzzle something out. What was going on in that head of his?

Lisa gave me a knowing look as she leaned against the well. "So what's our next step?"

Right. Focus on the library and deal with the butterflies in my stomach later.

"Clean the statues, find the wishing book, and officially sign up for the final ceremony of the festival." I frowned, glancing at Lisa. "That last one has to be done in person at the main festival grounds though. Will it be okay if we leave?"

She rolled her eyes. "We survived without you two for years, we can handle another day."

She might have said that, but her hands gripped her skirts a little too tight.

"You could come with us?" I offered. "Show the townsfolk how wonderful the story spirits are?"

Lisa froze. "I don't think that's a good idea, sorry."

"Okay, no worri—"

A dragon swooped by, completely interrupting us as it dropped a tiny knight in the well with a loud plop followed by frantic splashing.

"You damned dragons!" the knight shouted, but it came out a little gurgled as his armor kept dragging him down. "I'm a knight! Not a bath toy!"

I clenched my lips together, trying to keep my laughter inside as I scooped him out. Water dripped out of his armor like a sieve. He looked like a drowned rat.

Lisa took that moment to study some very important books, smiling just a bit while Roan chuckled.

"Let me help you with that," Roan said, laughter still in his voice.

The knight took off his armor, placing it along the edge of the well to dry as he searched the room for more dragons.

"They always get you when you least expect them," he said with grave seriousness. "Never take your eyes off the skies, that's what my King always told me."

The image of him dripping wet, but still trying to seem so professional was too much for me. A small laugh bubbled up and then more spilled out. The knight was a little red in the face, but then he joined in and laughed too.

"Want to help me get some payback, my loyal friends?" he asked.

"Depends what your idea of payback is." I crossed my arms, studying him. "If it has anything to do with fire around the well we just repaired, that's a hard pass."

Roan gave me a shocked look. "You would leave a knight's honor besmirched like that?"

Since when did he play along with the knights' antics? Last I saw, he was locking them in the lending libraries like they were in jail. Something had changed for him. I wasn't sure what, but I liked it.

"Of course I wouldn't," I said, holding my palm out to the knight. "Let's go get your justice."

The knight cheered and climbed onto my hand so Roan and I could chase down dragons with him. All in all, not a bad way to spend a day.

Chapter 20
Nyssa

In the end, none of the story spirits had felt comfortable coming with us to the festival except for the knight commander. And even he had only come after we promised that nobody would capture him in a jar again like a bug. He was currently hiding in Roan's jacket pocket, only visible when he peeked out to look at our new surroundings.

The Tales and Tomes Festival went on for an entire month and was the biggest story festival of the year, taking over the streets of the capital and spilling out into smaller cities beyond it. Thousands of authors spent the time writing new books while readers got to meet their favorite authors and join bookish events.

The whole thing culminated in a special ceremony held at magical libraries around the world where authors offered up their newly born books to the story gods and were blessed with good ideas for the year to come. The libraries were also blessed if enough people showed up, proving the public wanted them to thrive.

And I was going to make sure that our library was one of them.

As Roan and I walked onto the festival grounds, the sounds of groans filled the air. The festival only had a week left, so most of the writers were reaching their limits by now. Everyone started off all excited, but after pumping out the words day after day, their minds went a little mushy.

We entered the grounds by Nightmare Alley, the inspiration for many a horror novel. Haunting screams filled the air along with rattling chains and strange lights.

Roan frowned. "Is this what all festivals are like? It looks a little grim."

"Not exactly," I said, coughing as smoke tendrils coiled in front of me. "Maybe we should head over to the Enchanted Realm a few streets over, it's to the right of Lover's Cove."

Roan raised an eyebrow. "You've been here before, huh?"

"Of course, I'm a librarian."

Actually, I'd tried my hand at writing a novel once, but ended up just brainstorming ideas without getting any words on the page. The experience was amazing though. All these writers in one spot, cheering each other on, motivating everyone to just write one more chapter.

One more page.

One more sentence.

"You can't find another festival as bookish as this one," I said, excitement coursing through me as we left Nightmare Alley. "There are book themed crafts, food, plays, and a lot of authors even do book signings! It's my favorite time of the year."

"I love how much you love it here." Roan grinned widely, offering me his hand as if that was a normal thing between us now. "Mind showing me around?"

"Uhhh, sure. I'd like that." The back of my neck warmed as I slipped my hand into his.

If I didn't know better, I'd say this felt like a date. The idea sent butterflies racing through me. He'd been sleeping on the floor again lately, which somehow made me feel like we were even closer than before. Almost like him moving to the floor meant he actually had feelings for me and didn't want to cross any lines.

That was probably wishful thinking, and unhelpful too, because I needed to stay focused on the mission.

"Actually," I said slowly, "we need to sign the Misty Mountain Library up for the final ceremony first."

He curled his fingers around mine, tracing circles on my palm with his thumb. Warmth blossomed in my chest as we walked around the festival, hand in hand. Okay, maybe it was a little bit of a date.

As we made our way to the center of town, Roan's gaze kept wandering to the stalls.

"Don't even think about it," I warned. "We're in the magical food section. So unless you want a Mystic Mocha that'll keep you awake for three days and then knock you out flat or some Bard Biscuits that'll turn everything you say into song, I'd steer clear."

"Could be useful," he said, studying the menu. "Clarity Crystals are hard candy that bring focus to your mind and this Stamina Sourdough boosts your endurance." He turned to me, eyes sparkling. "The guild's chefs are always looking for new recipes, maybe they should visit."

The guild and Jade were two things I didn't want to think about today. Today was all about beautiful book magic that the library so desperately needed. And Roan...

"I'm going to go sign us up," I said, squeezing his hand before letting it go. "Why don't you get us some food? Normal food."

"Okay," he said, "but you're kind of taking the fun out of it."

I rolled my eyes. "Try the magical food too then. I'm not stopping you."

I wound my way through the stalls until I found the administration building and walked up to the counter.

"How can I help you?" a young woman with pencils stuck through her buns asked.

"I'd like to sign the Misty Mountain Library up for the festival."

"Of course, I'd be happy to help." She smiled a bit too brightly as she pulled some paperwork out. "Name of the library, address, and name of the writer who's sponsoring you."

"Name of the...writer?"

She frowned, fiddling with one of the pencils in her hair. "Yes, you need a writer to present their new book at your library, otherwise the festival would be kind of anticlimactic for people."

A sense of doom settled over me. I'd forgotten that key piece of the festival because my last library always had tons of writers visiting it, so having one was never in doubt. But a supposedly haunted little backwoods library like ours? Yeah, that might be a little trickier to convince anyone to bring their new book to.

"There are a few undeclared writers still," the woman said. "Maybe you could talk to one of them?"

Hope surged through me. "Can I have their names?"

"Well, we don't give out that kind of information," she said, leaning forward to whisper, "but once the writers are done with the noon writing sprint, you can ask around. I'm sure somebody would give your library a chance if it's nice."

If it was nice. I thought that it was the best library I'd ever been to, but I'd admit a lot of that was nostalgia and my personal connection to it. We'd all worked so hard to make it beautiful, but the rumors of it being haunted and the difficulty getting up the mountain might still be issues.

"Miss?"

"Oh, sorry," I said, "thanks for the information. I'll be back later."

She nodded and waved as I walked away, still trying to think of ideas. Would I be better off trying to find a local writer, one who would remember the library from their childhood like I did, or find a writer here where hopefully nobody had heard the rumors about it being haunted?

We could even do a little story spirit show-and-tell if the knight in Roan's pocket was up for it.

"Nyssa, over here," Roan said, waving me over to a table in the courtyard piled with all different kinds of food.

The scent of freshly baked bread washed over me, warm and toasty, mixed with delicate spices from a taco platter and some kind of meat and veggie skewers that the knight was drooling over. Then there were the desserts. Oh the desserts. He'd purchased tarts and cookies, pies and bars, a whole treasure trove of delicious-looking food.

My mouth was watering by the time I sat down, unable to choose what to try first.

"I wasn't sure what you liked," Roan said. "So I got a bit of everything."

"That was a very good plan." I reached for the bread, still warm to the touch. "We'll need to find some good food for our festival too."

"Think Mochi could do it?" he asked, munching on a fruit skewer. "I still have no idea where that food comes from, but it always makes me feel happy. Like he puts some secret ingredient in it."

True, Mochi's food did have a heartwarming quality. Nostalgic and warm, like this bread. I smeared an herb scented butter on a slice and took a glorious bite. It was so soft it practically melted in my mouth.

"Of course Sir Mochi could do it," mumbled a tiny voice from inside Roan's pocket. The knight climbed out, almost falling onto the table. He put his hands on his hips, all proud once he reached the table safely. "I'll just try some of this food and give him a full report so he can recreate it."

The knight carefully walked around the piles of food that were almost as tall as him. I slid an extra plate over to him so he could put his bite-sized pieces of food on it and he bowed in return.

"Thank you, Lady Nyssa."

Then he proceeded to try every single piece of food Roan had purchased. His happy little noises made me so glad he'd decided to join us. The other story spirits had said they were worried about traveling so far away from the library, but really I had a feeling they were worried about how people would react to them.

I had to show them that people cared about the library so they would give people a chance to care about them too. Once everyone got to know the story spirits, they'd love them like I did. It had been working out great so far with the few people we'd had one on ones with, like the apothecary, but now we needed a more widespread plan.

"This is so good," Roan said, closing his eyes in delight as he bit into a fruit tart. "If I'd known festivals had so much good food, I'd have come to one sooner."

"Wait, you've never been to a festival before?"

He shook his head, brushing a crumb off his lip. "My parents thought festivals were a place people went to spend money and drink, so they never let me go. And once I was on my own....well, festivals felt like a place you should go with friends, you know?"

Was that implying he didn't have any friends? I picked at the piece of bread in front of me. I knew he said he liked to move on before he got too attached to people, but that seemed extreme.

I wanted to say something meaningful, something to take away the kind of sad look on his face, but a theater troupe was setting up on the center stage and we wouldn't really be able to chat.

"Are there plays here?" he asked, leaning forward. The trace of sadness was gone, almost like I'd imagined it.

"Yeah, they act out famous stories throughout the festival. Based on the costumes and props, it looks like this one will be about the story of creation."

Roan sat at rapt attention as they announced the title of the play, only moving to eat some more of the good food. I smiled, happy we'd come here. Helping the library was great, but we needed to keep our spirits up too otherwise we'd be no good to Misty.

I pulled some squid ink pasta over to me and sat back to watch the show. The troupe used magic to enhance the story while actors played the roles of the three story gods: Terra, Solas, and Orion.

A narrator guided the actors through their parts. "At the birth of the universe stood three gods who yearned for a good story, and what do all good stories need? Settings, characters, and plots."

The knight sat down and tried to focus after noticing how intrigued Roan was, but he obviously cared more about the food than the play. I smiled, enjoying the moment with the two of them.

"Terra came first," the narrator said, "shaping the world out of magic, forming the mountains and rivers, the forests and plains. Her imagination formed the very land we walk on and grow food from. But a world without people was lonely, so Solas created gods, people, and beasts to roam the land, filling Terra's dream with life."

As the narrator spoke, illusion magic swept over the stage, showing the land being created and people walking across it aimlessly. Roan shifted his chair closer to me, smiling softly as his arm brushed against mine. My stomach fluttered. Yes, this was definitely a date.

"But simply living wasn't enough either," the narrator continued, "we had to learn and grow, struggle and love. So Orion wove our fate across the stars, giving each of us reasons to live and things to strive for. From their imaginations, our stories were born. From our minds, we create new stories to offer them."

As he finished speaking, the illusions grew brighter, glowing beautifully even in the daylight. I bet we could do something similar with the Demon Lord's shadows, using them to put on a play like these illusions. If I could get him to cooperate.

A gong sounded and the crowd cheered. I would have joined, but spotted some exhausted looking people coming into the courtyard as if they'd just been set free from some terrible hardship.

I knew who they were: writers. Mentally exhausted writers.

"Come on," I whispered, nudging Roan. "We need to get one of those writers to sponsor our library for the festival."

"That was not part of the plan," he said, laughter creeping into his voice.

"Well, it's part of the plan now," I said, sizing the writers up. "We're not going to get anyone famous, probably not even anyone experienced, but I bet we could convince a newbie to give our library a try."

"Do you think it'll work?" he asked. "Not trying to be mean, but the Misty Mountain Library hasn't been open in years. Will anyone really agree to bring their book there?"

He had a good point. Anyone who had heard of the library had probably either heard that it was closed or that it was haunted, neither of which were good for a festival.

"We'll just have to get creative," I said, "with a bit of good storytelling, you can get people to do just about anything."

He raised an eyebrow, swallowing a bite of food. "That's a bit manipulative, isn't it?"

"We wouldn't be lying or anything, just making sure we show off all the good points about the library." I nodded overtly at the tiny knight who was wolfing down pie. "Show people why our library is so unique."

Roan's mouth opened in an O. "Got it. Let's go nab you a writer then."

He was always willing to help with whatever I needed and he seemed to enjoy it too. I'd gotten so lucky the day he'd walked into my library. So very, very lucky.

The knight cocked his head at us. "Wait, so what's the plan?"

"Come with us and find out," I said, offering him my hand.

He brushed crumbs off his armor before climbing onto my palm. "You know, it's not exactly knightly to be carried around like this."

"Would you prefer to be on my shoulder, like a little spirit guide?"

Roan laughed. "I don't think that would end well."

"Sir Roan, don't talk like that!" the knight protested, but he was smiling as he did it.

Together, we walked toward the writers, ready to convince them that our library was the best in the world.

With Roan and the knight by my side, I felt like we really could do just about anything.

Chapter 21
Roan

We'd asked four writers to sponsor the Misty Mountain Library, but they'd all turned us down. Seeing Nyssa's excitement slowly die made me want to do something, anything, to bring her smile back a bit. I stopped to grab hot cocoa for all of us, hoping the creamy chocolate would warm her up and brighten her mood.

"This isn't over yet," I said as I sat down beside her. "We'll find the perfect writer soon, I bet."

"Cocoa, huh?" Steam curled around her hands as she took one of the cups from me. "I expected you to get one of those magical drinks from earlier."

"Hot cocoa *is* magical," I said firmly, before taking a sip. Warmth spread through my body, sweet and delicious.

I sighed with contentment. "Try drinking that and not being happy. I dare you."

She smiled softly behind the rim of her cup before blowing on it to cool it down. When she finally took a drink, her eyes closed for a moment, as if fully enjoying the rich chocolate flavor. I'd even asked for double marshmallows because those always added an extra special touch to a hot cocoa.

The knight hiding in her hair leaned forward, sniffing the air. He grinned, climbing down her arm so fast he almost fell.

"Yes, I got you some too," I said, pouring some into a bottle cap. "I hope this works for a cup. They didn't have anything in your size."

"That's kind, Sir Roan," the knight said, reaching up to grab the bottle cap. He drank deeply, apparently not caring that it was hot, and held the cap up for more. "It's delicious."

Nyssa's small smile turned into a grin. "Have I mentioned how grateful I am that you both came with me today?"

It was hard to be anything but happy when sitting next to somebody you cared about with a soothing hot chocolate. If only we were at the library so we could curl up under the book tree, then this would be perfect.

"It might take longer than you were hoping for," I said, "but we will find a great writer for the library."

She nodded, taking another sip of her drink and watching the people around us. Some chatted with friends while others looked like they were interacting with fans, signing autographs and handing out books. There were a few people off on their own too, just eating a meal and resting.

Overall, it was a pretty good vibe. Maybe we'd have to come back to this festival next year when we weren't on a mission to save the library.

I'd never planned anything that far ahead before, but being around Nyssa and the library just felt...right. I didn't think they'd hurt me like other people had, so maybe sticking around wasn't such a terrible idea. Maybe I could be happy here.

No, that was ridiculous. What would I even do? Be her jobless boyfriend? I was an adventurer, which meant being on the road. I could stick with jobs closer to the guild, but that would mean actually interacting with the guild and I definitely didn't want that. So what did that leave me?

"What's that?" a guy asked as he froze next to us, pen in hand. He stared at the knight, completely forgetting the journal he'd been writing in. "Is it a toy? Or some kind of magic?"

Instead of waiting for either of us to answer, the guy just grabbed the knight straight off our table. The knight's eyes widened as he dropped his drink, spilling it all over his armor. His eyes narrowed as he pulled out his sword, obviously ready for vengeance.

"Nobody spills a man's cocoa and gets away with it," the knight proclaimed. "I challenge you to a duel."

I'd have been more upset about being manhandled than the spilled cocoa, but I knew neither could be fun. I resisted the urge to grab my own sword and join the fight, but only because Nyssa was gripping my knee under the table, shaking her head slightly. She probably wanted to handle this calmly and quietly so we didn't draw attention.

I could do that. For now. I nodded and she relaxed, turning toward the stranger.

"You shouldn't just pick people up," Nyssa said, holding her hand out for the knight. "Give him back."

"Sorry, no offense intended," the guy said as the knight dangled helplessly by his cloak between the man's thumb and forefinger, feet kicking and sword swinging. "I was just curious what it was."

Nyssa's happy demeanor was turning into a glare, but she kept a smile on her face. "He's a story spirit from the Misty Mountain Library."

"A story spirit?" the guy asked as he dropped the knight onto the table, as if Nyssa was far more interesting than whatever the knight was.

I gritted my teeth, barely holding back angry words. Sure, I didn't always appreciate the knight's enthusiasm, but I'd never treat them like that. I set my arm on the table, motioning for the knight to stand by me if he wanted to. He saluted me and ran over, armor clinking softly.

"Our library has a special kind of magic," Nyssa said, phrasing it just like we'd practiced with the other writers who'd turned us down. "It can bring characters from books to life as story spirits."

Wait, she couldn't really be considering asking *him* to sponsor the library, could she?

"Nyssa —"

"That's awesome!" the rude guy interrupted. "Does that work for any book or just certain ones? I'm a writer, so it would be cool to meet my characters, you know?"

He ran his hand through his hair, smiling awkwardly as he continued chatting with Nyssa, but something about the way he looked at her set my nerves on edge. He reminded me of wealthy clients who'd found a new toy to play with and wanted to experiment, no matter the cost. Those were the ones who usually caused huge magical disasters.

He wasn't right for the library. We needed to end the conversation before he got any ideas, but the words hung in my throat. Was it really my place to tell her what to do? Sure, I'd been helping out, but I didn't plan to stay there. I should probably let her take the lead...

But the knight was still standing behind my arm like a barricade as he fought the air, muttering curses. The writer hadn't noticed at all, barely deigning to look at the knight like a real person. Nyssa had though, glancing at us with a concerned crease in her forehead.

"This has been fun," she said to the writer, "but we've got a lot to do still. I hope you tell all your friends about how wonderful the Misty Mountain Library is though!"

My shoulders relaxed. Of course she wouldn't have asked a guy like that to help us, I'd been worried for nothing. The knight climbed onto my shoulder as we got up to leave, but the guy grabbed Nyssa's arm.

"Don't you want a writer to sponsor your library?" he asked. "That's why you're here, right?"

Okay, he'd crossed the line now. Grabbing two people without their consent right in front of me was just too much.

"We don't need somebody as handsy as you." I glared at his tight grip on Nyssa's arm. "If you don't want to revisit that duel scenario, I'd think twice about who you touch."

"Agreed," Nyssa said, moving a bit closer to me. "Sorry, you're not the right fit for us."

He dropped his hand. "Fine, whatever. I bet the books don't even come to life and this was all a joke anyway."

"Oh, they come to life," I said, "but a guy like you doesn't deserve to meet them. Not after how you treated Sir Reginald the Third."

The knight gasped. "Sir Roan, you finally know my name?"

As the writer walked off, Nyssa leaned in close to whisper to the knight. "I caught him reading your book earlier."

"It was just sitting in front of me," I said, scratching the back of my head. "It doesn't mean anything."

"Oh, it definitely means something." Nyssa laughed, linking her arm through mine. "I think you secretly love the knights."

"Is it true, Sir Roan?" the knight asked. "Do you want to join our knightly ranks? We've been searching for our long-lost King and many think you might be him."

"Whoa, nobody said anything about that," I said with a laugh. The sun was beginning to set, casting the festival in a warm glow of oranges and yellows with just the barest hint of pink. We should get back before nightfall. Ghosts might not inhabit the Misty Mountain like the townsfolk thought, but that didn't mean trudging through the forest in the dark would be fun. "Let's head out for today. We can try again tomorrow."

Nyssa nodded. "Maybe bringing a story spirit was a bit too much."

The knight sighed so softly it wouldn't have been audible if he wasn't on my shoulder. Being small was probably already tough enough, but feeling useless had to be way worse. Nobody deserved to feel like that, especially when they tried as hard as the knight did.

"Sir Reginald the Third played his part admirably," I said. "If not for him, we wouldn't have known what a total creep that guy was."

The knight puffed up a bit.

"He was kind of weird," Nyssa said, frowning.

"Man, I was really worried when I thought you might ask him to sponsor the library," I said as we walked out of the festival courtyard.

"Really? Why didn't you say something then?"

I shrugged, glancing away from her. "It's your library, figured you should decide."

Nyssa gripped my arm a bit tighter. "It's your library too, you know. I see how much you care about the story spirits, whether you want to admit it or not, so you can speak up if you feel like something's off."

The story spirits honestly had been growing on me. From playing fetch with Cerbie, to the knights secretly training beside me, to Mochi always ready with a heartfelt snack. They were all so kind and genuine. Heck, even the Demon Lord had his good points, defending the library whenever he thought somebody might harm it. I might not like the guy, but I could respect that.

"Okay," I said slowly. "I'll say something next time something feels off."

"Good." Her smile was like the sun peeking out on a rainy day, bright and full of hope. "Now, let's head home."

Home.

I liked the feel of that word far more than I should.

Chapter 22
Roan

Moon lilies floated on the pond's surface behind the library, their glow dimming as the sun rose higher in the sky. The golem had asked me to wait here while he looked for downed trees to use on our super secret project: Mochi's Magical Munchies. It was a little gift for Nyssa to hopefully cheer her up after not finding a writer yesterday.

Enjoying the festival with her had given me a lot of ideas about how to make the library's portion of it successful. Good food and cozy drinks felt like a must and Mochi was the best story spirit for the job. He deserved a snack stand worthy of his food.

The red panda padded over by me, leaning up against the beautiful maple tree I was sitting under and gazed out at the forest. The clear mountain air was invigorating and the tint of red sweeping through the trees was picturesque as autumn sparked a change around us.

There was something so serene about this mountain. If only we could get the townsfolk to see it, experience its vibes, they'd come to the library every day just for the good view.

Mochi offered me a steaming mug of green tea, holding it carefully in his little paws as the earthy scent wrapped around me.

"Thanks," I said, taking the drink. "Are you ever going to show me how you do that?"

The panda swished his tail, chittering as another mug of tea suddenly appeared in his paws. I shook my head, laughing softly. This library, and the story spirits inside it, were really something special. I had a feeling Nyssa's dreams would come true very soon. We'd not only save this library, but we'd make it a place nobody could forget.

The slow plodding footsteps of the golem pulled my attention to the edge of the clearing. He lumbered out of the forest with an entire tree over his shoulder, the top dragging on the ground as he pulled it over by us.

"That looks perfect!" I said, getting up to help him with it.

The golem's eyes brightened. "Tree fell. Needs new life."

He'd been adamant about us not cutting any trees down and I was definitely not about to fight a forest golem over trees. So I was glad he figured something out that worked for both of us. Now onto the next part: turning it into a food stall.

I crossed my arms, staring down at it. I didn't actually know much about woodworking. Should we remove the bark first or cut it into planks somehow? The golem had hidden my axe, so I really didn't have much to work with.

"So...what now?" I asked, hoping the golem would take the lead.

The golem ran his hands over it, magically stripping the bark as it wrapped around his arm instead. Then he made a noise like a whistle, summoning the little dragons to join us. They flew over happily, landing on the downed tree with ease. Their flames warmed the air, drying out the tree so we could use it. Only a few spots got scorched too.

It was nice to see the story spirits working together. Soon we'd be able to cut up the wood and use it to build Mochi's snack shack.

"Any preferences for how it looks?" I asked Mochi, hoping somebody could translate his panda talk for me, but he was focused on the woods behind us.

The golem and the dragons were too.

I gripped the hilt of my sword. "Is something there?"

"Humans," the golem rumbled.

That's when I heard the rustling, as if somebody was pushing through an overgrown path. But I also heard something else. A thump thump that sounded far too familiar.

"Lending libraries?" I asked. "Are they leading somebody here?"

The thumping got louder, as if their stakes were hopping as fast as they could. Soon three little lending libraries leapt out of the trees toward us, followed by two women and a man. The people were breathing heavily and looked a bit worse for wear with small snags in their clothing and sweat mixing with dirt on their arms.

"Thank the gods," the man said. "We've been lost for hours. If these...whatever they are hadn't found us, we'd have been goners."

One of the women sucked in air, putting her hands on her knees. "We figured we'd just walk up the mountain like we used to, but everything's changed and the paths don't lead where we expected." She sank onto the ground, sighing. "I'm Isolde, that's Theo, and that's Anya."

"Roan," I said, releasing my grip on my sword as the lending libraries hopped around me like they were hoping for a treat after a job well done. I patted them on their roofs, making a mental note for Nyssa to switch their books out later. "Are you guys looking for the library?"

The man named Theo blanched. "The library? No way, not a chance. We don't want to be anywhere near that place. You know it's haunted, right?"

The lending libraries slowed, tilting to the side a bit as if confused. I scratched my head, glancing at the back of the library twenty paces away from us. Should I tell them? Or let them calm down first?

The golem and the dragons kept working on the wood as if nothing had happened, but Mochi went to hand the newcomers bottles of water.

"Oh, thanks," Isolde said, then froze, eyes widening. "You're a panda."

Mochi chirped, as if agreeing with her. He was, in fact, a panda.

The two women stared in fascination while the guy guzzled the water down, not even questioning that a red panda had handed the drink to him. Seriously, what were the three of them doing all the way up here? Especially if they thought the place was haunted?

"So, what brings you here?" I asked casually.

"Dragons," Isolde whispered in shock as her eyes landed on the tree finally.

"Dragons?" Theo laughed, shaking his head, utterly clueless. "No, we're here for paint supplies. This mountain has the best clay and plants. You can't find a moon lily within a hundred miles otherwise. We used to come here all the time, but it just got too dangerous."

"And now?" I asked, hoping the mood of the town had changed a bit. "You think it's safe?"

He sighed. "Sadly no, but we're desperate. All our supplies ran out weeks ago and we need to make more. An artist can't create without the proper supplies."

Anya had wandered over by him and was gripping his shoulder tight. "Theo!"

"What?" he asked, frowning at her.

She shook his shoulder, pointing at the golem and then at the library. I had to force myself not to laugh at his shocked expression, but honestly, where did he think he was? Isolde had calmed down a bit at least, opting to pet Mochi instead of adding to the chaos about to unfold. I could appreciate that.

"Welcome to the Misty Mountain Library," I said, spreading my arms wide. "Where the books come alive and cozy magic thrives. If you give it a chance, you might find something wonderful here."

There. I nailed it. I turned around half hoping Nyssa would be there to see, but she was probably still inside distracting herself with a good book. Guess this was on me then.

"I'm sure you have questions," I said, "but I can promise you the library is safe. I'm an S-rank adventurer, so you can take my word for it."

They visibly relaxed a bit, taking another gulp of water as they looked around. Theo's eyes landed on the moon lilies.

"You wouldn't mind if we took some of those flowers, right?" he asked, excitement obviously overtaking any fear he had a moment ago. "They make wonderful paint that shimmers at night. And there's usually some good clay around too."

"Let me check." I walked over to the golem, who'd already split the tree into planks and was getting ready to assemble it. "Hey golem, do you mind if these three take a few flowers?"

The rocks and plants in the golem's body seemed to groan as he stood up. "Flowers? My flowers?"

"Only a few," I said, holding up my hands. "It would really help make the library seem like a nice place."

The golem grumbled, ripping a branch off the tree. The loud crack made me wince. Maybe this wasn't a good idea after all. The golem loved those flowers.

"Sorry, but I don't think—"

I froze as I spotted Theo waist deep in the pond, ripping one of the lilies out by the roots. The other two looked like they were trying to stop him, but it was already too late.

"What do you think you're doing?" I snapped as the golem's eyes locked on the artists.

Isolde winced, but Theo just carefully put the flower in his bag like it was a treasure. A treasure so important he didn't seem to notice the golem taking a lumbering step toward the pond. He might be an entitled jerk, but I still couldn't let the golem vent its frustration on him.

"Hold on," I said, standing between the golem and the artists. "They didn't mean any harm and you're supposed to be on your best behavior, remember?"

Nyssa had discussed that with the story spirits, making them promise they wouldn't haunt or threaten any more visitors. But she hadn't counted on anyone stealing from the golem.

"Hey, Mochi? Maybe you should go find Nyssa," I whispered as the golem's eyes started to glow. Then I turned back to the artists. "Nobody gave you permission to take those. You need to get out and apologize."

"He's over-excitable, sorry," Isolde said, bowing deeply. "We'll pay for them."

As if that made up for hurting the golem's feelings.

"Money doesn't solve everything," I said. "Get him out of there."

"What's wrong?" the guy asked. "There are tons here so we'll just take a few and then find more in another pond. Nobody will even notice."

Nobody except the forest golem who was looking at them like they were termites devouring his trees. Seriously, how clueless and inconsiderate could this guy be? The golem took another step toward them, reaching out its long arm as if to snatch one of them. Memories of the golem lifting Nyssa into the air like a ragdoll came to mind.

"Don't even think about it!" I ran to catch up, heading straight into the pond to shoo Mr. Clueless out. "Remember what Nyssa said. No scaring patrons!"

The golem sighed. "No patron. Thief."

"I know," I said, "but you still can't scare him away."

Isolde's mouth dropped. "It talks?"

The golem ignored our conversation, grabbing Theo's shirt and lifting him into the air. I winced. Nyssa was counting on me to be able to handle the story spirits when she wasn't around and she was counting on them to behave for the good of the library. Right now, we were both failing miserably...

At least the golem had never actually thrown anyone off the mountain, just moved them somewhere away from what it cared about, so as long as they didn't upset it more we should be fine.

I pulled out my sword anyway, just in case I needed to climb the golem like a mountain again, but paused when the other two artists stormed over.

"Wait, we're not thieves," Isolde told the golem. "Or we didn't mean to be. What can we do to make it up to you?"

The golem glanced down at her as Theo hung limply in its grip. Oddly, he wasn't screaming or trying to get away. He was gazing out at the mountainside in wonder, excitement filling his eyes like he'd never seen something so cool.

"I need some paper and a pencil," he called down. "Paints too. All the colors we have. You should see the view from up here."

Isolde groaned. "He's gone mad. He's literally dangling from a golem's hand and all he wants to do is paint."

"He's amazing, right?" Anya said with a wistful look up at Theo. "But first you need to apologize before you get thrown off the mountain!"

It sounded like these two had their hands full with Mr. Clueless. He probably did things like this all the time, too oblivious to realize who he was upsetting until they pointed it out.

"Sorry," Theo said softly. "I won't do it again."

I shook my head, sighing. Artists were so intense when they got inspired.

"Ask the golem for help," I said. "It's the only one who can show you where to find good clay and plants that aren't in its gardens. It will probably show you the best views too if you ask nicely."

"Really?" Theo gasped. "Golem, you're the only one who can help us."

"I am?" the golem asked, then its eyes glowed brighter. "I am!"

As the golem lifted Theo to its shoulder, Isolde smiled just a bit. "So the golem isn't really that dangerous then?"

"Not unless you take its flowers," I said ominously. "But even then, the worst I've seen it do is gently set a librarian outside."

"I see." She pulled some paper out of her bag and handed it to me. "Then what are all these about?"

Terrifying drawings of the story spirits covered the pages along with detailed information of all the terrible things they'd do to you. Not that I believed any of them.

"Where did you get these?"

"They're posted all around town," Isolde said. "That's why we avoided coming here for so long until we got desperate."

The posters looked like badly drawn wanted posters for criminals and half of them didn't even look remotely like the story spirits. But apparently people still believed them because everyone we'd met so far was terrified of the story spirits. If we wanted to save the library, we had to get the real story out there instead of the one these posters told.

"None of these are true," I said before folding them up. "Do you know who put them up? Was it the adventurers' guild?"

It was probably Jade, but I didn't want to assume the worst of her. I wished we could go back to a time when we were friends, when we understood each other, but I wasn't sure how to do that anymore.

Isolde shook her head. "Sorry, it might have been the adventurers' guild, but I'm not sure."

I really should go talk to Jade soon. If she had put up those flyers, it meant she was determined to undermine us. She was stubborn and never gave up on something she believed in, so until we won her over, she'd keep scaring the town away. There had to be some way I could reason with her, make her see the beauty of this library.

First, I had some patrons to win over though.

"Why don't you join Theo on the golem and see if that view is really worth it?"

Isolde grinned. "I think I'll do that, thanks."

She hurried over to where Anya was already being lifted up and the golem picked her up too.

"Room for one more?" I asked the golem, wanting to be close in case there were any more misunderstandings.

"You too?" The golem asked, bouncing happily. "Roan too!"

Then my feet left the ground as it whisked me into the air. The artists laughed as the golem took us around the mountain, showing off all the wonderful things they might never have noticed from the ground.

Chapter 23
Nyssa

The golem stood in front of me, regaling me with the great story of how he reprimanded the thieves who tried to steal his flowers. The three thieves in question didn't really look ashamed though, their cheeks were rosy and their eyes were bright. They'd showed up at the library on the golem's shoulders, looking like they'd just taken the ride of their lives.

"Care to explain?" I asked Roan.

"Well, let's just say the golem showed them a whole new world," he said, sheepishly rubbing the back of his head. "One full of *his* flowers."

"Was that the whole mountain?" I asked softly and when Roan nodded, I sighed. "Golem, we've been over this. You can have some gardens, but not the whole mountain." The artists perked up at that, so I turned on them next. "And you, this is a library. You can't just steal from the grounds. Didn't anyone ever teach you manners?"

"Sorry," one of the women, Anya I think, said. "It won't happen again."

The other woman, Isolde, glared at Theo. "Definitely won't happen again."

I stared at the three of them, bracing my hands on my hips. This was a great opportunity to get their help with our PR issues if we handled it properly.

"Golem, if they help us get patrons to the library, would you mind showing them where to pick flowers without disturbing the land too much?"

"Patrons? Library wants those..." The golem stared at the great book tree before letting out a raspy breath. "Fine. Golem will share."

"Excellent," I said with a smile. "Then will you three help us out with a little project in return?"

"Of course!" Theo said. "How can we help? A portrait maybe? Or a sculpture for the entryway? Maybe lawn art?"

Roan made a calm down motion with his hand. "I think the golem's got the lawn handled. I'm guessing she wants help with those."

He nodded at the so-called wanted posters they'd brought with them and at the ones Roan had gathered from town while the golem was giving them a tour. We'd been working so hard to repair the library so everyone could enjoy it, but we just kept running into new roadblocks. It was so frustrating.

"I can't believe the adventurers' guild would stoop that low," I said, shaking my head. "What did we do to deserve that?"

The Demon Lord glared at one of the posters of himself. "Right? How dare someone make me look so...unsettling."

My lips twitched. That particular poster made the Demon Lord look like he belonged on the cover of a dark romance novel, terrifying but handsome at the same time. It was the only one with enough detail to show that the artist had actually come face to face with the Demon Lord.

Before I could ask about that situation, he picked up another poster. "Now this one shows promise." He pointed at the big sharp teeth drawn on his face like children's art. "It has a fearsome aura, just like I deserve."

I almost laughed, but his face was dead serious. He really thought that was a better poster than the other one. Which made me a little sad for him. Why would he feel better about looking scary? Especially when it did nothing but hurt the library at this point.

"Why would anyone make these?" I asked softly. "Was it because of those scare tactics you guys told me about earlier?"

The story spirits froze, like I'd caught them doing something bad, then glanced away from me.

"Was what you did really that awful?" I asked. "I won't judge you. We just need to know what we're dealing with."

They'd made it sound fun last time I'd asked, almost like ghost stories around a campfire, but I didn't think anyone would go to all this trouble if they weren't worried for real. Not even somebody like Jade, who was full of herself sure, but she also seemed to genuinely want to protect the town. Roan seemed to think so too when I'd asked about him.

Shadows swirled around the Demon Lord. "My job is to terrify people, and I do my job well."

I glanced at Lisa, hoping she'd elaborate, but she wouldn't meet my eyes. Mochi was nowhere to be seen and the dragons were hiding in the stacks. A gloom settled over the library so fierce that the books themselves started quivering. So the town wasn't crazy for being afraid of the mountain. Whatever had happened, their fear was valid.

I rubbed my face, slightly frustrated. They'd been hiding something from me.

"Okay, so last time you mentioned nobody trusting Mochi's snacks," I said slowly, "and the Demon Lord making Cerbie's shadows chase people. That can't be everything, so what am I missing?"

Lisa sighed. "That's how it started, with Mochi and his snacks. He wanted to invite people in and make them feel welcome, but the townsfolk took it all wrong. Then the golem tried handing out flowers and people ran in terror thinking it was going to crush them. No matter what we did, everyone kept misunderstanding."

"Ummm...," Isolde interrupted, "but it wasn't just the panda and the golem right? There was a witch luring kids into the woods with sweets. She'd sing sweet songs that put you under her spell, leading you up the mountain until you were too lost to find your way home."

Theo nodded. "And I heard those snacks were poisoned. If you ate one, you'd never eat anything else again."

I glanced at Lisa, vaguely remembering her mentioning singing in the woods. "Was the witch in the woods you, by any chance?"

"Me?" she shrugged, glancing away. "Who could tell?"

Which meant it was definitely her. I sighed, rubbing my temples. At least the artists were too distracted to realize what Lisa had alluded to as they repeated more and more out of control versions of the stories. None of this sounded that terrible still though, not until they got to the part about the traumatized kids.

"Wait, go back," I said, "what happened to the kids?"

"Well, story goes that some kids came up here for a test of courage one night," Isolde said, "daring each other to go inside the haunted library. Except, when they went inside, the ghosts attacked them. They ran through the woods all night, desperately trying to find their way home until they stumbled into town covered in scratches and dirt, so scared they could barely speak."

"And all they did was step inside this library," Theo whispered, gazing around as if ghosts were going to jump out at him. "Makes you wonder what happened that night, right?"

No matter how you spun that story, it sounded like the story spirits went a little too far if the kids were that terrified. But I didn't think they'd really put anyone in danger, so it had to be a mistake, just another one of their tall tales.

"There's always two sides to every story," I said, glancing at Lisa. "What really happened?"

She crossed her arms, leaning back into her chair as if she needed distance between us. "Well, that little test of courage wasn't what they said. The kids came up here sure, and they came inside too. The library was so happy to have patrons again, so we were going to do our best to welcome them."

Her voice was quiet and full of unease, like the bad part of this story might actually be as bad as it sounded. I worried my lip, wishing I didn't have to hear it. If the story spirits had hurt children, there was no coming back from that; this library really was doomed. But I didn't think they'd do that.

Roan stepped closer to me, a silent supporter. I took a deep breath, preparing for the worst.

"And what happened then?" I asked.

"Those little monsters started throwing rocks and breaking windows." Lisa gripped her arms so tight her fingers went white. "We were shocked and the library was devastated. Kids were supposed to be full of magic and wonder, the ones who loved the library the most, but they turned on us, laughing at how pathetic the library was. They broke the library's heart along with its windows, shattering any hope we had left. You have no idea how painful that was and I just...couldn't watch it anymore."

The Demon Lord gripped her shoulder. "You did the right thing." He stared me in the eye, voice low with anger. "We chased those kids off, making sure they'd *never* step foot on this mountain again. If the townsfolk couldn't appreciate the library, then we wouldn't let any of them come back. We vowed to protect the library from its worst enemy: humans."

I swallowed hard, anguish strangling my voice. How could anyone do that to the library? Sure, they didn't know it was sentient and they were just kids, but still. Vandalism was an awful thing for everyone involved. It took away something people loved and tainted it.

"You didn't hurt them though, right?" I whispered.

"Of course not," the Demon Lord growled. "We're not the monsters here."

I'd known deep down that was true. They were protecting the library in the only way they knew how: by keeping everyone away. But they'd kept the truth about how bad it was from me and that wasn't going to fix anything. The library would fade away at this rate and be reborn somewhere else. Is that what they really wanted?

Roan stepped closer, as if lending me his support. Frustrated tears pricked my eyes. He'd helped me so much and it might all be for nothing. I couldn't let all this be a waste.

"We're sorry," Lisa said, standing up to join me. "We never thought we'd find somebody who cared this much about the library. About us."

The golem nodded. "Sorry."

I took a breath to steady myself and forced a smile. "It's okay. That was a long time ago and everyone makes mistakes. You were just protecting the library. If we apologize, I'm sure the town will understand."

Lisa winced. "Well, there's more. After the first test of courage, other groups of kids tried to outdo them, proving they were even more courageous. And we kept chasing them off. That's when the town hired the adventurers' guild and things really did get out of hand. That's around when you showed up, actually."

Ah, everything was clicking into place now. I'd thought the town was really overreacting to the situation, but if their kids were scared, then they had to take it seriously. So basically, I'd been fighting an uphill battle this whole time without knowing the full story. It didn't matter that the story spirits hadn't physically hurt anyone, because they truly did scare them. That would take a while to overcome.

"Thanks for telling me all that," I said, forcing myself to be hopeful for them. "I know it's hard, but we can make this right. We've already changed a few people's minds, like the apothecary and these artists." I glanced at them, hoping they'd agree. "Maybe they can help us explain to the town?"

"Of course," Theo said, nodding. "Good art is complex, just like this situation. People will understand that. Plus, the kids never mentioned vandalism or doing anything wrong, so that'll put things into perspective a bit."

"Good, so..." I faltered, not really sure what the next step should be here.

How did we apologize to the town if they didn't want to talk to us? If we could get them to come to the festival, then maybe we'd have a chance. We could make the day a meeting for both sides to come together and bond. I knew the library would want that, no matter how hurt it was, because I'd already seen it opening up to Roan and me.

There really was hope, not much, but some. We just had to put in the work.

I glanced around, taking in all the story spirits' pained expressions. None of them had actually enjoyed scaring people, no matter how they'd made it sound last time. It was just a means to an end, a way of keeping the library hidden and safe, away from the people who'd hurt it. But the library wasn't alone anymore. We were all here for it.

It was time for real change.

"Okay then, let's do something to fix this," I said. "If the town has fear-filled posters of you, then let's make joy-filled ones instead! Once they meet you, I'm sure they'll understand where you're coming from. Or at least, be willing to listen. We just have to get them here and a festival is a great time for new beginnings."

Lisa finally lifted her gaze, smiling softly. "Right. We'll apologize and welcome them to our wonderful library."

"Exactly." I turned to the three artists still sitting in the corner. "Will you help us? We need to make these posters colorful and heartfelt to ease people's fear."

They nodded and Theo even hopped up with excitement. "This sounds like a challenge worthy of our skills!"

Roan sighed. "This is going to turn into chaos, you know that, right?"

"Maybe," I said with a laugh, "but what's wrong with a little fun chaos?"

He put his arm around my waist, pulling me close as he whispered in my ear. "If you're here? Nothing at all."

My heartbeat pounded in my ears as my face warmed. He'd never touched me like that before, so sure of himself. I leaned into him for a moment, enjoying the feel of him next to me.

I wished we had more time to ourselves, but the library needed me too much right now. I sadly pulled away from him to gather up pens, pencils, crayons, paint, paper, and whatever else the library had.

The mood eased as everyone gathered around tables in the middle of the library, talking about what kinds of things to draw. Turns out the Demon Lord was actually pretty skilled at drawing, but everything he drew was terrifying.

"Maybe you should just help the knights..." I suggested, but he glowered at me and decided to supervise from afar.

Lisa on the other hand was drawing flower-filled images that the golem was fawning over. "Those are beautiful!"

She beamed. "I have a few skills I haven't shown you yet."

All in all, it was going pretty well, until the knights dragged a small bucket of paint over for Cerbie so he could put pawprints on the posters. His little pawprints were adorable, until he ran away after a dragon and those little blue pawprints ended up all over the floor.

"Cerbie!" I shouted, running after him.

Roan laughed as he picked up a cloth. "I've got it. You worry about the rest of them."

The knights shrugged and started using the crayons as swords for mock battles, fighting across the table in great waves. I sighed, glancing over at the actual artists hoping they were faring better, but they were lost in the stacks looking for inspiration. Really it seemed like they were just snooping, but hey, maybe they'd produce something beautiful.

All in all, today felt like good progress. The story spirits had finally opened up to me about what they'd done and we were working on a way past it. As long as everyone tried their best, I was sure we could get through this.

Chapter 24
Nyssa

Chaos only lasted so long thankfully, because these posters really needed to get done. The Demon Lord had taken on a supervisory role, sternly keeping the artists from wandering off and the knights from fighting, which was working pretty well. Grumpy Demon Lord for the win, I guess.

Roan had taken the golem outside about an hour ago to finish up some secret project they wouldn't tell me about. I was curious, but Roan seemed really excited about it so that made me happy enough for now. At least we'd managed to create a few piles of usable posters. The others I'd just keep as mementos of our arts and crafts day.

"What do you think, Misty?" I asked as I leaned against a bookshelf. "There are three new people in the library and everyone's working hard to help out. I know they're not really patrons, but that's gotta feel good, right?"

The great book tree glowed softly as a book with a vibrant yellow cover flapped over, landing in my hands like a sign. A smile tugged at my lips.

"I'm taking that as a yes," I said, hugging the book to my chest. "I'm glad. We'll keep trying our best to make this festival work."

It was the only thing we could do right now, and deep down, I really believed it would all work out. The library's magic was slowly being restored and the town wouldn't let this library fade away, not once they realized it was full of wonderful story spirits and remembered all the happy times they'd spent here. I couldn't be the only one who'd had a great childhood between these shelves.

Lisa flexed her hand like she had a cramp and the knights were slumped over, nothing but crayons holding them up. Maybe it was time to call it quits.

"I think that's enough," I said, joining them at the table. "Don't want to overdo it or anything. The posters look great, so we'll put them up around town and see if it helps."

"Does that mean"—Theo glanced around the room, leaning close to whisper—"we're good with the golem? That it'll show us where to pick flowers now?"

Isolde swatted his shoulder. "We don't even know if these will help yet. Let's ask after the festival, once we know how things turn out."

I was starting to like her more and more now that she was enjoying the library so much. I'd seen her earlier, wide-eyed and full of excitement exploring the stacks. It wasn't much, but she was one more person we'd won over. One more person who would say good things about the Misty Mountain Library.

"Of course," Theo said, nodding. "We'll tell everyone to come here for the festival too instead of going to the library in town. Once they hear about the golem yanking me off the ground and running around to show me the mountain, they'll be hooked."

I winced. "Maybe let Isolde tell the story?"

Her and Anya grinned. "We will. You can count on us."

They stretched and stood up, meandering over to talk to Lisa and the knights. I should probably serve everyone tea or snacks or something after all their hard work. I headed toward the stairs that led to the small kitchen upstairs when a noise froze me in place.

A soft knock at the main door followed by a creaking sound as it opened.

"Hello?" a woman's voice called out. "I'm here to return a book?"

Wait, somebody was here to *return a book?* That was something so normal, but extraordinary at the same time. It was almost like we were a regular library! I hurried toward the door, but paused when I sensed the unease coming from the story spirits. They glanced at each other warily, whispering things I couldn't hear.

They were probably nervous about random people showing up. Especially after the kids, adventurers, and even those artists who had all tried to harm them in one way or another.

"It's okay," I said, "I'll go talk to her and if she's not actually here to return a book, I'll send her away. Nobody's going to hurt the library again, not while I'm here."

Lisa nodded. "Let us know if you need anything."

I gripped her arm as I passed by, trying to promise her it would all be all right. Then I made my way to the entrance to find a woman around my age with bright red hair, taking a half step into the library, then back, as if she couldn't decide what she wanted to do.

She didn't look afraid though. No, I recognized that look in her eyes.

Pure unadulterated wonder.

I'd seen the same look in my own eyes whenever I caught a glimpse in the mirror. The library had that effect on people who loved books.

"Welcome to the Misty Mountain Library," I said, holding out my hand. "I'm Nyssa, the head librarian."

The woman finally stepped inside fully, glancing around as if waiting for something to happen. Then she shook my hand. "I'm Willow. Nice to meet you."

"So, you said you have a book to return?" I asked, trying not to sound too excited at the idea of helping an actual patron. Our very first one! "Did you check it out before the library closed? Those late fees are going to be astronomical."

She laughed with me, wandering farther into the library. "I'm actually returning it for my Gran so she doesn't have to climb this mountain again. She said a librarian lent it to her a few days ago. Was that you?"

I glanced at the book clutched in her hands, noting the colorful dragon cover. "Do you mean the apothecary?"

"Yeah, she told me some crazy story about dragon nip and said I should read this book before I returned it for her." Willow laughed again as she handed me the dragons' book. "I think she just wanted to give me ideas for the story I'm writing and knows how much I miss this place."

Wait, so the apothecary had not only sent us a writer, but also somebody who missed the library? No way, that felt a little *too* perfect.

"You're a writer then, huh?" I asked as I took the book from her, checking it into the system again. "It must be fun having somebody like your Gran help you come up with ideas. She seemed really nice."

Willow raised an eyebrow at me. "Gran said she did nothing but grumble at you until the very end."

"Well, she was still nice," I murmured as the back of my neck warmed up. "We've got a bit of a reputation, but she was willing to look past that. So she's pretty awesome in my book."

She stared at me for a moment, her gaze calculating, then nodded as if she'd made up her mind about something. "Okay, so the real reason I'm here is because Gran thought you might need a writer for the festival. And she also thought that you might be a little desperate, desperate enough to let me sponsor the library even though this is my first book. But I promise I put my heart and soul into it!" Her words tumbled out faster and faster as a blush burned across her face. "So...think you need somebody like that?"

I blinked. So she was a writer, but not a very experienced one it sounded like. Most people's first books were terrible though, so that didn't really mean much and she'd kept going. That showed a lot about her as a person. Plus, the festival didn't require good books, it just required stories in general. Getting a famous author just helped draw more people in. It had no other effect on the blessing.

"Sorry," Willow said, taking a step back. "I was practicing that the whole way up the mountain and then when it came time to say it, a bunch of words just came out. I love this library, so it would mean a lot if you let me be the writer for your festival."

Her smile was so warm and bright, full of such genuine happiness that I couldn't help but believe her.

"You're fine, don't worry about it," I said, motioning for her to follow me deeper into the library. "If you really want to sponsor the library though, there's something you need to know first. Our library's unique. The stories here... come alive."

Willow smiled. "I love when stories do that, like you can see them in your mind."

"No, they really come alive," I said, "like the characters can talk to you."

"Oh, you're one of *those* people," she said with a small smile. "Uhh, my characters have never talked to me, but it seems like a cool way to write."

I shook my head. "No, that's not what I meant. The books in this library magically come to life."

"Okay..." She paused, staring at me like I was speaking a different language. "Maybe I should just head back to Gran. I'm the only one helping her at the shop, so... yeah."

I ran my hand across my face, fully realizing I was messing this all up. How was it so hard to explain that the story spirits existed?

"Just show her already," the Demon Lord said as he casually leaned against a bookshelf with a sinister grin. "Showing always works better than telling."

Willow's eyes widened. "You have...horns?"

"And more." His grin widened, showing off all his teeth like he was trying to mimic that poster from earlier. "Want me to give you a tour?"

I sighed. "We're trying to welcome her, not scare her off. Go find Lisa."

"No, no, it's fine," Willow said, moving ever so slightly closer to the Demon Lord. "What are you?"

She sounded curious instead of fearful and something about the way she was looking at him made me wonder. Did she, maybe, like dangerous men?

"Willow, meet the Demon Lord," I said. "Demon Lord, meet the wonderful writer who so graciously decided to stop by."

I gave him a *hint hint* look, trying to make him realize how important she was without saying it. We needed a writer for the festival, so he better behave.

"Hello, nice to meet you." His voice was gravelly with only a hint of disdain, but it was the best attempt I'd seen at him being welcoming.

I wanted to cheer him on, but he'd probably snap at me and ruin all these good vibes.

"So, about that books coming to life thing," Willow said as she reached toward the Demon Lord, dropping her hand before she actually touched him. "Sorry, but are you saying he's from a book? I mean, demons don't exist, so if he's a Demon Lord, then...he's gotta be from a romance novel. Nobody else would write a demon this handsome."

The Demon Lord's usually gray cheeks got a little bit rosy before his shadows curled around him, as if he was shrouding himself in darkness. I clamped down on my laughter and grabbed his book from the table.

"He's a character from a pretty famous fantasy series actually," I said, showing her his book.

Her eyes widened. "Wait, I love that series! The Demon Lord hasn't been an on-page character yet though, so I didn't recognize him. This is actually happening then? The books in this library are *alive*?"

"Yeah, there's other story spirits here too if you want to meet them."

"There's more?" she snatched the book from me, flipping through its pages.

"A lot more."

"Show me," she said, gaze roving over the library searching for them. "Story spirits are such a cool name for them, like you're seeing the souls of the books themselves."

"That's exactly what I was thinking!" I grinned, happy somebody finally got it. "The story spirits are more than just illusions. They have thoughts and feelings, just like you and me."

"That's awesome." She smiled at the Demon Lord. "I think I'll take you up on that tour now."

His eyes widened. "Wait, what? I'm sure Nyssa will show you around. She's the librarian, not me."

My shoulders shook with silent laughter at the idea of these two, one bright and full of happiness and the other dark and trying to avoid everyone. Maybe she was just the kind of person we needed to get the Demon Lord out of his shell.

"By all means," I said, "show her around and make sure to take your time. You did offer her a tour after all."

He glared helplessly at me, as if begging me to save him from this human, but I just shook my head.

"Fine," he said with a dramatic sigh as Willow made a happy noise and hooked her arm around his. "This is the Misty Mountain Library. We've done a lot of repairs lately to make it as glorious as it once was."

I bit my lip, honestly loving this far too much.

"I noticed that," she said, turning back to me. "Last time I was here it was pretty rundown. You guys have done an amazing job."

"Oh yeah, you said you've been here before, right?"

She nodded. "I used to spend a lot of time here as a kid. Gran would drop me off while she was gathering herbs on the mountain."

"Wait, really? Same here. Maybe we met back then and never realized it."

Willow laughed. "That would be really cool."

As the Demon Lord showed her the different sections of the library, the new windows, and the repaired roof, I started to wonder if he was stalling for some reason. We'd gone in circles, cleverly avoiding the middle area where the rest of the story spirits were.

"What's going on?" I whispered at him as Willow knelt down to look at some books on the bottom shelf. "Just show her the story spirits already."

His eyes narrowed. "And risk another spilled cocoa incident?"

I winced. I hadn't realized he'd heard about that, but of course he had. They all trusted him to defend them and the knight had still been upset when we returned from the festival.

"I don't think she'd treat any of you like that," I said, "but I honestly can't be sure. Sometimes you've just gotta take a chance on people. The library needs a writer and I think she'd be a good fit. Don't you?"

The Demon Lord studied her as she sat cross-legged on the floor, flipping through books with the joy of a child. If I didn't know better, I'd have sworn he was smiling just a little.

"Maybe," he said, "but I'm going to keep my eyes on her."

"That sounds fair," I said, resisting the urge to tease him. I'd never seen him interested in anyone before, not enough to give them a tour and possibly smile at them. "Hey, Willow?"

She glanced up, putting her finger in the book to hold her page. "Yeah?"

"I'd love it if you sponsored our library for the festival."

"Really?" She leapt up, barely holding onto the book. "That's amazing! I won't let you down. I'll go home and write right now. My book will definitely be done by the time the final ceremony starts."

"Wait, you're not done writing it yet?" I asked, suddenly nervous. "The ceremony is in less than a week."

The Demon Lord sighed, but before he could say anything, Willow shook her head. "It'll be fine. I'm almost there. I promise."

With that, she backed up, bowing and smiling like a woman overflowing with joy. Then she seemed to realize she still had a book in her hands, because she turned around and put it back on the shelf. Then bowed again.

"Thank you."

"No, thank you," I said, chuckling. "I can't wait to read your book. I'm sure it will be great. And say hi to your Gran."

She frowned. "Speaking of Gran, she wanted me to remind you to fix the mountain path."

Now it was my turn to sigh. "Will do. It's on my list for tomorrow."

Not that I had any idea *how* to fix it, but my to-do list would never get done if I let things like that bother me. We needed easier transportation so that's what I'd get. Hopefully Oren had found something by now since he'd left in a hurry like he'd had some great idea.

With Willow gone, there was only one thing left to do: share the news with the other story spirits. The Misty Mountain Library had found a writer!

Chapter 25
Roan

I felt a little useless when it came to poster-making, but there was still something I could do for the library: settle things with the adventurers' guild once and for all. Nyssa might be an optimist, but I knew that no matter how hard we worked to repair the library and change the town's mind, if the adventurers' guild saw the library as a threat, we'd keep running into issues.

So why was I once again standing in front of the Mistfall Adventurers' Guild unable to open the door?

My hand hovered over the handle, willing myself to just walk inside and talk to them. It wasn't that big of a deal. What they thought of me didn't mean anything anymore. This was a job, nothing more.

Except, the closer I got to Nyssa and the story spirits, the more it reminded me of how warm and comforting this guild used to be. How this was the first place to truly welcome me in after my parents had abandoned me, not just as a dishwasher or an errand runner, but as an adventurer in my own right.

This was where I'd gotten my start, where I'd grown into my skills. This was the first place I thought I'd been wanted at after everything had fallen apart. Which was why it hurt so much coming back here, knowing that Jade and her father had just wanted me for my skills. I mean, sure, that's why I was hired, but at some point it had gone past that for me. I thought I'd become part of their family, but they still just thought of me as Jade's trainer.

Maybe I'd been so desperate for people to care about me that I'd just imagined the family vibe. Either way, it was in the past and I was ready to move on. To find a new adventure.

I pulled the door open, stepping into the cacophony of noises that a guild hall always had. People laughing, shouting, drinking, or just playing cards. Guilds were always full of people and oddly, it felt kind of comforting today. It reminded me of the chaos the story spirits created every day.

The noise dulled as I walked in and one adventurer came up to greet me. "It's been a while, Roan."

My eyes widened. I didn't think anyone besides the guild master and Jade would remember me after all these years.

"It really has," I said, wishing I could remember who he was. "I'm, uh, looking for the guild master."

"Upstairs," the adventurer said, patting my shoulder as I passed him by. "It's good to see you again."

"You too," I mumbled.

A few other familiar-looking adventurers nodded at me, smiling and clapping me on the shoulder just like the first one had. I honestly hadn't expected anyone to remember a kid from so many years ago. Had I been close to these adventurers? I'd been so focused on training Jade that the rest of my time here felt a bit fuzzy, like all childhood memories did after a while.

But they clearly remembered me and that meant something. Maybe there was more I was missing, more that I didn't realize when I was here.

I knocked on the guild master's door. "Hello? It's Roan."

The familiar sound of a chair creaking was followed by the door opening moments later. The guild master stood in front of me, frowning.

"I'm surprised you're back," he said, motioning for me to come inside. "I figured Jade had pissed you off again. Last time that happened, it took you almost a decade to step foot in here again."

His eyes softened as he eased himself back into his chair, his body creaking with age. He'd seemed like an undefeatable hero when I was younger, but now he felt like an elderly man about to retire. So much had changed while I was gone.

"Sorry about leaving like that," I said, taking the seat across from him. "I didn't mean to just disappear."

He raised a bushy eyebrow. "Didn't you? I thought that was the whole point, to cut ties with us."

I winced. "Well, yes, but still. I could have let you know I was doing okay or something."

"It's fine, you had your own path to take." The guild master nodded, smiling warmly. "I kept up with your exploits just fine and now you've returned as a famous adventurer. Your parents would be proud. It was their loss not staying around to see the man you'd become."

"Why do you keep bringing them up?" I clenched the handles of the chair. "You did that when I was young too, like talking about them would somehow lessen the pain. I don't want to talk about them."

"But they're the reason for everything, Roan. I know they're why you trained so hard that your body and mind broke over and over until you hardened beyond the point of breaking. I was trying to teach you to bend, but that was never something you could do. Until now, I think. Coming back here twice feels like a big step." He leaned forward, staring at me with that intense look that had always glued me to my chair. "It's not your fault that they never came back. It's theirs. But you can't keep avoiding everyone else because of it."

I ground my teeth as memories clouded my thoughts. Them waving goodbye, promising to come back soon. Following their missions in the news, seeing them do great things without a stupid kid like me hanging around. Training until I passed out each night, just wanting to impress them. Tracking them down and seeing how happy they were without me.

I blinked faster as tears welled up in the corners of my eyes. I could have talked to them, could have made them see who I'd grown up to be, but they didn't deserve that. They were my past and I wouldn't let the pain of their absence ruin my future anymore. It was time I let myself be happy.

"I know I can't keep avoiding people, that's why I'm here," I said, relaxing my grip on the chair. "I've been working at the library on the mountain the past few weeks. I need you to talk to Jade, convince her that it's not dangerous. To make her stop harassing the people there."

A muffled snort from outside the door made me flinch and rub my eyes. No way would I let her see me about to cry. "Jade, what the hell, are you eavesdropping out there?"

"No?" she mumbled, then threw the door open, waltzing in like she owned the place. "Well it's not like you gave me much choice. You refuse to talk to me."

"Me not wanting to talk to you doesn't give you the right to barge in," I said. "You're so full of yourself."

The guild master sighed. "Can't we just have one civil conversation? You used to be as close as siblings."

"I was delusional," I said harshly, "just wishing for a family anywhere I could find it."

"I'm going to let you two work this out," the guild master said as he stepped outside. "Don't you dare leave this room until you do. I'm old and I'm tired of this."

The click of the door shutting behind him sounded far too loud. Guilt gnawed at my stomach. I'd been trying to upset Jade, not him. He'd done his best by me, taking care of me when I needed it most. So what if he just wanted me around to train his daughter? He'd still wanted me.

Jade smacked me on the back of the head. "Look what you did. Grow up, you're supposed to be an adult now. How can you still be mad at me for one stupid thing I said?"

"One stupid thing?" I snorted. "Try all the stupid things. You're so stubborn and always need to get your way. Like with the library. You're working so hard to ruin things for them for no reason."

"No, I'm protecting the town," she said coldly. "They're what's important right now. It's not my problem if the library shuts down. It's dangerous, so maybe it deserves to be shut down."

"You have no idea what you're talking about," I said, "but even if it was dangerous, I'm there to make sure nothing bad happens. I know you don't like me, but you've always respected my abilities. Can't you just trust that I'll keep everyone safe for you?"

"You? Keep everyone safe?" She laughed, the brittle sound of it making my shoulders tense up. "You'll be gone in no time, just like always. You abandon everyone and everything you get close to. So no, I don't trust that you'll keep anyone safe. The only thing I can count on you for is to run away."

I swallowed hard, remembering Nyssa's conversation with me under the stars. About how me leaving before I got attached was kind of like me abandoning people before they could do the same to me. Was she right? Was that really what I'd been doing this whole time?

No, Jade told me to leave and now she was just trying to cover her own ass.

"You didn't want me here," I said. "You said nobody wanted me here, that I was just a pity case. That the only reason anyone teamed up with me was so that they'd feel good about themselves."

She rolled her eyes. "I was jealous, you idiot. You were doing so much better than I was and my father kept praising your name. I didn't think you'd take it so seriously. I tried to apologize an hour later, but you'd already run away."

"No, it had to be more than that," I said, my chest tightening. "You hated me being here. You thought I was a terrible trainer, always getting in your way."

"No, I thought you were an amazing trainer," she said, slumping into the guild master's chair. "I turned out pretty badass, didn't I?"

That was true, but I wasn't sure I'd had anything to do with it. She was hot-headed and inexperienced when I left, but now she was cold and bloodthirsty, far from inexperienced. Somebody else did that. Probably her sheer force of will, if I was honest. She was so determined to get stronger that she wouldn't let anyone hold her back. Not even herself.

"How could you not care enough to fight me about it?" she asked softly. "To yell at me or tell me how wrong I was? It's like you didn't even care."

Oh I cared. I cared so much I'd fled with tears in my eyes, shame burning me to my core. I'd felt like a fool, getting close to them when that's what they'd thought of me. I never stayed anywhere for longer than a few weeks after that. I never got close to anyone. I never...

Jade's gaze fell to the ground as she scuffed her boots against the floor. "You left without even saying goodbye. You just took off. That's not how families work, Roan. You're supposed to talk things out."

"Well how was I supposed to know that?" I asked, shaking my head. "My family wasn't exactly close."

Awkward silence stretched between us with nothing but the noise of the guild master's chair creaking as Jade leaned back in it. She'd wanted me to stay? To yell at her? All this time and she'd just been a jealous kid, wanting her father's attention. I could relate to that.

I sighed. "I'm sorry. I shouldn't have left like that."

"Damn right you shouldn't have," she snapped, then gave me a weary smile. "I missed you, you know."

I clenched the chair again, glancing away from her. "I'm sure you were fine without me."

"Yeah, right." She laughed, falling back into her chair. "I got my ass kicked so hard day after day. Every mission I went on was a slog and I barely made it out. I never realized just how much you handled when we went out together, just how much you did for me so I could focus on training. I'm sorry it took you leaving for me to notice."

I dared to look at her, and for once, there wasn't a trace of that mocking smile of hers. She was being honest.

"Well it looks like you got better somehow," I said. "You've become an amazing adventurer, just like I always knew you could be."

She let out a breath, then smiled. "If you're really planning on sticking around, maybe we could start over. See if there's a friendship here left to salvage."

"I'd like that." The tension in my shoulders eased. I think I'd been wanting to work things out with her ever since I left, but I just couldn't bring myself to admit it. "I'll be around for a while. To help the library."

"For the library, huh?" Jade grinned. "Sure it's not for that cute librarian I saw you with last time?"

"Oh shut up," I said with a laugh. "I just meant I'll be around."

"You know," she said, leaning forward with her arms on the desk, "we're looking for some new trainers. You'd be perfect for the job and it would keep you close to the library."

Now that was a good idea. I leaned my elbows on my knees, thinking. Maybe I didn't have to worry about people using me for my skills and I could pass them on instead. I'd helped Jade when we were younger and had enjoyed it, for the most part, so maybe I'd be a good trainer...

"I'll think about it," I said. "But for now, can you help me convince people the library isn't dangerous?"

Jade sighed. "Fine, but I want to meet those story spirits again. See what they're really about."

"Deal. You should come to the festival, it's our grand reopening."

She smiled softly. "Hearing you say things like that makes me happy. It sounds like you've finally found a place you feel comfortable at."

We kept talking for a while as her words sank in. I really did feel more comfortable at the library than anywhere else. Maybe it was time to finally tell Nyssa that I was going to stay. That I wanted to see what we were to each other.

"Sorry, but I should get going," I said. "I have to get back to the library."

Jade smiled knowingly at me and nodded. For the first time ever, I had somewhere I wanted to run *to* instead of away from.

Chapter 26
Roan

After a few days of hard work, this library was finally looking festival ready. Mochi was laying out snacks on the new snack bar, which Nyssa had absolutely loved, while the golem hung strings of lights from the ceiling. It was all coming together and I couldn't wait for people to see it.

"Want to help me clean the story gods' statues?" Nyssa asked, holding a bucket of water that looked like it was dragging her down.

"Only if you let me help with that," I said, nodding at the bucket.

I held my hand out, grabbing the handle with her to share the weight. Our fingers brushed against each other, sending a spark through me. Every little touch was like the first time, full of excitement and anticipation. I wanted to explore that feeling, revel in it even, but the only thing on Nyssa's mind was the library. Maybe once we finished up her to-do list, we could go on another date and I could finally tell her about my decision to stay.

Tiny roars, like what you'd hear from kittens trying to be big cats, pulled my attention up. Some of the dragons had gotten caught in the new string lights, flying so fast they must not have noticed the golem hanging them. With all the changes we'd been making, the dragons were often getting caught in something and causing a ruckus.

Nyssa clicked her tongue against her teeth, sighing.

"Hey golem?" she called out. "Mind helping the dragons out again?"

The golem turned slowly, tilting its massive head as if trying to find the dragons. They were so small and it was so big. They probably looked like flies.

"Over there," I said, pointing at the new lights.

The golem's eyes lit up. "Okaaaay."

Each step it took rumbled through the library, but soon the dragons were free and flying around its head like happy little birds. Not that I'd ever call them birds to their faces. Those dragons were a handful and I didn't want all our hard work getting burned down accidentally.

A smile stretched across Nyssa's face as she watched the dragons. "I love this library."

Honestly, so did I. All the craziness sort of felt normal now, like this was just how magical libraries were supposed to be. The wild magic had made the library better and that was such an amazing thing to see.

"Think the library will bring even more stories to life?" I mused out loud. "Maybe we could suggest one."

Nyssa's eyes widened. "You want *more* story spirits?"

"Maybe?" I said, watching Cerbie gobble up half the snacks Mochi had put out, only for Mochi to cuddle up next to the pup and put out even more snacks. "They're growing on me."

Nyssa let go of her half of the bucket. I opened my mouth to protest at the sudden weight, but she hugged me so tight that I almost dropped my half too. My heart raced as I stared down at her, our lips just inches apart as she started to pull away. The urge to kiss her was almost too strong for me to overcome. Her eyes were shining with happiness as she squeezed my arms before pulling entirely away.

The moment was gone before I could even do anything about it. That had been happening a lot lately.

"I'm so glad you like it here," she said, her voice breathy. "It means a lot to me."

"Me too," I whispered as I dipped a rag into the water and started cleaning the stone statues. "I've never...I've never felt like this before. Being with you and all the story spirits feels so warm, like maybe I belong here or something."

My face was hot by the time I finished, so I scrubbed the statues even harder, focusing on that instead of what she might say back. I really did love it here, more than I'd ever loved being anywhere else. I had thought the guild was home when I was a kid, but maybe I never really understood what that meant until now.

Home wasn't just the place you slept or the people you worked closely with. Home was the place that made you feel safe and comfortable. The place where you could relax and be yourself. I glanced up at Nyssa.

Home was the place full of people you cared about.

"Roan," Nyssa said, her voice low as she took the wash rag from me. "You know that you're welcome to stay as long as you want, right? You do belong here. If you want to."

My heart swelled and I took her hand without even realizing it. I looked down at our intertwined fingers, feeling a little shaky inside. All of this felt too good to be true. Like it could all go away in an instant. That was old me though, the one who ran from things before even seeing where they went.

I'd already stayed here far longer than anywhere else and I knew deep down that I didn't want to leave. For once in my life, I wanted to call someplace home and fully experience what that meant. I wanted to stay.

"But I'm an adventurer," I blurted out instead of just telling her what I really wanted to say. "I um, I have to get back to that eventually."

"So?" She squeezed my hand, smiling. "Just because you come and go doesn't mean you don't belong here. Make this the place you come back to between jobs."

Those words were like salve on a wound. I had a place that I could come back to, one with an amazing woman and wonderful story spirits. Maybe this was all the adventure I needed.

"And what if," I paused, pulling her closer, "I didn't want to be an adventurer anymore?"

Nyssa slid her hands around my neck. "Well, then you could stay here and wrangle the story spirits with me. Or start over with something entirely new. You helped me when I needed it most, so I'd like to return the favor. I'm here for whatever you want to do."

The guild master had offered me a training job for new adventurers and it was sounding better and better the more I thought about it. I would still get to help people, but I wouldn't have to travel far away to do it. I could stay right here for as long as I wanted.

I held Nyssa tight, closing my eyes to enjoy the way her hair smelled like the golem's flowers and how her hands toyed with my hair. This was the life I wanted. Something warm and satisfying, where people worked together on even the smallest things and there was constant, but happy, chaos.

A life where I wasn't alone.

"Okay," I said, leaning my forehead against hers, "I'll stay then."

Her lips pulled into a grin, promising me the warmth and comfort I'd been craving all wrapped up in this beautiful woman. I'd never dreamed going to a library book sale would end up like this, with me finding somebody who could change my entire life, but I was so glad it had.

She pulled away, biting her lip. "Maybe we should..."

I tried to focus on what she was saying, but a bubble was casually floating toward her and in this library, bubbles were never just bubbles. Memories of that ridiculous bath where I'd been pinned down by magical bubbles gnawed at my mind. I thought we'd taken care of that though when we'd repaired the laundry crystals.

The bubble grew larger, shimmering in the light just like the other ones had.

"Everything okay?" Nyssa asked, turning to look behind her. "Oh, no wonder you got distracted. Those bubbles really did a number on you, huh?"

"No," I said, a blush burning my cheeks. "It's just weird seeing one now. What if something's broken again?"

Her lips twitched. "Guess we should check it out then."

Wait, I'd had Nyssa all to myself and I let a bubble get in the way?? I sighed. What's done was done. There would be plenty more time for us to be alone, especially now that I'd agreed to stay, because this was my home now.

Home.

It was funny to even think about, but it felt so right as I gripped her hand, following her down a trail of bubbles. Nyssa and this library were definitely all the adventure I needed.

The bubbles seemed to be coming from outside where a thin man with glasses and suspenders fiddled with some kind of device. I groaned. Oren was back and he'd brought a bubble machine.

"Hey Oren," Nyssa said, joining him by the machine, "what treasure did you bring us this time?"

She winked at me as she said the word "treasure" like she'd actually enjoyed our last bubble encounter. Maybe she had, but I did not want to repeat it. Her and I with a hot bath to soak away our troubles? Great. Magical bubbles that would pin you down? Hard pass.

Oren turned some dials on the machine, almost like he was tuning it for something, then stood up with a smile. "There. Should be all ready for a test."

"A test?" I shook my head, taking a step back. "Whatever you've got planned, we don't need it."

"Are you sure?" Oren asked, readjusting his glasses. "Nyssa said you were desperate for a way to get patrons up the mountain."

I blinked, looking from her back to him, trying to make sense of that statement. Her furrowed brow made me think she had no clue either.

"And a bubble machine is somehow the answer to that?" I asked, a pit forming in my stomach. I'd seen far too many people play around with magic and the pieces were starting to fall together. "No, you wouldn't. Nobody would do that."

Nyssa tilted her head. "Wouldn't what?"

"Make people fly...on bubbles?" I could barely get the words out, but when Oren started grinning like a fool, I just shook my head. "No. That can't be a real thing. Who would even make something like that?"

"Well...," Nyssa glanced at Oren and then away quickly, fiddling with the edge of her shirt. "A novice relic engineer?"

I thought he was just a researcher, but now he was meddling with relics too? I pinched the bridge of my nose, feeling a headache coming on. I said I'd wanted an adventure, but this was just plain dangerous.

"Hey now, of course nobody's going to fly on bubbles," Oren said, waving a hand at me. "That would be silly and dangerous. They're going to fly *inside* bubbles. Safe and sound, protected by a perfect bubble shield."

Nyssa raised an eyebrow. "Well, they did seem pretty sturdy before..."

"Not you too!" Then her words sank in. "Wait, why would you link the bubbles from before to these? Did you give him that wild magic infused laundry crystal to play with?"

"For research, yeah," she said, shrugging. "Seemed like a good idea at the time."

The two of them started chatting about what dials did what, about how the bubbles could change shape and size, and about how the connection between start and end point was the key to making sure the bubbles didn't fly off course.

The old me would have dragged them both in to the guild, but the new me? Eh, maybe I should just let them do their thing and see where it went. A few bubbles couldn't be that bad, right?

An icy chill swept down my spine, remembering that bath. They could definitely be that bad, but maybe Nyssa was right and I just had an aversion to bubbles at this point. If this could actually help the library, I should at least consider it, right?

While I debated, Nyssa stepped inside a giant bubble.

"Hey, wait!" I called out, but she was already rising up in the air, a gleeful smile on her face as she waved at us.

"It worked!" Oren exclaimed, practically jumping for joy.

"Why do you sound so surprised?" I asked. "Is this your first trial?"

"Don't worry." He waved his hand at me again, like it was no big deal. "I tested it loads of times on myself, but this is the first time I've used it on anyone else."

Nyssa landed back on the ground and the bubble popped immediately as it touched the device. She rushed over to Oren, grabbing his shoulders and pulling him into a hug. Together they danced and cheered.

"It really worked!" she said, happiness tinging her voice. "This is the coolest thing ever. Even if people are worried about the library, they'll want to visit just to ride the bubbles."

"I was hoping you'd think that," he said. "Nobody else seemed to think it was a good idea."

I had a feeling his colleagues had told him he was crazy, but now wasn't the time. Not with how happy Nyssa looked. Would people really enjoy riding inside giant bubbles though? I pictured the apothecary staring disapprovingly at them, but if she didn't have to get sore walking up the mountain, maybe she really would use them.

"Want to try it out?" Nyssa asked, a teasing note in her voice.

"It can't possibly be safe."

Not that I was trying to avoid them or anything. I was just being cautious, that was all.

Oren frowned. "If you're worried about it popping, there's no need. These bubbles are so strong I doubt even a sword could pop them. The only thing that worked was applying magic like the device I'm using."

"Not even a sword, huh?" I asked, resting my hand on the hilt of my magic-absorbing sword as I stared at Nyssa. "Wonder what gave you that idea."

Her eyes widened. "I swear I didn't tell him about the bath. I mean, about anything. Just the crystals!"

Right. Just the crystals. I sighed, pulling her close. "If I'm doing this, you're coming with me."

"What?" she yelped as Oren surrounded us in a bubble. "Can this even hold two people?"

"Of course, it's perfectly safe," he called out as we drifted into the sky about ten feet.

"If you were too scared to go alone," she said as she leaned into my side, "you could have said so."

"Maybe I just wanted you all to myself."

I grinned, wrapping my arms around her as we gazed out at the library's courtyard through a shimmering bubble film. Nothing in the world compared to the magic and wonder of this library, except for the woman who'd brought it back to life of course.

She kept nudging me to look at things, pointing out the golem's gardens or the little lending libraries hopping around. It was honestly adorable. I pulled her closer, kissing her temple.

"Let's go on a date when we have a chance."

"I'd, um, I'd like that..." Her cheeks grew rosy. "Very much."

I cupped her face in my hand, staring into those beautiful brown eyes of hers as she held my gaze. I leaned down to kiss her cheek, hearing a tiny gasp escape her lips, before focusing on the scenery again.

"The bubble's growing on me," I mumbled.

She snuggled closer, molding into my side like she belonged there. "Me too."

Chapter 27
Roan

I led Nyssa toward an ancient cave hidden away at the edge of a forest that I'd found on one of my adventures. It had a wonderful hot spring inside and beautiful crystals that I couldn't wait for her to see. We'd finished all of the library repairs, decorated it beautifully, and were as ready as we could be for the festival.

This trip was a surprise to help her relax, because she had more than earned a day off. Whatever happened tomorrow was going to happen no matter what we did today, so she might as well feel amazing instead of worn out like she was now.

"What if the dragons cause their usual chaos," she asked, glancing behind us as if the library was somewhere back there, "and destroy all the decorations or something?"

"Jade and Oren won't let that happen," I said. "Working hard is a good thing, but so is taking care of yourself. You seem to miss that step sometimes, so please, let me take care of you."

She worried her lip, glancing between me and the cave. "I appreciate that, but Jade and Oren don't exactly, well, get along. What if they're the ones who destroy the library?"

"That's a good point...," I said, but stopped when panic filled her eyes. "I'm kidding! They're both adults. They can handle babysitting the story spirits for a day." I paused, waiting to see if she'd change her mind, but then sighed. "Okay, if you really don't want to do this, we can go back."

Her eyes softened. "But you have a whole surprise planned, don't you?"

"Yeah, but it'll be just as good another day." I smiled, taking her hand as a warm breeze drifted out of the cave carrying the scent of minerals and magic.

She frowned at the cave's entrance. "But now I'm curious. What's in there?"

"Oh, just the most luxurious hot spring you'll ever find," I said, keeping my voice light and teasing. "But we should really go check on those dragons."

Her eyes had lit up at the words hot spring. I told her she'd need a swimsuit for this outing, but I didn't say what kind of water we'd be going in. She hovered at the entrance, gaze landing on a shimmering crystal flower that had almost managed to escape the cave.

"And that?" she asked curiously. "Is it some kind of magic?"

I grinned, knowing she was hooked now. "Those flowers were why I got called here a few years ago. A student had been experimenting with crystal magic and ended up creating living crystals that wouldn't stop multiplying." I leaned closer, whispering in her ear. "The whole cave's full of them, but we should really get back and help Oren."

"You're terrible, you know that," she said with a laugh as she tilted her head to look at me. Her lips almost brushed against mine, but she just smiled and tugged my hand. "Come show me this surprise of yours."

I'd set light stones up around the cave, which turned on as we walked by, guiding us to the hot spring and shining off the crystals just enough to make them glitter. The soothing sound of water bubbling from the spring bounced off the crystals, creating the perfect natural background noise.

This was one of my favorite places to hide away from the world, my own secret escape. I'd never told anyone about it before, preferring to have the place all to myself after difficult missions, but Nyssa was different. These feelings I had for her weren't fleeting, they were growing stronger every day, and I was so happy to share this secret with her.

"This place is beautiful," she said, gazing at the shimmering flowers coating the walls and ceiling. "It's crazy to think this was all some big accident."

That look of wonder on her face made all the setup worth it. I pulled her close, hugging her from behind as she leaned her head back against my chest to study the ceiling. The crystal flowers were so concentrated there that they looked like a crystal chandelier, with light globes enhancing the effect.

Nyssa ran her hand along my arm. "Maybe somebody taking care of me isn't so bad after all. Thank you, Roan."

"I'm just glad you like it. My favorite cafe delivered dinner too. I figured we could eat and relax in the hot spring for a while, if you wanted to."

"A cafe delivered here?" she asked, face scrunched up in disbelief. "How'd you convince them to do that? We're so far away from everything."

I shrugged. "I saved the place from a bunch of monsters once when they decided the cafe's food was a bit too tasty to resist."

"Seriously?" She turned to get a good look at me. When I nodded, she shook her head, smiling. "These adventures of yours would make an amazing story. You should really write them down one day."

"I'm not really good at that." I motioned for her to follow me to where the food was set up. "Maybe if a writer needed some inspiration, I could help, but I don't think I'd do the stories justice."

She glanced sideways at me. "I bet you'd do a better job than you think. I'm always interested when you talk about them."

My face warmed, and not just from the humidity of the hot spring. "Maybe I'll give it a try sometime. For you, I mean."

Steam curled through the air, dampening her hair as she smiled at me. I felt myself reaching out to tuck a strand behind her ear, but paused when I almost ran into a metal bowl on the ground. It looked like one of the domes the cafe used to cover plates so the food stayed warm.

I glanced up at the table in horror, seeing the plates uncovered and food scattered everywhere. Two small golden brown cookie slimes with chocolate chips speckled throughout their bodies bounced on the table, their mouths open wide to gobble up the rest of our dinner.

"Hey!" I called out, groaning as the slimes gulped down another chocolate chip cookie, which was the cafe's best seller and their favorite food. The slimes froze when they noticed me, jiggly bodies quivering as they avoided my gaze. The perfect guilty puppy act, but I knew they'd devour everything the moment I turned away. "Sorry, Nyssa. They must have stowed away with the delivery man."

"So...you know these slimes?" Nyssa pressed her lips together as if she was trying not to laugh.

"They live at the cafe. It's basically a slime sanctuary." I shook my head at the cookie slimes. "You know you're not supposed to go on deliveries, right?"

The slimes glanced at each other, bouncing slightly as if they were nodding. They hopped off the table with the saddest sighs I'd ever heard. No, I would not be swayed by that. Not even a little bit. One of the slimes looked back at me, golden eyes big and shimmering.

"It's fine," Nyssa said, smiling as she leaned down to reach her hand out to a slime. "You're hungry, right? I'm sure we can share the meal."

The cookie slime brushed up against her hand and then leapt into her arms. She fell back, laughing as she cuddled it. The way her smile lit up the cave made my heart swell. I could watch her play with slimes all day and be a happy man. She seemed to make the best out of every situation, not letting things get her down. That must be hard to maintain though, which was why I'd wanted her to be able to relax and not worry about anything.

"I really wanted today to be perfect for you," I said softly, kneeling to pet the other cookie slime. "You always work so hard. I wanted to do something nice for you."

"You know, I think you're the one who needs to relax," she said, giving the slime one last pet before standing up and offering me her hand. "You brought me to a gorgeous cave with a hot spring, adorable slimes, and good food. What's left of it anyway. The point is that you cared enough to plan this whole day for us and that means the world to me."

I felt a big goofy grin stretching across my face as I followed her to the hot spring, my stomach fluttering as she removed the hoodie she was wearing over her swimsuit and stepped into the water. The light from the crystals glowed against her skin, reflecting off the water and teasing me into looking longer than I'd meant to.

She was beautiful and the fact that she was happy just being here with me, despite our ruined dinner, had my heart pounding in my chest. I wanted to keep making her happy for as long as I could.

"Are you going to join me?" Nyssa asked, a faint pink blush spreading across her cheeks. "Or just stand there all by yourself?"

"Sorry, got distracted." I pulled my shirt over my head and joined her as fast as I could, glad I'd worn my swim trunks.

The water was hot as I sank into it up to my shoulders, resting against the warm rocks near her.

"Distracted, huh?" She smiled, scooting a bit closer until her bare legs brushed against mine and my pulse really started racing.

"So..." I paused awkwardly as my brain refused to think of anything to say. I was too focused on the beads of water dripping down her skin or the way her eyes sparkled with mischief as she looked me over, her fingers running through the water in a slow, hypnotic motion.

"So," she said, smiling deviously, "is this what all your adventures are like? Finding cool caves and saving students in over their heads?"

"Sometimes," I said, barely managing to find my words again, "other times I've been sent to dispel wild magic, investigate strange occurrences, bodyguard merchants, or clear out some dungeons before they surge and overflow. I've even saved a few kittens from trees. It all depends what people post jobs for."

Nyssa grinned. "Oh, I can so picture that. Roan, savior of kittens."

"Hey, I do what needs doing," I said, shrugging. "Honestly, just getting to see the world and meet so many new people is what I really love. There's always something interesting happening if you look for it."

"Oh?" Nyssa asked, averting her eyes. "Are you sure you want to stay at the library and give up adventuring then? Like I said before, you can always just come back between jobs if you want. I don't want you to miss out on something you really enjoy doing."

The air felt heavier with each word, like she was trying to give me a way out if I wanted it, but that was the furthest thing from my mind. This felt too important for her to misunderstand, so I shifted, taking her hand in mine under the water.

"Nyssa, I love being at the library. It's full of adventure all on its own, so I haven't missed going out on missions at all. So many amazing things happen and there's tons of people to meet when they stop and visit. It's wonderful."

Especially since she was there. Not only had I found a place I wanted to call home, but a woman I wanted to share it with. The words I really wanted to say stuck in my throat. There were so many things to love about the library, so many things that made me never want to leave.

"I'm glad," she said softly as she looked at me through her long lashes, "because I love having you there."

I swallowed hard. We'd never really had *the talk* about where things between us were going or how we really felt. Maybe that was my fault since she'd been assuming I'd be on my way eventually, but I didn't want her to worry about that anymore.

"I was serious about staying," I said, shifting closer. "Meeting you changed my life, opening me up to whole new possibilities. I'd always thought that keeping my distance was the best way to protect myself, but you and the library showed me that even if you're hurting or abandoned, that there will be people who stay by you. People who care and will fight to show you how much you matter to them."

I rested her hand on my chest, right above my heart. "I'm willing to put in the work to get to know you better, to show you how much I care. I want to be a part of your life, a part so solid that there's no doubt I'll be there for you if you ever need it."

"You already are that." Her fingers pressed into my skin as she wrapped her arm around my neck, pulling me to her. Her soft lips pressed against mine, filling me with a warm fuzzy sensation I never remembered having before.

Was this...what love felt like?

I deepened the kiss, wanting her to feel just how much this moment meant to me. How much her welcoming me into her life and wanting to keep me in it mattered. I never realized how much I'd craved a place to call home, but now that I had it with her, I never wanted to let it go.

She'd opened up a new world for me and I wanted to do the same for her.

I pressed my hands into her back, anchoring her to me as she shifted to get closer. Nyssa surrounded me, encircling me with warmth and happiness. When our kiss finally broke, we were both rosy cheeked and breathing unevenly.

Light danced in her eyes, sparkling as she smiled at me. My heart felt so full that there was only one thing I could say.

"I love you."

Her fingers froze as she stared at me, her smiling growing bigger with each moment until it was like she was so full of happiness that she couldn't contain it anymore.

"I love you too," she said, her voice barely a whisper.

Then she kissed me again as the steam from the hot spring curled around us, blanketing us in our own little space. It was just me and Nyssa, bound together by our own dreams and wishes. A moment so perfect it went beyond anything I could have planned.

My love for her was new and precious, but this was only the beginning. I couldn't wait to see how we'd grow from here.

Chapter 28
Nyssa

I woke up as the first rays of sunlight peeked through the window, snuggling closer to Roan to stave off the autumn chill. He was fast asleep and looked so peaceful I didn't have the heart to wake him. We'd gotten back pretty late last night, and he'd worked hard planning the perfect date for me, so he deserved as much rest as he could get.

I smiled, brushing a stray strand of his hair back, my fingers light on his skin so I didn't wake him. Nobody had ever treated me to something as thoughtful as that date. My entire body felt relaxed, as if the warmth of that hot spring had sunk into my body and released the tension that was building up since I got here.

Today was the most important day this library faced, the final ceremony of the Tales and Tomes Festival. Usually,

I'd be downstairs frantically making sure everything was perfect, but for some reason, I couldn't seem to pull myself out of bed. More specifically, I couldn't pull myself away from Roan.

I never let people help me, not with anything that really mattered at least. I was a bit too much of a perfectionist for that, but Roan had been helping me since the moment I met him. From buying me all those books, to helping repair the library, to taking care of my well-being, Roan was always there.

"Thank you," I whispered, hoping I could return the care he'd shown me.

When he'd told me about his rough past, my heart had ached for him, and it made me beyond happy to hear that he considered this library home now. He was too good a man to wander the world alone, afraid of getting close to anyone. I wouldn't let him down. I'd make sure he knew exactly how amazing he was every single day.

Roan shifted in his sleep, pulling me closer. A smile tugged at my lips as he wrapped an arm around me. The longer I stayed here, cozy and warm in bed with him, the more I wished he was awake to continue what we'd started in that hot spring.

Which meant I should get up and check on the story spirits or something so he could sleep. There'd be time for all that and more later, because Roan wasn't going anywhere.

My smile turned to a grin at that thought as I slowly got out of bed. Roan sighed, turning onto his side, his hand falling off the bed as if he'd been reaching for me. I shook my head, pulling the blankets up to his shoulders so he'd be warm enough without me before getting ready for the day.

I never thought I'd find somebody like Roan, somebody who would fight for what mattered to him, but was also happy to just curl up with a book or play with the story spirits. His strength gave me the confidence I needed to get this library running again and today was the day it all paid off.

The Tales and Tomes Festival was finally here! Patrons would be filling these stacks in a few hours, filling the library as if we'd never been closed. The story gods would surely see how much this library meant to the town and give it their blessing too and then everything would be perfect.

My footsteps quickened down the stairs, as if I was a child on Frostfire morning rushing to open my gifts. The festival lights were shimmering in beautiful arches and the book well was decorated with bright blue flowers. Everything was ready to go, except, something felt off. I couldn't put my finger on it, but the more I looked around, the more wrong everything felt.

It was the silence. I'd never heard the library this quiet before.

My gaze swept over the bookshelves, expecting to find dragons roosting on them or the golem's head peeking out over one, but found nobody. Were all the story spirits sleeping?

Wait. My gaze flew back to the shelves. Not a single book was on them.

The bookshelves were as empty as when I first got here, as if all the books I'd purchased had just disappeared. I gasped, racing to the shelves holding my most precious books, the ones Roan had bought me, but those were gone too.

The library was empty.

"No, no, no," I whispered in horror as I went from bookshelf to bookshelf, seeing nothing but barren shelves. "What happened?"

Silence blanketed the library like an impenetrable fog. This was not happening, not on the most important day of the year! No matter where I looked, everything was empty and gone. As if the story spirits had never been here. As if I had never been here.

No. The library had been full of books last night and they couldn't just disappear. This was probably just a bad prank the story spirits were pulling on me.

"Very funny guys," I called out half-heartedly, "you can come out now."

Silence.

If the story spirits had done it, they weren't coming clean like I'd expect. No playful Cerbie jumping at me, no cocky Demon Lord gloating about something, and no Lisa helping me put things back together.

Lisa. She'd never have let anyone get rid of the books a second time.

I searched the library, checking every area I could think of, hoping they'd be piled up somewhere, but every door I tried to open was locked tight. I rattled the knobs, trying in vain to open them, but they were stuck. It reminded me of my first day here.

Okay, this was going too far. I hurried upstairs to wake Roan up. He turned over in bed, taking my hand as he snuggled under the blankets a bit more.

"Morning, beautiful." His voice was still husky with sleep, but he cracked an eye open to really look at me. "Why are you already dressed and ready?"

"I need your help. Something's wrong."

His eyes snapped open as he reached for his sword leaning against the nightstand. "What's going on?"

"No, nothing like that," I said, urging him to drop the sword. "It's the library. All the books are just...gone. We need to find them before people start showing up."

Roan sank back onto the bed, rubbing sleep out of his eyes. "What did the story spirits say?"

I swallowed hard. "I think they're gone too."

"Let's go find them then," he said, taking my hand. "If they're back in their books, maybe we can lure them out. I'll get Cerbie's ball, you can brew some of Lisa's tea, we'll find the books, and it'll all work out."

His confidence eased my nerves. I nodded. "You make it sound so simple."

"Simple or not, we're going to make it work." He leaned forward to kiss me, his lips light as a feather, before we headed downstairs.

We searched again, trying the doors I couldn't get into, but they still didn't budge. Luring the story spirits out hadn't really worked either, especially since I still didn't know where their original books were. It was like everyone was hiding from us, but why would they do that? They cared about the library just as much as I did, maybe more.

So why would they disappear on the most important day?

I sank to the floor, resting my back against a bookshelf as I stared out at the library. The decorations mocked me. No matter how prepared we were, the festival was doomed without books. The library had to realize that.

Unless...that was the point.

I stood up slowly, making my way to the great book tree. The library had been nervous about patrons coming back, so nervous that the story spirits had even chased people away. I thought we'd moved past that, but maybe the feeling of abandonment was too painful to really ever go away.

"If something's wrong, you can talk to me, Misty." I rested my hand against the great book tree. The bark was rough beneath my fingers. "Did you maybe hide the books because you're worried about the festival?"

The book tree shivered and a few leaves fell to the ground.

"I'll take that as a yes," I said, leaning my forehead against the tree's bark. How could I not have realized that sooner? Of course the library would be worried after how people had treated it in the past. "But what other option do we have? If we don't go through with the festival, you're going to disappear."

My words were barely above a whisper. I didn't like saying things like that, but it was true. If the Misty Mountain Library didn't get the story gods' blessing this year, it would fade away and be reborn somewhere else where people would appreciate it more. But the library had to realize that we already appreciated it.

That I wouldn't let it down.

"I know this is hard," I said, "but I'm here for you. So are Roan and the story spirits and even Willow. You remember her, right? She's so excited to present her new book today and she chose this library to do it at."

The book tree shook harder as more leaves fell. Putting more pressure on it wasn't helping. Roan joined me, raising an eyebrow as if asking if I needed help. I shook my head. This was between me and the library.

"Look, if you really don't want to participate in the festival, we can call it off."

I took a deep breath as everything in me resisted the idea. I wasn't the one in pain, so I didn't have the right to push my opinions on the library. But I really hoped it would change its mind.

"Think of the story spirits though," I said, "do you think they'll still exist if you disappear?"

The book tree's branches swayed with uncertainty and Roan nodded like I should keep going. I felt a little bad guilting the library into seeing my point of view though.

"It's up to you," I said, standing up to join Roan. "If you really don't want to go through with the festival, I won't force you. I know that some of the townsfolk hurt you, but that's all the more reason to give them the chance to make it up to you. To show you that they still care, like I do. I'll make sure nobody hurts you again."

"We both will," Roan said, placing his hand on the tree.

I added my hand next to his. "If you're scared, let us protect you. Count on us and we'll do everything we can to make this festival the best it can be."

The book tree's branches swayed softly as the creak of a door opening pulled my attention to a nearby closet. Books tumbled out, like a great wave, floating just above the ground so they didn't get damaged.

"The closet? Really?" I asked wryly. "Okay, let's get everything back on the shelves."

The books flapped in the air, soaring to their original positions. Everything might just work out after all, as long as the town really did show up. A sense of nervousness tightened my stomach, but I chose to ignore it because the library needed me to be confident right now and put on a brave face.

The final ceremony of the Tales and Tomes Festival would be starting soon.

Chapter 29
Nyssa

It was finally time. Festival-goers would be traveling out to their favorite libraries to celebrate not only everyone's hard work the past month writing their new books, but every new book that had come out in the past year. This part of the festival was to honor books and the story gods who inspired people to write them. They'd bless the world's writers for another year of great stories too.

And bless our library with all the magic it needed to thrive again.

My hands shook as I grabbed the door handle. Once I opened these doors, everything would change. We'd be open to the public again, welcoming people in on a daily basis hopefully. Unless nobody showed up and this was all a complete failure...

I took a deep breath, squashing those thoughts down. Everything was going to work out. We'd put too much work into this for it to fail.

The doors pulled open smoothly, revealing a bright sunny day perfect for travel. Willow was already outside, playing with the lending libraries as they hopped around with excitement.

"Hey," I said, waving to Willow. "I hope you haven't been here long."

"Only....an hour or so?" She glanced away sheepishly. "I'm pretty excited. I never thought I'd be sponsoring a library or that I'd even finish my book in time and it's all so exciting that I thought a walk might help." Her eyes widened. "Oh, and those bubbles are amazing! I can't believe how easy it was to get up the mountain in one of those. So cool."

At least some people liked the bubbles. I'd have to let Roan know they were a hit.

"You could have come inside," I said.

"No, you guys looked busy." She put a book back inside one of the lending libraries. "Plus, these lil' guys were happy to show me all the books they have available and I got distracted."

We'd decorated them with hanging lanterns that swayed beneath them as they hopped, glowing softly to help lead people to the library. We'd also filled them with books until they couldn't fit any more and they'd been hopping around excitedly ever since.

I patted a few of them on their little roofs. "Thank you for keeping her company. You did great."

They wiggled back and forth, opening their doors to show off their books. I really loved how happy they were every time we gave them something new, so I went inside and found a few more to trade out with the ones they already had. They hopped in circles, almost like a dance.

"They are so adorable," Willow said, smiling at them. "Seriously, this library is amazing."

"It really is." I grinned as I sat on the bench outside. Roan and I had moved it closer to the library after our little stake-out that had gotten us inside the first day. There were so many memories here and so many more to make. "So how did your book go? You said you finished it, right?"

As Willow joined me on the bench, she told me all about her new book and how hard it was to finish. She almost gave up a few times, but powered through because she loved writing and just wanted people to enjoy her story. I hoped for that too, to show her that all her efforts were worth it. Working hard had to count for something, right?

Over an hour passed by as we chatted and played with the lending libraries, my gaze going to the bubble transport more and more to see if anyone was coming up the mountain.

A knot began to form in my stomach. I'd expected the artists might stop by or even Willow's Gran. Somebody. Anybody.

But no one did.

The golem joined us outside, planting and replanting some of its flowerbeds. By the time it had moved three beds around, my anxiety was at an all-time high. They were counting on me to bring people here, to save the library. I'd gotten their hopes up, making them believe we could pull this off.

I clenched my hands against my thighs. This was all wrong. We'd worked too hard for nobody to show up and see our progress.

"We need to do something," I whispered, avoiding looking at the library that had put so much faith in me. "I can't..."

Let it end like this.

Wait, end? How could I think like that? I shaded my eyes as I gazed up at the sky. The sun wasn't even high yet. There was so much time left to turn this around.

Willow frowned as she followed my gaze. "Is that a pegasus?"

I squinted, staring at the bright blue sky so hard my eyes watered. But yes. It was a pegasus. With a very friendly rider waving at us.

"That's the courier from Arcadia Books!" I jumped up to greet him as they landed softly on the grass. "Welcome to the Misty Mountain Library."

The young man grinned as he slid off the pegasus. "I told you I'd be back. Every time I pass over this mountain, I'm so curious how the library's going. I wanted to wait until your official reopening though and boy was it worth it." His eyes widened as he walked up to the golem. "Hello, I'm Jasper. Nice to meet you."

Jasper held his hand out to the golem who held out his pointer finger in return. The courier grinned and shook it vigorously before admiring the plants.

"Somebody came!" Willow exclaimed, grabbing my arm as a grin spread across my face.

We had our first patron of the day and he wasn't afraid of the golem at all.

"Do you want to go inside?" I asked Jasper. "There's so much more for you to see."

"Yes, ma'am," he said, tipping his hat at me with a kind smile. "I want to see everything."

A warm happy feeling settled in my chest, driving all the worry from a few moments ago away. Willow and I led him inside to find Roan hard at work keeping the other story spirits entertained. Seeing him like that, so at home with the story spirits compared to how he was when he first came here, filled my heart. How could I possibly fail with him by my side? We were a team, reviving this library together.

Roan turned with a smile as a small green dragon landed on his head. "Hey there."

"Hi," I squeaked out, trying not to squeal over how adorable such a strong adventurer looked with a tiny dragon on his head. I cleared my throat, gesturing at Jasper. "This is Jasper, the courier who brought us all those books a few weeks back."

"Welcome to the Misty Mountain Library," Roan said warmly. "We're all very glad you're here. The books were wonderful."

Jasper nodded, his eyes practically shining with wonder as he tried to take it all in at once. Lisa wandered over, leading him to a chair just in case he was a bit too overwhelmed, but he seemed fine.

"This is amazing," he said. "I never dreamed that stories could really come to life like this." He frowned at me. "They are characters from books, right? That's the rumor I heard around town. Well, one of the rumors at least."

I resisted the urge to wince at the idea of rumors and forced a smile instead. "Yes, they're books brought to life with story magic. We're a one-of-a-kind library, the only place you can talk to your favorite stories in person."

Roan smiled, nodding slightly at me like he was telling me I was doing a good job. Butterflies danced in my stomach. Everything was riding on us getting more patrons, but finally getting one was a little nerve-wracking too. I was glad it was somebody like Jasper, so full of joy and love for books.

"It's such a shame not many people are here to see this," Jasper said, shaking his head. "If they knew what they were missing out on, really knew, they'd be racing up the mountain to get here. But I bet it's hard to tear anyone away from Lady Thistlebrook. You should have seen the lines waiting to meet her."

I froze. "Wait, what about Lady Thistlebrook?"

"Oh, uhhhh...," Jasper busied himself petting Cerbie. "The library on the other end of town got her to sponsor them so everyone's going kind of crazy. They've never had somebody so famous there before."

She was one of my favorite authors, so any other day I'd have been overjoyed to hear that she was at a library nearby. I'd have grabbed my favorite book of hers and raced into town to get it signed, no matter how long the line was. But today wasn't any other day. Today was the Tales and Tomes

Festival, the one day that this library needed to be full of people, to prove that the town wanted it to keep existing.

I sank onto a chair as the weight of Jasper's news really sank in. The only reason that library had even popped up there was because nobody was coming to this one and it sensed the town's love for books was still strong. Add that to Lady Thistlebrook's fame and we didn't have a chance.

After all the repairs we'd done, after all the people we'd talked to, after everything, it was going to end like this. I really thought that all we had to do was fix the library up and let people know it was open. I assumed people would rush to see the story spirits, to see this library full of life again. That's what I would have done...

Tears pricked my eyes. I tried to blink them back, but I'd been going and going for so long on sheer optimism, believing that we could do this if we just worked hard enough, and now it was all crumbling around me. Even if we got patrons, it probably wouldn't be enough to show the gods that this library really mattered to anyone. They'd think it could serve the world better somewhere else.

I was going to lose everything I'd fought so hard to protect and I'd be letting everyone down in the process too.

"I'm so sorry." My vision blurred as my tears flowed down my cheeks. "I got all of your hopes up for nothing. I didn't even really think about the other library or trying to get somebody famous here. I genuinely believed that the library being repaired and full of story spirits would be enough. People probably still don't know what they really are though and that's my fault. I should have gone into town more often, should have worked harder to show them how amazing the story spirits are, should have —"

"Stop," Roan said, kneeling by my chair. "This isn't your fault."

I squeezed my eyes closed, unable to look at his kind smile. He'd finally found a home here and that would all be gone soon. He'd probably go back to adventuring and I'd... find another library?

No, I didn't want to work at another library again. The Misty Mountain Library was my home.

The Demon Lord's shadows snapped at my ankles, the only thing I could see while I hid from everyone's gazes.

"Stop crying," he said, blinking a bit faster himself. "You're making everyone else sad too."

Lisa sighed. "Give her a break. She deserves to have a good cry if it'll make her feel better."

I took a deep breath, swallowing hard as the tears of frustration I'd been holding in for weeks just kept falling. This was my dream. I'd quit my job, left my apartment, basically given up everything for this one opportunity. It couldn't just end like this.

A glowing light drew my attention to the stacks as a book flew off the shelf and opened its cover. Bright like shined from the pages, just like when the story spirits came out of their books, except I didn't recognize this story.

"Hey Misty, what's going–"

Torrential rain fell from a dark gray rain cloud that was now covering the ceiling.

"Save the books!" I shouted as I threw myself over the displays we'd set up.

Apparently the library needed a good cry today too, but its tears were a lot more of an issue than mine. The Demon Lord sighed as he grabbed a blanket, tossing it unceremoniously over me and the books while Lisa ran off to presumably look for a better solution.

Rain beat against my back, drenching me and everything around as Roan leaned over me to try and shield some of it. I glanced up at him and caught a small smile on his face.

"Are you seriously smiling right now?" I asked.

"Yup, because this goes to show that Misty cares about you just as much as you care about the library. Your tears brought Misty to tears too and it's pretty wonderful to have a friend like that."

I blinked up at him. "Do you really think that's what this is?"

"Of course it is," Lisa said as she rejoined us with the tarps we'd used to cover the broken windows earlier. "You were here for us when we needed you most and now we're here for you. What's a little rain in the grand scheme of things?"

She placed the tarps around us carefully, covering everything she could that was in range of the rain. Somehow it had missed all of the bookshelves and was just focused on me, while the other story spirits stood at the edge of the downpour perfectly dry. Maybe they were right and this was just some sort of show of solidarity?

"Thank you, Misty," I said, staring up at the stormy cloud while big fat rain drops hit my cheeks. "Now that we've let all the bad vibes out, let's work on a solution. Together."

I glanced at the rest of the story spirits, at Cerbie who was wagging his tail ready to race over to me at any moment, at the golem who was trying to shoo the rain cloud away, at all of them just surrounding me with warmth.

I'd never felt so much love from so many people at once and I wasn't going to waste a single moment of it. It seemed Misty agreed because the rain started petering out. I was drenched though, my hair sopping wet.

Roan handed me a towel with a reassuring smile. "Well, that was refreshing, right? Just what we needed to wake us all up."

"You have a weird sense of refreshing," I said with a chuckle.

As the storm disappeared back inside its book, so did the water thankfully. Every drop dissolved back into the story as if it was never here. Our books would be fine.

I walked over to the great book tree, sitting down beside it and motioning for the others to do the same. Together we crowded around the tree, sitting on the ground like kids waiting for story time. Cerbie padded over to me, resting his heads on my lap. I pet his soft fur, feeling my anxiety melt away as he cuddled up against me.

"Now is not the time to give up," I said firmly. "Now is the time to show the world how amazing everyone here is. Sorry I doubted that for a minute."

Lisa smiled, handing me a warm cup of tea. "I'm glad you're back to your usual self. Now, what's our plan?"

The tea smelled like spiced chai, invigorating my senses with each breath. I took a sip, enjoying the warmth spreading through my body. This was exactly what I needed after getting out of a downpour. I glanced at Jasper, who was awkwardly looking around the library like he wasn't sure if he should join us or not.

"Come on, take a seat," I said, motioning at an open spot on the rug. "What you said about the story spirits gave me an idea. That other library might have a famous author, but *this* library has the very souls of its books. That's something special and beautiful, something nobody else has." I ran my hand over the smooth bark of the tree. "And we have you too, Misty, the best and kindest library anyone could ever ask for. Do you think you have enough magic to summon another story spirit?"

We'd spent weeks recharging its magic, but after hiding all those books earlier and then summoning a rain cloud, I wasn't sure what the levels were at. I still saw buds on the trees that hadn't formed into books yet and the leaves were green. It had more magic than when we came here, but nowhere near the magic it should have.

There was only one way to fix that: fill the stacks with patrons.

"What are you planning?" Lisa asked.

"Just a little adventure," I said with a grin. "I'll need to find the perfect book for it though. Think you can help?"

Roan nodded. "I'm always up for an adventure. What are we looking for?"

"Something with a character who can fly," I said slowly, "and is big enough to transport all of us and the townsfolk."

Lisa's eyes lit up. "Oh, I love that idea."

"We're going to get people here," I said firmly, standing up to browse the stacks. "This is going to be the best festival the library's ever seen."

Willow peeked around a bookshelf. "I think I've got an idea for what book to use..."

She held out a fantasy novel about a town that lived on the back of a flying whale.

"Oh, that's perfect." My grin widened as I held it up to the book tree. "What do you think? Do you have enough power to summon a flying whale?"

The book tree glowed faintly. Not bright like it was when I was a child, but bright enough to help us now. We were going to win over the town and save our library. Even if I had to ride a whale through the sky to do it.

Chapter 30
Roan

I fully supported Nyssa and her desire to get people to the library, but I also knew just how hard it was to get over feeling abandoned by the people you cared about. Her plan of dragging patrons here with showy theatrics felt... off. Like the townsfolk wouldn't be coming for Misty, they'd be coming for the flying whale. And that just didn't sit right with me, not after what they'd done.

If my parents suddenly appeared back in my life without a big apology, I doubted I'd even be able to look at them. What if the library felt the same way when Nyssa brought those patrons here? It was obviously apprehensive about the festival already, so it didn't seem too far-fetched to think about.

"Are you really okay with this?" I asked Misty, hovering inside the library while the rest of the group walked outside chatting about flying whales. "I'm sure it hurt that people didn't show up on their own."

The library didn't react, but maybe it was conserving energy for the big whale summoning. The stakes were high and I didn't want the library to fade away, but I also didn't want it to be even more sad with people visiting it out of pity or selfish reasons.

It deserved to be happy and loved after all these years alone.

"I can ask her not to do it," I said softly, leaning against a bookshelf. "Nyssa's kind and was so excited about getting people to visit the library. I didn't want to question her, but I just can't stop this nagging feeling that something's off."

I clenched my hands as memories of my parents waving goodbye surfaced. They promised to be back soon, but instead, they started a whole new life without me and never looked back.

"I've been where you are," I said, "and if it was me, I'd feel like they only came back because they got something out of it. Not because they actually felt bad about abandoning me."

A few books rattled on their shelves. I leaned my head back, watching Nyssa page through the book in her hands. Her smile was so warm and bright, exactly the thing we needed to heal our broken hearts. She'd given me a place to call home and I'd be grateful to her for that for the rest of my life.

But we'd worked so hard to win people over the correct way, that it felt wrong to parade the story spirits around now. We already showed the town that the story spirits weren't dangerous and we'd gotten all the guild missions taken down. There was no reason for anyone to avoid the library anymore.

So what if there was a famous author at the library in town? Everyone knew this library hadn't been part of a festival in years. They had to know what that meant. Maybe not this year, but sometime soon.

Did they just not care? Or were they still afraid deep down?

Whatever it was, I didn't feel right not saying something to Nyssa. Maybe we could land the whale outside of town and give people one last chance to come visit on their own. I bet that would make a big difference to Misty.

"Give me a minute," I told the library, walking outside to join the others. "Hey Nyssa, can we talk?"

"Sure, no problem." Nyssa tilted her head, her smile faltering as she studied me. "Is everything okay?"

Before I could answer, a commotion arose among the story spirits. Four children who looked to be in their early teens or a little younger floated up the mountain path in giant shimmering bubbles, full-out grins on their faces. One by one, the bubbles pressed against the transport station and popped, releasing the kids. They jumped around, celebrating their victorious trip up the mountain, asking if they could do it again.

I glanced back at Misty, hoping the library was excited to have visitors. Maybe we just needed to give the town more time.

"Hello," Nyssa said, greeting the kids, "welcome to the Misty Mountain Library. We're so happy you're here."

Cerbie growled, hackles raised, while Lisa had an uncharacteristic glare on her face. All the story spirits were on guard and the only happy people here seemed to be me, Nyssa, and Willow.

Which meant we were missing something.

"Everything okay?" Nyssa asked, glancing between the kids and the story spirits. "They won't hurt you, it's fine."

"They're the ones who did hurt us," Lisa said, her glare turning icy. "These are the children who threw stones, broke windows, and told tall tales to the town."

The boy in front winced. "Yeah, that's why we came here today actually. To apologize."

"Our parents were talking about this library earlier," another child said, "about how they'd love to visit it again, but after what happened to us, they just couldn't. The more they talked about it, the worse we felt. We're sorry for making the town hate you…"

The other kids nodded, but were huddled together like they were afraid. They'd done something wrong and were trying to apologize, even in the face of this big angry group of story spirits. That was admirable.

I smiled as these kids did exactly what I thought the adults in town should have been doing. They'd come all on their own, visiting the library to make amends. They were happy to be here and had chosen Misty over any other library.

"Calm down everyone," I said, putting my hand on one of Cerbie's heads. The dog's growls ceased, but he stayed alert. "They're just kids and this is a festival, remember? It should be a time of new beginnings. Let's hear them out at least."

Misty needed to hear what they had to say, even if the story spirits didn't want to. The library was the one who'd been truly hurt.

The boy nodded at me. "My name's Cliff. A few months back we did....a stupid thing."

"And then an even stupider thing," another child added. "After we got chased off, we were so scared and afraid that people would get mad at us for breaking the windows, that we lied to our parents and said it was all the ghosts' fault. That they hurt us."

"We didn't know it would get so out of hand," Cliff said, hands clenched into fists. "We didn't—I didn't mean to..."

The kids stared at the ground, unable to meet anyone's gaze. Nyssa pulled them into a big group hug.

"Thank you for apologizing," she said, "that's what you should always do when you do something wrong."

She raised an eyebrow at Lisa and the other story spirits, obviously hinting that it was their time to apologize too. This wasn't a one-sided problem after all. Cerbie tilted his head, staring up at me as if asking what to do now. I pet him, not really sure how much he understood about the whole thing.

The three-headed pup slowly moved forward, pushing his nose against the little boy's arm. Cliff flinched, but then relaxed when Nyssa started petting Cerbie and the dog flopped over on his back, rolling around in the grass.

The kids' lips twitched, smiling as they knelt by the dog. I'd have to give him so many treats and new toys for that, breaking the ice in a way nobody else could manage.

"So much for the hellhound," Cliff laughed as Cerbie's tail thwapped against his leg. "It was so dark that night. All I heard was the barking. We'd already spent the past hour scaring each other for our test of courage and really hadn't expected to find anybody here. It just made it all scarier."

Lisa sighed. "We're sorry we scared you. We were upset and handled it badly. We care about this library so it hurt to see anyone damage it. But that's no excuse for us to have scared children, chasing you in the dark like monsters."

One of the younger kids started crying as he ran over to Lisa. "I didn't even want to be here. I'm so sorry."

Her eyes softened as she too pulled the boy into a hug, patting his back softly. "It's okay. It's all over now."

As they continued talking, reassuring the kids and each other that everything was fine, I glanced back at the library. Was this enough to reassure Misty that the town cared? That they'd just been misled and afraid?

The library's door swung open, as if saying they were allowed inside if they wanted to. The tension eased from my shoulders. This was what Misty had needed all along. Somebody from the town to care enough to apologize and make amends.

I smiled, happy for the library. It deserved this and so much more. Once we got more people here, its heart would heal even more. Just like mine had.

The tiny knights climbed onto the dragons, flying in big circles around the kids. Their eyes were as wide as saucers as they followed the dragons around the yard.

"Are those...dragons?" Cliff asked dumbfounded. "There were dragons up here and we never knew?"

"There's a lot of wonders up here," I said, "as long as you treat them well, they'll do the same."

"Why are they so tiny though?" he asked. "And the knights too?"

I frowned. "Honestly, I've been wondering that myself. Lisa, why are they the only story spirits who are so tiny?"

"Because there's so many of them," she said, motioning to the large group of knights and dragons. "The more spirits that come out of the same book, the tinier they are." She shook her head, smiling at me. "It's nice to see how far you've come, asking questions about the spirits you once called creatures."

"I'll ask even more if it makes you happy," I said with a laugh.

"There will be time for that later," Nyssa said, standing up and opening the book she'd set aside. "I think it's about time to summon this whale now."

The book glowed with golden light, shimmering as the pages flipped on their own. The kids froze, transfixed by the magic as the sound of a whale's song filled the area. The sky whale soared out of the book, high above us.

It was breathtaking, a sight no human had ever seen before. This library was a place where the impossible became possible, and I loved every minute of it.

"It's beautiful," Nyssa said breathlessly. "Thank you, Misty."

I eyed the giant whale curiously. "How are we supposed to get on it though?"

She frowned, looking around until her gaze landed on the golem. "Think you could help us?"

The golem lumbered over, reaching its hand down for Nyssa to climb on. She grasped its vines firmly before glancing back at the rest of us.

"Anyone else joining me?" she asked. "It's time we showed the town exactly how amazing we are and that there's nothing for them to fear."

Willow leapt forward. "Me, definitely me. How could I turn down riding on a sky whale?" Her eyes widened as she clasped her hands over her chest. "These story spirits are so amazing."

"They really, really are," I said, smiling as I climbed up next to Nyssa.

Now that Misty was happy, I could help Nyssa with a clear mind. Her plan to win over the town would work, I could feel it.

Lisa stood beside the kids, glancing back at the library. "I'm going to stay here with them, make sure everyone's okay."

"Actually, I'd like to go," Cliff said, looking a little uncomfortable as he scuffed his boots in the dirt. "If you're going to talk to the town, there's a few things we should probably explain to them."

"Mom's going to be furious," another kid moaned. "She hates when we lie."

"Yeah, but she can't be *that* mad when she sees a giant whale, can she?" Cliff asked, grinning at the new story spirit. "She'll forgive us, as long as we're honest about it and take responsibility. That's what she always says."

The golem leaned down, offering another hand to the kids who climbed on with wide eyes. Eventually the Demon Lord stepped forward from wherever he'd been lurking.

"I won't help you," the Demon Lord grumbled, but then shook his head. "I mean, I'll be of no help to you. They'll probably just be scared of me."

"Oh I don't know about that," Willow said, smiling at him.

If I didn't know better, I'd have sworn he blushed. Huh, so he did have other emotions besides grumpy. Who knew?

The dragons flew up to the sky whale as the golem lifted us up. The golem had gotten better at moving smoothly, so I barely even got dizzy as it deposited us on the sky whale's back. A far cry from that stomach-churning ride I'd taken with the artists.

The moss on the sky whale's back was soft and lush, pillowing my feet like it was made of magic. I could feel the whale breathing beneath us, moving slightly as it floated in the air. It was amazing and strange at the same time.

Moments like this were why I loved being an adventurer, but loved even more that I could still have those same adventures without even leaving home now. It still hurt that my family had abandoned me, but I think I was finally moving past it. Allowing myself to care about people again, to risk getting close to them, was the first step to healing.

I had a new family now, one full of love and kindness, and I couldn't be happier.

"We'll be back soon," Nyssa yelled down, waving at everyone, "and we'll bring lots of people with us."

They waved back as the whale slowly turned, angling down the mountain. Nyssa threw her arms wide, embracing the wind as it swept over us. I wrapped my arm around her to steady her.

"I can't believe we're really doing this," she whispered, leaning her head against my chest. "Thank you for being here. It helps with my nerves."

"Always," I said, kissing her temple.

The sky stretched out ahead of us like the ocean, with the city sprawling below like tiny toy houses. As the whale swam through the air, everything got bigger and bigger until we could see people pointing up at us with shocked faces. A group of kids raced after us, their parents screaming at them to come back.

Nyssa waved and shouted, "Come to the Misty Mountain Library today and see even more wonderful things!"

She was the true wonder here, confidently shouting from the top of a flying whale with her hair blowing in the wind and nothing but joy in her eyes. She was more beautiful than a magical bubble and more amazing than a flying whale. She made the impossible possible and I loved her for that. She never gave up, so neither would I. I'd spend every moment protecting that smile of hers and filling her days with as much joy as I possibly could.

The kids reacted to her voice, racing through the fields and spreading the word to other kids. Perfect. We needed as much word of mouth as we could get. The more people talking about the unbelievable sky whale flying through town, the better.

"This is awesome," Willow said with a grin. "Thank you for choosing me to sponsor your library."

"Thank you for accepting," Nyssa said. "We wouldn't be here without you."

This festival was the starting point, the moment where we showed the world exactly what the Misty Mountain Library was made of.

We drifted over the town as the dragons flew down with flyers in their mouths, nudging them at anyone and everyone they saw.

"Meet us at the town square," I shouted down over and over at the people we passed, "we have room to carry a lot of people. Come celebrate the Tales and Tomes Festival with the Misty Mountain Library!"

When we flew over the other library in town, Nyssa ducked down. I raised an eyebrow at her and she shrugged.

"I don't want them to think we're stealing patrons," she murmured, giving me a guilty look. "I mean, I know that's part of the point, but it still feels weird!"

I laughed, pulling her close. "This town's big enough for two libraries, you know. Especially if they're being run by people as amazing as you."

The sky whale groaned as it lowered itself as close to the ground as it could. I ran my hand over the moss on its back, hoping it knew how much this meant. Nyssa helped me toss a ladder she'd found over the side of the whale, so the kids could get down and go talk to their parents like they said they would.

Then we invited anyone who wanted an adventure to join us.

At first it was just a few curious teenagers, but then people showed up by the dozens. People of every age, some looking like they'd dropped everything just to come here, covered in flour or paint or with paperwork still clasped in their hands.

All of them had the same look though, eyes wide and full of wonder.

It was hard not to feel that way on the back of a sky whale. As more and more people climbed up, I felt sure that we'd succeed. This had to be enough people for the library to get the story gods' blessing. If we took any more, they might not even fit comfortably inside the library.

Once everyone was aboard, Nyssa and I moved to the front of the whale, sitting down so I could run my hands along the smooth skin around its face. Its kind eyes looked back at me, making a beautiful song-like noise. With this one amazing story spirit, my new home was going to be safe and sound for years to come.

"Thank you, we're ready to go when you are."

The whale groaned its song out as it turned slowly, drifting in a wide half circle over the town. Squeals of excitement came from behind me and a few screams. This was a moment nobody would ever forget.

"Let's go home," I said, hugging Nyssa tight. "The Misty Mountain Library is waiting for us."

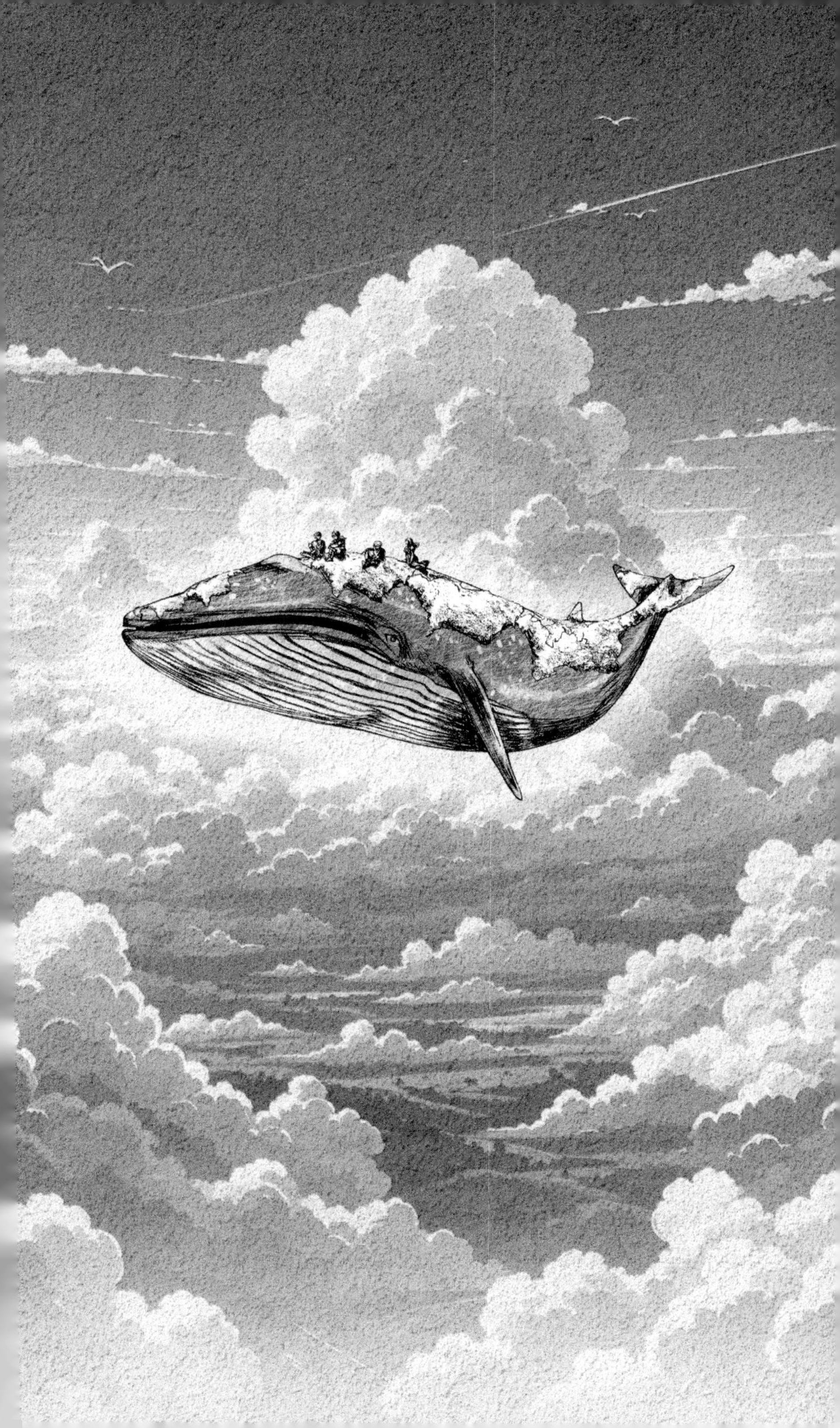

Chapter 31
Nyssa

The cool wind whipped through my hair as we soared through the sky, listening to the whale's beautiful song as we made our way home. Bubbles surrounded us as we got closer to the library and a few more people milled about. I spotted Oren talking to the apothecary, the artists who'd stolen the golem's flowers, and even the contractors who'd been terrified of Cerbie!

They'd followed us up the mountain when they saw the whale passing by. Add them to all the people on the whale with us and this festival was going to be a success. My chest warmed as I turned to Roan.

"We did it," I said as a grin stretched across my face. "Look at all these people."

"You're amazing." He wrapped his arms around me, taking the chill of the wind away. "The story spirits and the library will be happy."

I leaned back against him, enjoying the view as the whale settled down near the library. The flight had been so steady we hadn't even needed to hold onto anything and the kids were cheering as Willow lowered the ladder.

Lisa stood in the courtyard with the golem and the Demon Lord while Mochi sat behind his snack shack with Cerbie. None of them moved, as if waiting to see how the people with us would react. For a moment, I thought it was going to be a standoff as the townsfolk's eyes widened, taking it all in.

Then Mochi broke the ice by bringing one of the little boys from earlier a stick of cotton candy.

He carefully took the fluffy blue sugar like it was a great treasure before turning to a woman behind him. "See, mom? They're nice!"

The woman's arm was wrapped around her son tightly, like she still wasn't sure what to do here. I glanced at Lisa, who shook her head like we shouldn't step in. This was all Mochi right now and I believed in the red panda.

Mochi produced a matcha boba tea and held it up to the woman, chittering happily.

"How'd you know that's her favorite?" the boy asked, his voice full of shock. "Aren't they amazing, mom?"

"Thank you," she told Mochi with a small smile as she took the tea. "Maybe they're different than I thought..."

With that, the others seemed to think it was safe enough to move again, and everyone started mingling. I let out a breath. This was actually going well! To be fair, it was hard to be terrified of a cute red panda handing you snacks.

"Welcome to the Misty Mountain Library everyone," I said loud enough to be heard over the mumblings of the crowd. "We've got festivities outside ranging from Mochi's Snack Shack to golem rides and bubble magic, then in about an hour we'll be starting the book ceremony inside. Feel free to look around until then." I motioned at Lisa. "This is our other librarian, Lisa, and she's actually one of the story spirits too. If you have any questions, feel free to ask one of us."

Lisa's eyes shined bright as she smiled. "Hello, it's nice to meet you. Let me know if you need any help."

That set the conversation off. Everyone had questions and soon there was a mix of awe and laughter as the story spirits welcomed the townsfolk into our world. The library wasn't the scary place they'd all imagined. It was full of magic and wonder.

Willow wandered over to her grandmother as the apothecary played with the little dragons, who seemed far more excited than usual. I grinned as the older woman slipped them some dragon nip out of her pocket, like she was keeping a secret stash just for them. The dragons flew in circles, their flames a rainbow of colors.

"I'll keep an eye on them," Roan muttered, shaking his head, "don't want them getting too out of control."

"Bring the knights with you," I said, nodding at the tiny soldiers camped out on the bench nearby like there were too many big people around. "Don't want them feeling left out. Or getting stepped on."

Roan saluted me with a smile as he marched over to the knights. They hopped to attention as he drew near, listening to everything he said like he was their new commander. Or their King.

A sense of rightness settled in my chest. This was how the library should always be, bright and full of people. A large bubble drew my attention as more patrons flew up the mountain. It was Jade and some other adventurers with an older man. Unease tightened my shoulders.

I hurried over to the bubble transport, meeting them right as their bubbles popped.

"Don't even think about causing trouble," I told Jade. "Not today."

She held her hands up with a crooked smile. "Hey now, that's not my goal in life, you know. We just wanted to see how things were going."

"Really? That's not code for *prove everyone's in danger* or something, is it?"

"No, it's really not," she said, glancing over at Roan and the knights. "He already settled things with us. We're good."

Her gaze traveled past him, to the people climbing onto the golem's shoulders, then to the ones playing fetch with Cerbie, and even past the ones getting snacks from Mochi. She shook her head as she smiled. "This place really is something else. Mind if we take a look around?"

The others with her had already started exploring, so there wasn't much point in saying no. The elderly man had made a beeline for Roan, who was smiling and shaking his hand. It seemed like everything really would be okay here.

"Look, I heard about the kids," Jade said quickly, "about how they exaggerated their story. All the missions got taken down at the guild too. So there's not really much for us to do here. Just consider me a curious patron hoping to get a good snack from a certain red panda."

That seemed fair enough. She'd been protecting the town with the information she had at the time. I'd have done the same for the library. Plus, if Roan and her really were good, there was nothing left for me to be upset over.

"Then by all means, go visit Mochi's Snack Shack." I pointed it out to her. "He's got a knack for finding exactly what you want to eat."

"Thank you," she said, pausing as she passed me by to mutter, "I never had it out for you, you know. I was just doing my job."

She might have seemed rough around the edges before, but maybe deep down, she was actually a good person.

"I know, we were all just doing what we thought was best," I said. "I'm glad this worked out."

"Same here. You make Roan happy and that makes me happy too," she said, nodding at Roan and the older man who'd come with her. "I'm glad he finally settled down. It means a lot to our guild and my father, the guild master."

Ah, so he was the guild master then and he was actually helping Roan lift tiny knights onto the dragons so they could watch out for each other. I grinned, hoping that meant we really wouldn't have any problems with the guild anymore. This whole festival felt like a coming together of town and library, a time to heal old wounds and overcome the divide.

"Now, where's that panda again?" Jade asked. "And why exactly is a panda running a food stall?"

"Because this is the Misty Mountain Library," I said with a laugh, "a place where anything's possible."

She grinned and went over to Mochi, grabbing three cinnamon rolls and taking them to Roan and the guild master. It felt nice seeing the three of them together. Roan deserved all the friends and family he could get.

After a while, I wandered over to Willow who was clutching her bag tight. "You ready? It's almost time for the story ceremony."

Her fingers whitened on her bag. "Uhh, sure. Totally ready."

"You'll be fine," her grandmother said. "I believe in you."

"Me too," I added. "Plus, it's not like gods ever say anything terrible to anyone. They're honest, but in a kind way from what I've heard."

Willow sighed. "I know, but literal gods are going to be reading my book. What if they hate it?"

"The gods will know how much time and effort you put into it." Her grandmother directed a dragon to land on Willow's shoulder, as if giving her some extra support. "That matters just as much as the actual content of the book. So let's go offer your story to the gods and thank them for inspiring us each year."

"Okay." Willow took a deep breath and nodded. "Let's go."

"Everyone," I called out to the crowd of people outside, "we're going to start the ceremony soon. Please follow us inside."

Excited murmurs spread through the crowd as people asked about Willow and what kind of book she was writing. Usually libraries asked popular authors to sponsor them, but Willow was perfect for us. Having her offer her story to the gods helped her just as much as she was helping us. We were a team.

The stacks were full of patrons as we made our way to the magical book well, which was clean and glowing faintly after all of our efforts. The shimmering water cast a beautiful glow on the story gods' statues next to it, illuminating them with the magical vibes they deserved.

Terra, the goddess of worldbuilding, held a giant pen in her hands, drawing rivers through the air with her imagination. Solas, the god of characters, held tiny people in his cupped hands like he was giving us a gift. Finally, the statue of Orion held a massive book, as if he was reading the tales of everyone here. He was the god of fate after all, giving every character's life a dramatic plot all their own.

Standing in front of these statues was awe-inspiring.

I bowed low. "The Misty Mountain Library honors the story gods, Terra, Solas, and Orion. You created our world from your imagination and need for a good story. Those stories shape our lives and fill our minds with joy. Today we'd like to give back in our own way. With our own stories."

Willow approached, easing her book into the well with reverence. The water glowed brighter, accepting her offering. I smiled at her as Lisa and the others handed out paper and pens for the patrons to write down their story too. It was an important part of the festival, writing down what happened in the past year and what you hoped would happen next.

I eyed Roan as I took my own piece of paper, writing down the story of how we met and how we restored this library together. I even dared to write that we'd end up happily ever after, like every good love story.

His eyes met mine as he wrote his own story down, and I wished I could take a peek, but that was frowned upon. Everyone's story was their own, to share or keep private. This was about telling the gods, not other people.

When it looked like most people were done writing, I stepped up to the statues again, holding my paper high and then setting it inside the story well.

"We share our stories with you," I said warmly, gazing at the gods' statues, "so that you can stay connected to us and enjoy the world you created. Thank you for giving each of us the spark of a great story."

I moved to the side as Willow, Lisa, Roan, Oren, and everyone else here dropped their stories into the well. The light grew brighter and brighter with each offering. This well connected us to the gods, merging all of our stories together.

A beautiful golden light pulled my attention to the great book tree. Its branches grew larger as new books sprouted all over, from tiny buds to full books in a matter of moments. Its warmth shone over all of us, blanketing the library in magic as the story gods blessed us.

My heart soared as the crowd cheered. We'd actually done it. We'd saved the library!

My grin was so wide my face started hurting, but I didn't care. We proved that the town cared, so the gods had given us their blessing in return. They believed in the Misty Mountain Library, just like we did.

I pushed through the cheering crowd to get closer to the tree. My hand brushed over the bark, feeling the warm magic surge beneath my fingertips.

"Thank you for believing in me, Misty," I whispered to the book tree. "This was only possible because you trusted us and I'm so glad you did."

The book tree's branches curled around me, draping me in leaves and new books. I breathed in the earthy scent of trees and paper, letting it bring me back to memories of my childhood. The library was exactly like it had been before, full of magic and patrons.

No. It was better now, because now it had story spirits too and would never be alone again.

When I first got here, I was so worried about failing and determined to do everything myself. I thought things needed to be absolutely perfect if we wanted to succeed, but now I realized that some of the best stories happened in those moments of imperfection when everyone banded together to achieve a goal.

I never would have been able to make this festival a success on my own. I needed the story spirits and Roan, the library and everyone in it.

I'd never felt more at home than when I was here and that feeling had only grown since I'd returned. I'd found a family at the library, and together, we'd made it a home.

This was the Misty Mountain Library, and I was its librarian.

EPILOGUE
NYSSA

A few months had passed, but the magic of that festival was still going strong. Not only the magic the story gods had blessed us with, but the magic of people gathering to show their support and love for the library. People visited daily, browsing the shelves and checking out their favorite books.

It was like that wild magic storm had never hit the library and we'd never closed our doors.

Kids were huddled up in the new children's section anxiously awaiting story time with the knights, who always went all out when they told a story. Fans crowded around the Demon Lord, no matter how much he tried to shoo them away. A group of teens was asking Lisa for romance recommendations.

All in all, the library felt healthy and full again. Everything felt exactly like I remembered, but better. Because the library was my home now, and the home to so many other amazing people.

Cerbie bounded through the stacks, chasing a ball Roan was not supposed to be throwing inside.

He smiled sheepishly at me as he bent down to pet the lovable dog. "Sorry. He just really wanted to play."

"Yeah, yeah," I said with a laugh, "I think it's you who wants to play."

"Me? Never, I'm a grown adult. A famous adventurer!"

"And a big softie for puppy dog eyes." I nudged his shoulder, smiling at him. "Why don't we go read for a bit? Recharge the library?"

He nodded, motioning for Cerbie to follow us. "Come on, boy, we're going to go read for a bit."

Cerbie raced him to the great book tree, curling up in the exact spot we always chose to read. I grabbed a couple of books Roan had mentioned wanting to read as he stopped by Mochi for two mugs of steaming hot cocoa.

We snuggled up beneath the book tree, cocoas in one hand and books in the other. This was how I wanted to spend my days, with him by my side surrounded by books.

He draped a blanket over my legs, leaning down to kiss me softly. His eyes sparkled as he gazed at me. "You really are amazing, you know that, right? Look what you've accomplished in just a few months."

"What *we've* accomplished," I said, kissing him again before he pulled away. He tasted sweet, like chocolate. "You changed my life the day you came to our book sale."

"Money well spent," he said, snuggling closer. "I'd buy every book in the world if it meant you'd smile like you are right now."

A blush burned across my cheeks as I took a sip of cocoa to hide it. "You don't need to buy anything, just... be here."

"Always," he whispered as he kissed my cheek, then cracked open a book. "Ohhh, this looks like a good one. Thanks."

I nodded as Cerbie settled next to Roan, resting his heads on our legs. This was everything I'd ever wanted and more—family and friends, love and laughter, a community bonded over books, all of us writing the next chapters in our own stories.

This was my happily ever after.

See you soon

Continue the story with Willow and the Demon Lord in the next book Myths and Manuscripts!

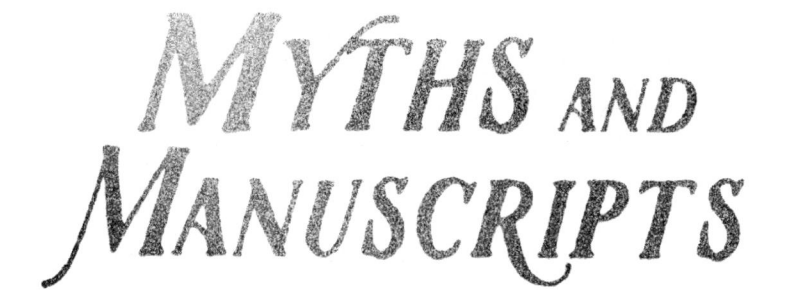

Myths and Manuscripts

PANDORA PIERCE

PANDORA PIERCE

writes cozy fantasy stories where magic, friendship, and playful mischief come together to warm your heart. If you enjoy lighthearted adventures without the stress of looming danger, her new books offer the perfect escape—filled with laughter, joy, and plenty of charm.

Pandora also shares this cheerful spirit on her Twitch streams, where her playful energy shines through just like in her stories. Her goal is to bring a little light into the world by creating tales that feel as comforting as a warm cup of cocoa.

Website and Merch Store: www.**pandorapierce**.com

Printed in Dunstable, United Kingdom